NIGHT CALLER

The next thing I knew the phone was ringing and it was dark. My eyes were crusty
again, and I was able to open them only part
way. I didn't know where I was at first. It
was only after I realized which direction the
ringing was coming from that I woke up to
the fact that I was on the living room couch.

The answering machine clicked in before I
could get to the phone. Then I heard a deep
muffled voice. It was a voice I had heard before. He had told me he was watching me.

"Good evening, Mrs. Kirk," the voice said. "I
know they're all gone, and you're alone."

IF LOOKS COULD KILL

RUTHE FURIE

AVON BOOKS ◆ NEW YORK

IF LOOKS COULD KILL is an original publication of Avon Books. This work has never before appeared in book form. This work is a novel. Any similarity to actual persons or events is purely coincidental.

AVON BOOKS
A division of
The Hearst Corporation
1350 Avenue of the Americas
New York, New York 10019

First Avon Books Printing: July 1995

Printed in the U.S.A.

RA   10   9   8   7   6   5   4   3   2   1

IF LOOKS COULD KILL

Prologue

I woke up gasping, my heart pounding in my chest and echoing in my ears. My demons haunting my dreams. Adrenaline charging through my system.

But as I fought my way out of sleep, the thumping didn't stop. Was I really awake?

The crash next to the bed made me sure I was conscious and made me wish I still was dreaming. My back was cold and wet with sweat.

I pulled my knees up almost to my chin and covered my head with my arms. The next blow would fall on me, I was sure.

The thumping was next to the bed. I was crying.

Nothing hit me. The bumping went on, in the same place, no louder, no closer.

"Oh God." Now I knew what was happening. I got out of bed on the side away from the lamp and turned on the overhead light.

"There, there, Horace."

My dog lay on his side, frothing, clawing. There were no demons in my room except the ones that flashed through my poor dog's head while he was having a seizure.

"At least you didn't get cut when the lamp fell, old boy." I spoke to him, but he was lost to me.

I had to work around the thrashing legs to clean up

the glass. Then I remembered to check the clock; the vet told me to time the seizures.

"Poor guy. It's OK. I love you."

Then the dog's bowels let loose. I cursed and ran for some tissues to clean up the mess.

I had a garbage can full of glass, lamp parts, and poop at three in the morning. My dog was still writhing on the floor when the phone rang.

I knew only one person who didn't care if he woke me up. I heard my own voice, "Hello, this is Fran. I'm sorry I can't answer right now. Please leave a message after the tone."

"Pick up the phone, you bitch. I know you're there. I wanna talk to you. Who do you think you are anyway?" Then a string of obscenities. The outraged, drunken voice of my ex, Dick Kirk. "I'm gonna get you this time, you bitch." More slurred curses blistered the phone line until the answering machine finally cut him off.

The dog was twitching; I was trembling again. The demon of my dreams had fallen off the wagon, and everything that was wrong with his life was my fault. Again.

"Damn. I have to call the cops." I put the garbage can in the hall and hurried to make the call.

Dick wasn't supposed to come anywhere near me. Or call me, for that matter. More than a month before, in February, he had come to my house and left Horace and me unconscious. Men on that kind of roll get more violent. I didn't know whether I could live through anything more violent than that last time.

The parole officer told me Dick had turned over a new leaf after his stay in the local jail. Some new leaf.

Before I could call the precinct, the phone rang again, and Dick picked up where he left off. I turned the volume way down. When the machine cut him off, I called the cops.

"This is Fran Kirk at 45 Maple Street. There's a restraining order . . ."

"Bret Hauser, Fran. Is he there?" That was Sergeant Hauser of the Cheektowaga Police. He kept track of my case.

"No. He just called me twice, screaming and yelling. He said he was going to get me."

"Did you hang up on him?"

"No, the answering machine cut him off. I didn't pick up the phone."

"Good. Was he drunk?"

"Sounded drunk."

"Leave the machine on. Don't talk to him."

"Fat chance."

"If he shows up, call us."

"But last time he broke in."

"I'll send a car by every half hour or so."

In a half hour I could be dead. "Thanks," I said, hung up and sighed. I wished they would park a car in front of my house until Dick was off the binge. I knew they would come when I called, but last time I didn't get a chance to get to the phone.

Sergeant Hauser had urged me to get the thirty-eight. It was cleaned and loaded in the night-table drawer. Black, shiny, and silent. I'd been going to the practice range faithfully. My aim was good, but that was when I was shooting at a target that wouldn't bleed.

"Even if you never use this to defend yourself," Hauser had said, "you'll feel better. They don't call these things equalizers for nothing."

"But handguns are designed to kill," I'd protested.

"Yeah? Well so is Dick Kirk." He had looked at me as though I were a stupid child.

Most of the time, though, the sergeant was sympathetic. Once he said that it must be awful to have a threat like Dick Kirk hanging over my head. He even joked about not asking me out because he didn't want to get on Kirk's list. I thought it was a joke.

I didn't have eyes for the sergeant anyway. And even if I had, I wasn't much for come-ons. I never learned much about that game. Passive. That's what Polly, the leader of the battered women's group, called me when I first went to the group. Passive.

If Dick broke in again, maybe he would back off if he were confronted by a gun. Maybe.

Horace was still lying on his side, breathing hard. The spasms were shorter and less frequent. It had been a half hour since the attack started. The longest seizure yet.

A car door slammed and my heart started racing again.

I grabbed the gun. It felt heavier in my hand than it had when I was target shooting. I walked through the dark, down the hall to the living room and lifted one slat of the miniblind just enough to peek out.

No cars at the curb. All the cars in their driveways.

I saw someone on the front porch across the street. *A neighbor just got home,* I thought. I breathed deeply and went back to the bedroom.

Horace hadn't budged. He needed to get to the vet. I called. The vet's answering service gave me an emergency number of a clinic several towns away.

"Yes, we're here," the woman on the line said. And after she told me that the condition could be life-threatening if he didn't come out of it, she said, "We'll be looking for you."

I pulled on jeans and a sweater.

"Don't die on me, buddy." I knelt by the dog and stroked his side. Horace weighed about forty pounds. Carrying him wouldn't be easy, but I could manage that weight as long as he didn't start thrashing again.

I plotted my exit: Check the attached garage before carrying Horace out through the door from the kitchen. *Should I carry the gun? When will the squad car come by? Should I wait or call the precinct again?*

Muster your forces, I told myself (one of Polly's maxims). *Don't be imprisoned by fear, but don't be foolish* (more of the world according to Polly). My breath was coming fast and I felt light-headed. Hyperventilating.

"One thousand, two thousand, three thousand. Breathe slowly. Crying won't help. Call the precinct."

My fingers shook as I pressed the buttons. *Could I shoot a gun in this state?* I wondered.

"Cheektowaga Police, Sergeant Hauser."

"It's Fran Kirk again."

"He's there," the sergeant said, alarm in his voice.

"No. The dog . . ."

"Did he hurt the dog again?"

"No. I have to take the dog to the vet."

"Now?"

"He's not coming out of his seizure. I'm afraid . . ." I couldn't hold back. I started sniffling, and I hated myself for it.

"There, there," the sergeant said. "I want you to wait right there. We won't be long. Our boys are busy on a break-in about a mile from your place. As soon as I can get a car free, I'll send one."

"But Horace . . ."

"It won't be long."

"But the dog could . . ." The line went dead. Every nerve was raw. I was sure the line had been cut. Then, in a few seconds, the dial tone sounded.

I hung up and went back to the dog; he was lying still as death.

"Horace," I shouted, "Blink your eyes or something."

His heart beat against my hand as I held it against his chest.

"Dick Kirk did this to you. And you're liable to die now because of him. I've got to get you some help."

I inhaled, feeling more resolute. "Well, here goes nothing," I said. But Horace, who usually wagged his tail when I spoke aloud, lay comatose at my feet.

I pulled on a winter jacket with large pockets, put the gun in my right pocket, my wallet and keys in my left.

Dick has probably drunk himself into a stupor by now, I told myself.

The light in my attached garage blazed over the car, gardening tools, garbage cans, and ever-ready snow shovel. Everything was where it should be. There was no noise. I wrapped my fingers around the gun and checked the car. *So far, so good.* I left the door open so I could put Horace on the back seat.

The dog was dead weight.

"You're supposed to be protecting me, old boy," I whispered as I plodded back toward the garage. "And here I am risking my neck to save you. But I guess that's fair." The memory of the night Horace was injured flashed through my mind. When Dick swung at me, Horace went for his leg and hung on with his teeth. Dick bashed the dog in the head with a chair and knocked him out. That was the first time I saw Horace having a fit. I thought he was dying that night. We both had a close call.

I staggered out the door and down the steps to the car. "Uhh," I grunted and let the dog down onto the back seat.

Then I heard the breaking glass and turned toward the sound at the back of the garage. A hand was coming through the broken pane.

I didn't grab the gun. I jumped into the back seat and scrambled into the front, where I pushed the button that locked the car doors.

The hand fumbled for the lock of the door knob. I knew that hand. I had seen it close up, just before it smashed my face. Now it was already bloody and it hadn't hit me yet.

I fumbled for the garage-door opener. I knew the script. It had been played out before. Where was the opener?

Start the car!

The engine rumbled. Something was going right.

Hit the horn! Yes. Hit the horn. What had I been told

about a car? A ton and a half of lethal weapon. I could move it back and forth. Where was the damn opener? I was leaning on the horn. Someone would hear. Someone would call the cops. In time, maybe.

The back door of the garage swung open just as my fingers found the opener under the seat.

The big overhead door slid slowly up as Dick lurched toward my side of the car in a staggering frenzy. I looked into the gleaming blue eyes in the livid face and didn't recognize the person behind them. He wrenched a spade off the hooks on the garage wall, raised it over his head and smashed it on the car roof. I saw his mouth shape the word, "Bitch," and heard the thunk of metal on metal. I looked up, half expecting the spade to come through the roof.

"Don't," I cried, leaning on the horn. I put the car in reverse and gunned the engine. The car squealed backward.

Dick got in a whack across the grille and kept coming at me, screaming and cursing.

Where were the neighbors? Where were the cops? I was still banging away at the horn. It didn't stop Dick. It seemed to stoke his fury.

I saw a dark car at the curb and cursed myself for not checking the street again before I came out of the house.

As I stopped to switch gears and go forward, Dick bashed in the passenger side window and the glass flew across the seat and hit the side of my face. I brushed my cheek with my hand and found pieces caught in my hair.

Dick thrust his arm into the car. I gunned the engine again.

"I don't care if I drag him down the street," I said out loud. "He's not going to beat me again."

The hand slid back out the window and Dick shouted a creative mixture of four-letter words describing my mother and parts of my anatomy. There was more banging. More broken glass. I was sweating and blubbering.

My heart pounded so loudly that I hardly heard the engine, which was roaring because I had slid the gear all the way to first.

"Damn car. What's the matter with you?" I screamed when I realized how little acceleration I was getting. "Oh." I shifted to the right slot.

Then I felt the pressure on my shoulder. *He got in through the back,* I thought. All at the same time, I screamed full out, reached for the gun, jammed on the brakes, and turned to face him.

My life changed in that moment: I was ready to shoot him down.

But I didn't. Horace had come to and was wagging his tail as if the world was all sunshine.

"Thank heaven. Good boy, Horace." I patted him on the head.

But I was stopped and Dick wasn't. The black shadow had lumbered up to the car and the bloody hand was inside again.

I tightened my grip on the gun and shot once out the front window. "Get back," I screamed.

His face appeared in the frame of shattered glass. His eyes were watery, his skin bright with broken blood vessels, the lines etched deep beside his mouth. He was looking straight down the barrel of the thirty-eight.

When he took his eyes off the gun and lifted them to my face, I don't know what he read there, but a pained expression came over his face, so tormented I could almost see the boy I knew.

"Back off," I said, hearing a firmness in my voice born of desperation more than strength.

The hand receded and I shifted into drive, without a false move this time, and peeled out. The car smelled of gunpowder.

Horace whimpered and jumped into the front seat, pressing his body against my side. I petted him all the way to the precinct. It was as if he never was that writhing mess on the floor.

*   *   *

Sergeant Hauser wasn't at the precinct when I got there. And I saw no cops on the way to my house either. *So much for police protection. You're born alone, you die alone, and you fight off wife beaters alone.*

The sergeant was at the break-in, the young desk officer told me.

"That must be some break-in," I said. "I hope you can get to my house to keep my ex-husband from trashing it the way he trashed my car."

The desk officer fumbled with papers and worked the radio. It looked like he was manning the precinct by himself. I heard a lot of conversation about a break-in and numbers that cops use to describe the kinds of emergencies they're dealing with.

I stood on one foot and then the other waiting for him to give me some attention. He was obviously handling more than he could cope with. *Cutbacks,* I thought. *Everybody's cutting back.*

I cleared my throat.

"Sorry," he said. "You're obviously all right now. I've got to handle the emergencies first."

"Triage?" I said.

"Huh?" he said, and went back to manning the radio and the phones.

Ten minutes later, Sergeant Hauser walked in. "Ah," he said. "You're here." The sergeant was lean, more than six feet tall, and had thinning dirty-blond hair and a big bony face.

I started to tell Hauser about what happened. I was going to add a few complaints about not getting police protection, too. But before I got into it, the sergeant interrupted.

"I just came from your place, Fran. Your ex is dead."

My knees turned to jelly and I sat on the bench across from the desk. "But he was alive. He was trying to get in the car. Did he put his arm back in? Did I drag him? I couldn't have shot him. He wasn't anywhere near . . ."

But I was sure that I had killed him. My head was running movies of his face in the ragged glass. The face of the boy, the hurt, damaged boy I had married ten years before.

His troubles are over.

"It looks like he bled to death." The sergeant was talking to me. "We'll take your statement and then you can go home."

I numbly told my story and the desk officer wrote it all down. He looked sympathetic as I wept through my encounter with Dick Kirk. At one point, he said, "The guy's an animal."

"Amen," said Hauser.

After I answered a few questions, I called the veterinary clinic to let them know I wouldn't be coming, and then Hauser offered to drive me home.

"My car is still working," I said. "I think I can drive.

"But I'd be happy for an escort," I added as I saw the sergeant's mouth turn down. Why did I feel I had to please him? The question came right from one of Polly's sessions on dependence.

I got into my car, which was practically on the front step and parked at a crazy angle, and waited for Hauser. Horace had been waiting for me, sitting next to my thirty-eight on the front seat where shards of glass were clustered in the creases of the upholstery.

The dark car that drove up and stopped looked like the car that had been at the curb when I backed out of my driveway with Dick in pursuit. But Hauser was in it.

Had he watched Dick chase my car down the street? Had he seen Dick bashing my car with the shovel? Why hadn't he stopped Dick?

The sergeant got out of his car and came over to me. "Are you all right?" he said.

"You, you were there . . . at the house. I saw your car."

The sergeant pressed his lips together. Why did I get

the feeling he was hatching a lie? "I, ah, had just arrived on the scene when you backed out of the driveway. It took me a minute or two to realize what was going on."

I didn't believe him. Cops have better instincts than that. Besides, how much intuition does it take to know what's going on when a guy is whacking away at a car with a shovel?

He had been sitting in that dark car, watching, and waiting. But for what? Then it hit me like white light. Pure and simple. He had been waiting to rescue me.

"I'll see you at the house," I said, and started the car. I ran through Polly's lessons, wondering what was happening now.

The sergeant followed me, his flashers startling the dark, to my block, where red lights flickered and flashed and neighbors stood in clumps along the street. In the middle of the street, a blanket was draped over what had been Dick Kirk.

Lit red, then dark. Red. The body under the blanket. Dark.

Where I fired the shot, I thought. *He must have been losing blood all the while. When he looked at me, was he dying? Why didn't someone see him and try to help? Dick bled to death. Where was the sergeant? Dick was still alive such a short time ago.*

Hauser, I thought, as he came up beside my car, where I sat watching the street as if the scene were playing out on a TV set.

"I guess the coroner hasn't arrived yet," he said.

"Did you see Dick fall?" I asked.

"I can see you're upset, Fran," he said. "Nobody is going to blame you."

"Did you see him fall?" I asked again, tears welling up.

"Yes." He sighed.

"He was alive."

"I told you nobody would blame you."

"You could have saved him."

"No," he said. "I couldn't have."

"Didn't anyone try to help him?"

"One of the neighbors brought out a blanket. Nobody wanted to get too close. Who knew what he would do next?"

"Didn't anyone call an ambulance?"

"When the ambulance came, it was too late."

I shivered. *My rescuer and concerned neighbors,* I thought. They stood around clucking like hens in a barnyard while the life had oozed out of a man lying in the road.

Whoa, I said to myself. *Mrs. High and Mighty. How close would you get to a man lying in the street? A man who was raging just moments before? Aren't you glad to be rid of Dick? Would you take it all back if you could?*

I struggled with my feelings of guilty relief. My head ached, wrestling with the rights and wrongs. But Dick was alive. Had the sergeant waited until he was dead to do anything?

"I have to go inside," I said. "I'm feeling sick."

A half hour later, my stomach was empty, my face was sweating. I was wrapped in a robe, sitting in my living room opposite Hauser, Horace lying on my feet.

"Can I get you a drink?" the sergeant asked.

"Probably couldn't hold it down."

"I'll leave an officer out front for the rest of the night," he said. "If you need anything, holler."

Now there's manpower to station a cop outside, I thought. *Now that I don't need it.* "Thanks, Sergeant Hauser," I said.

"Bret," he said. "I'll call you tomorrow. Maybe I can help you with the details. You know. The funeral."

"You could call his mother," I said. "I'll give you the number. He's my ex. I'm not his next of kin."

The sergeant looked surprised, but he said, "OK.

Good thinking. I'll call you tomorrow.'' He had a yearning look in his eyes.

"No.'' I said and looked back at him without blinking. There was something bothering me. Something about people who wanted to help. It had to do with control. I felt as if I was smothering. I knew I'd been turning my life over to other people and now I wanted to try it by myself.

"You're different now,'' the sergeant blurted out in a voice that sounded like a complaint. He was no longer relaxed and sitting back but was wriggling uncomfortably and scratching the arms of the chair.

You betcha, I thought, but I said, "People change.''

"I'll call you tomorrow,'' he said, getting up. The rest of what he wanted to say was written all over his face: *Tomorrow, when you come to your senses.*

"I'll still be different,'' I said.

The muscles in the side of his face bulged as he gritted his teeth, and he walked straight as a rod when he left.

Once he was gone, I cried. Not for him, not for myself, but for the wasted life that was Dick Kirk. The dead are easy to cry for; they can't come back and do something that would make you regret your tender feelings for them. He could never again sully the happy memories of young love, first love.

I slipped into slumber on the couch while I was weeping and watching the flashing light through the blinds. Some time during the night they came and bore the body away.

One

"Oh, Fran, don't you think you should come to the funeral?" my ex-mother-in-law said for the third time, this time tearfully.

"Marsha," I said, "I can't do it."

"But why?" she asked, again.

"I told you. You read the story in the paper. Dick was trying to kill me."

"You were married to him for ten years, Fran. Surely that must count for something." More tears.

"I'm going to hang up, Marsha," I said.

"You bitch," she lashed out.

"That's what your son called me, too," I said and put down the receiver on the old Mrs. Kirk. I couldn't share her grief, and she couldn't share my pain.

I was still called Mrs. Kirk, too. I had kept the name, sort of by choice. But not mine. I had been bullied: "I'll sign the papers if you keep the name."

Most of my life I'd not been very strong—a psychological wimp, a pushover. But I'd been working on stiffening my spine.

And I had made one decision. I wasn't going to that funeral. I was still trying to figure out why it wasn't my funeral. So were the cops, other than Sergeant Hauser, who had been strangely silent while I was asked the next day about shooting my gun "during the incident."

Once the medical examiner had determined that Dick didn't die of a gunshot wound, the questions stopped. I wondered whether Hauser had told his colleagues that he watched the "incident."

But I had survived.

It was the first time since the battered women's group had been meeting that one of us had had a crisis and come out of it without broken bones or wounds that needed hospital care.

And now the man who had cowed me for so long was dead. I once thought that it would be a victory to outlive him. But that wasn't the way it felt. Maybe I was growing up, at last.

I turned on my answering machine, in case Marsha called back. As I hit the switch, I remembered that the messages from my ex on the night he died were still on my tape. I stopped and played it forward, ". . . bitch. I know you're there . . ." I pressed the button to erase it all. I couldn't really start over. Ten years were gone.

It was Monday and I started looking for a job in earnest. I could have limped along without working; when I got married, my mom had set up a trust fund, which kept Dick and me going most of the time. Mom fixed it so I couldn't touch the principal. That was probably the only way to keep it out of Dick's fingers. And from his fingers to those of the nearest bartender.

My mother had been dead a year and I missed her. For a while, I thought that Mrs. Kirk could substitute in the mother department. Maybe even commiserate; I'm sure Dick learned what he knew about beating up his wife from his father. But Marsha Kirk and I had an unsurmountable obstacle between us: Dick. Even dead. Her son, my tormentor.

Now I had to get a job. But I had little in the line of office skills: I could file and I could type thirty words a minute and, of necessity, I knew about private investigating, which was Dick's business when he was sober. Many were the stakeouts when Dick slept off a drunken stupor and I did the watching, the picture taking, the logging of the time and place. But how could I write that on a resume?

One ad that Monday called for a "Gal/Guy Friday" and didn't ask for special skills, just "some typing and flexible hours," so I circled it. But I put off calling. There were probably a lot of better-qualified people— better typists who were more flexible—who had already called. I had been humiliated enough and didn't need more rejection.

The phone rang again, and Marsha's voice sounded conciliatory. Then she gave me the other barrel:

"Since you're the beneficiary of the insurance policy, the least you could do is go to the funeral of the man who was trying to provide for you."

I hadn't heard about an insurance policy. I ran to the phone and had my hand on the receiver, ready to capitulate. I was saved by the doorbell. Really.

It was Polly. "I'm making a house call," she said as Horace made a fuss over her, wagging and whining and licking. Polly gave him a big greeting, petting him, cooing at him, and scratching his favorite spots, behind his ears and on his chest. "I'm sorry I didn't come sooner. I was waiting for you to call."

"I'm glad you came," I said. I felt like hugging her, but I didn't. Feelings were hard for me to act on. "I didn't call, because . . . well, because I didn't get beat up this time."

"I'm glad," she said.

"Glad I didn't call or glad I didn't get beat up?"

"Yes," she said.

I thought I knew what she meant.

I made a big batch of coffee and got a couple of boxes of cookies from the pantry. Polly liked cookies, and she looked it. She told us once that she hid herself under the fat, that it was protection from advances by men. Her face was quite pretty, lit by her pale blue eyes and surrounded by her blond pageboy. But the glamour stopped at the neck.

We sat at the kitchen table for an hour and I told her about Friday night, when Dick had broken into the garage and Horace had had a seizure. She listened and ate.

"How's Horace now?" she asked.

"OK. The vet says he might have seizures the rest of his life. But there is a possibility that the injury will heal and the seizures will go away."

"Let's hope so," Polly said. "Then you won't be running around in the dead of night."

When I told Polly that Marsha had been badgering me to come to the funeral, she asked, "Do you want to go?"

"No," I said. "He wanted to kill me. Why should . . ."

"You don't have to convince me," she said.

Of course, I didn't have to convince Polly. What I had to do, as Polly was reminding me in her own oblique way, was convince myself and speak my mind.

Then I tried to tell Polly how it felt, not having someone threatening me anymore. A sort of freedom, but unfocused. Polly put another cookie in her mouth and nodded her head.

"You'll get used to it," she said. A crumb dropped from her mouth.

Then I showed Polly the ad for the job in the paper. I knew what she would say. I was angling for her to give me a shove in the direction I wanted to go. She didn't let me down.

"I think you should call right now," she said.

"What about settling all the other stuff? You know, how I feel, before I start something new."

"Life doesn't wait for you to settle things. This ad looks like a lifeline to me."

Lifelines were one of her favorite topics. Things that drop in your lap sometimes and haul you along.

I had to dial the number twice to get it right. When I

heard the answering machine on the other end, I hung up.

"A machine," I said.

"You can leave a message," she said.

I dialed again.

"I'm calling about the ad for a Gal or Guy Friday," I said. My voice quivered. "I'm a gal." What else do I say, I thought. "But I don't know how Friday I am." I giggled, thinking I was witty. Then the words came easier. "My name is Fran Tremaine Kirk. I type, but not fast. I can work flexible hours. I haven't any kids, just a dog. No husband either." Then I left my phone number.

"You did fine," Polly said. "But it's none of their business about kids and husbands. They're not supposed to hire or not hire because of things like that."

I felt disloyal to other women. Polly was always the feminist, or rather the womanist. Womanist was her new cry.

The phone rang and we waited to see who it was. A man's voice said, "This is William Lightfoot. I just got your message. I like your voice. You're hired."

I dashed for the phone. "Hello, I'm here. This is Fran Kirk. I'm hired? Just like that?"

"Weren't you married to Dick Kirk?"

"Yes." I was glad he couldn't see my face, which felt like it was turning scarlet.

"Didn't you two run a private investigating office on the South Side for a while?"

"Dick had the license. It was his business."

"Right. I used to be married myself."

"Do I know you?"

"I used to talk to you on the phone about some of the Sunset Insurance cases."

"Oh," I said, vaguely remembering him, but mostly recalling the way the business was falling apart while Dick was on one bender after another. It got to the point where I did the work myself and hoped no one would catch me operating without a license. "But Dick Kirk's dead now," I said.

"I know. I read about it in the paper. Where were the cops?"

Good question, I thought. "At a break-in," I answered.

"You mean another break-in." He laughed. "The other people probably had an alarm system hooked into the precinct. Well, when can you start?"

I caught my breath. "Tomorrow morning," I said, thinking on my feet. The sooner I found a job, the sooner I'd have another excuse not to go to the funeral.

He gave me an address and told me he'd see me at nine o'clock in the morning. I hung up and looked at Polly. She was grinning.

"That was a take-control thing to do. Tomorrow morning! Super!" Polly said.

I didn't tell her that I was not exactly thinking of taking control. It was more like wiggling out.

"When he first mentioned Dick, I thought 'there goes the job.' He knew about the investigating business and he'd heard about Friday night. He said he had talked to me on the phone about some insurance cases."

"Well, maybe you got something good out of that marriage after all." Polly smiled viciously.

Excitement was bubbling into my throat and making me gasp. "Here goes nothing," I said. "Oh God, I'm hired. I'm hired." I laughed and clapped my hands. I didn't know then that my life was going to get a lot more complicated.

"I guess when we meet tomorrow night you'll want a full report about the job," I said. The battered women's group met every Tuesday.

"You'll have to tell the others about Friday night. It will be a boost for them to hear how you came out of it in one piece."

Suddenly, I thought about the others and how some weeks the pain in the room was splashed around like blood. Some of us were regulars and others made appearances when they could or when they wanted to or when they needed to.

There were never more than seven of us at the meetings, which were at the County Services Center.

"I think Natasha is coming tomorrow," Polly said.

Natasha didn't come every week. Her boyfriend used to show up when he got his monthly paycheck, take her out for a nice dinner, then take her home and beat her till she threw up. She was a great beauty, half Thai and half black. We kept telling her she could do better than the creep she put up with.

"Friday was payday," I said, some of my joy subsiding.

Polly nodded yes.

"I wonder what I should wear to work," I said. I had had a few jobs during the ten years I was married to Dick Kirk. Most of those I had quit rather than show up for work with bruises.

I started for the closet, but in my flustered state of mind, halfway there I remembered the typewriter under the bed and pulled it out.

"What are you doing?" Polly had followed me into the bedroom. She had a handful of cookies.

"Maybe I should practice typing."

"I have to go soon. I can help you pick out your clothes. I can't help you practice typing."

Most of the time, I wore jeans or sweatpants. The skirts were all at the back of the closet—old, dusty, and the wrong length. Polly and I laughed when I put one on. It looked like something out of an old movie.

"I shouldn't have told him I'd come tomorrow," I said. "I need new clothes." I was panicking. "I might not want this job."

"Keep an open mind and let's shorten one of those skirts," she said.

We picked out a gray twill that would look almost

fashionable once it was shorter. Polly pinned it up and started hemming while I tried on sweaters.

"A blouse," Polly said. "Sweaters show too much boob."

"But they're all so loose," I said.

"They cling."

"Were you always this bossy?"

Polly laughed out loud, and kept on laughing.

I realized how far I'd come since that first night at the group six months before. And I started laughing, too.

I got out the blouses, though, and found one that I could wear with a cardigan.

Polly was still smiling. "How are your nylons? Got any without runs or snags?"

"Shoot! I forgot about stockings." I dug into my bottom drawer and pulled out a plastic bag full of twisted, wrinkled panty hose in a variety of colors. I had one tan pair with a run on the thigh.

"That run might show when we shorten this skirt," Polly said. She was mothering me.

Finally we settled on a pair of gray hose and black flats. I didn't have any pumps with high heels. Dick was five ten and at five seven I was as tall as he was when I wore heels. He never liked that, so I wore flats. My next new pair of shoes, I thought, would be patent leather spikes.

Before Polly left, I put on the outfit.

"Very preppy," she said.

I was in a good mood, excited as I watched Polly drive away. And then I saw a car, which wasn't one I'd seen before in the neighborhood, pull out from the curb and go in the same direction as Polly. I shivered. Was he following her?

I wrote down everything I could remember about the car and put the paper by the phone. I gave her a half hour to get home.

She hadn't seen a car following her, she said, but she would keep her eyes open.

Marsha called again later. When I answered, she told me that Dick had two insurance policies "for his girls." She actually said that and believed it. Maybe he did, too. Each was for five thousand dollars, she said, expecting me to be impressed.

"That ought to pay for the bodywork on my car," I said.

She ignored that and went on to say that she wanted me to help her greet people who came to the wake. She claimed that she didn't know most of his friends.

I didn't tell her that I didn't think he had many friends left. "His friends would know all about the divorce and won't expect to see me there."

She grumbled, but I was done arguing.

I found her next topic a bit more disturbing. She said she had heard that Dick had died under "mysterious circumstances."

"Mysterious how?" I asked, not wanting to bring up my own suspicions about Hauser.

"I don't know exactly," she whispered, as if someone were listening, "but I'm going to find out."

"Are you going to order a complete autopsy?"

"No. That's not the mysterious part. I know what killed him. I'll let you know what I find out." She seemed intent on being mysterious herself.

There was no more talk about the funeral. I did send flowers, though, and signed them "Once Upon a Time."

Two

I had a lousy night's sleep. Horace got nervous after the third time I got out of bed for a drink. He probably thought Dick Kirk was going to come and kick him around again. I was alternating milk and water.

Finally, sometime after five, I fell into a deep slumber that was interrupted by the alarm, which was set for seven, but which rang for about a half hour before I finally was roused.

"Damn." What could I skip? Not a shower or the shampoo and blow-dry. And I'd need coffee to keep me from slipping into a coma.

The roads were clear and dry, not to be taken for granted in western New York in late March, so it would take me twenty minutes to get to Mr. Lightfoot's office in Buffalo. The makeup would have to give. I'd settle for lipstick and a little mascara instead of the production number I had planned.

When I was dressed and standing in front of the mirror, I looked like I was in costume. The reflection was so unlike me, so starched and curled. Horace sniffed around my clothes as if I were a stranger.

"It's still me," I said.

I closed the bedroom doors and put up a gate in the doorway to the living room to keep Horace off the furniture. Wads of white hair dropped off him. I gave him a dog cookie and went out to the garage, where my car's new windows were conspicuous for their lack of dog-nose prints. The dents on the roof and on the passenger side were still there, giving rise to a vision of Dick's face, full of rage as he raised the shovel over his head.

I made it to 423 State Street in plenty of time and found a place to park on the street. It was a commercial neighborhood, the kind that goes dead after the businesses close. Number 423 was a narrow gray-brick two-story building with a driveway on each side. On the first floor there was a flashy beauty salon done in Art Deco and called Looks. The curved glass windows of Looks wrapped around the front, and peach velvet benches interspersed by potted palms lined the windows.

The only entrance was a big chrome door in the center of the building that seemed to lead into the beauty parlor. I decided to ask someone in Looks how to find Mr. Lightfoot. Once inside, I was in a glass foyer with the beauty parlor wrapped around it. At the back of the foyer were the mailboxes and a stairway hidden behind more palms.

Sure enough, there was a mailbox for William Lightfoot along with one for Billy's Dating Service, one for P.B.W. Catalogue Sales, and another for something called Probabilities. I rang the bell under the Lightfoot mailbox and started up the stairs. As I got closer to the top, I heard phones ringing.

There was only one door at the top of the stairs, so I knocked. I heard a deep voice inside, but no invitation to come in. After a couple more knocks, I turned the knob and walked in.

The deep voice was coming from a thin man who was lounging rather than sitting in an office chair. He reminded me of a cat the way he curled himself so easily in the chair and against the desk. His dark hair was tied in a ponytail and his face, rising up from a long neck festooned with a black bow tie, had a tan that looked as if it were recently acquired. He was holding a phone in each hand and talking to both at the same time. He had a long, thin head and deep-set eyes under bushy brows, and his thin-lipped large mouth opened onto square yellowed teeth. The well-set jaw and strong cheekbones pulled all the elements together. *Handsome,* I thought.

"Lakers and five, Mets and one, Yankees and three." He looked up at me, his face crinkled into a dimpled smile, and he hung up. Meanwhile another one of the half-dozen phones was ringing.

"Are you Fran?" he said with that dimpled smile again.

"Yes."

"Take that desk, answer the phone on the right, say 'Billy's Dating Service.' Ask for their names, addresses, phone numbers, and when they need the date. Find out when they can be called back. If they give you a hard time about anything, anything at all, you say, 'Hold on,' push the three button and hang up the phone. Got it?"

I nodded.

"If this phone rings," he said, indicating a phone on a stand next to the desk, "take down the catalogue number, the item number, and the credit card number. If they ask you questions, tell them to call customer service."

I was too nervous to do anything except what I was told. I sat at the desk and plunged into the world of Billy's Dating Service and P.B.W. Catalogue Sales. By noon I had a stack of papers with information on people who wanted dates and others who wanted items from the catalogue of which I didn't have a copy. A number of folks had been plugged into the three button, some who made lewd suggestions and others who wanted some prior wrong made right. If they called back screaming, they were plugged into three again. The three button, which I couldn't resist listening in on, was tied into a recording that gave out an address to which written complaints could be mailed.

Mr. Lightfoot, at least I thought it was Mr. Lightfoot,

hadn't introduced himself. I was waiting for him to talk to me about the job, the hours, the pay. I wondered whether I was being tested. But he kept talking numbers on the other bank of phones.

At noon, promptly, Mr. Lightfoot turned off the phones and connected the answering machines. "We've got almost an hour to eat and get our business out of the way," he said, walking to the back of the office where there was a small refrigerator.

I found it hard to take my eyes off him. Even in his cowboy boots his walk was so smooth and light I was put in mind again of a cat.

From the refrigerator he pulled out a tray of wrapped sandwiches and a couple of quarts of juice.

"Tuna, peanut butter and jelly, and ham and cheese," he said, pushing the tray toward me. "Hand me those sheets you did." After looking them over, he said, "Great. Everything's here."

"I did what you told me to do," I said.

"Fran," he said, "you don't know how many people can't do as they're told. You have no idea." More dimples.

I took a breath. "Does this mean I'm hired?

"Of course. Now let's get the other stuff done. Fill out this thing for the IRS."

I cleared my throat and he looked up. My heart was beating triple-time. "What's the pay?" I asked.

"I'll start you at three hundred dollars a week, and we'll see where we go from there."

I made a face. I didn't know what kind of face. It wasn't that the pay he offered was too low, it was that I was overloaded. I didn't know what I looked like.

"OK," he said. "Three-fifty."

In my confusion, I smiled and we made a deal. The scrunched-up organ that was my heart opened up with a new sense of power. I didn't know what was happening to me. But the world was a nicer place.

"By the way, call me Billy. I'm William Lightfoot," he said after I had filled out the forms.

"OK, Billy," I said. "Your sandwiches are good."

"By Friday they get a little stiff," he said.

"Thanks for warning me," I said. "Maybe I'll pack my own for Friday. Is that what you meant by a Gal Friday?" I smiled.

He chuckled. Then he got back to the business of filling me in. While he talked, I took in the rest of his outfit. Besides the bow tie and the boots, his costume consisted of tight jeans, a shirt with a pleated front and French cuffs, and a black leather vest.

When he was done and I was just about to ask, he told me, "The bathrooms are downstairs in the beauty parlor. Just walk through to the back."

I got up to go and he said, "We turn the phones back on in ten minutes."

I walked in the door of Looks and headed toward the back. No one bothered to look at me except a young woman by the shampoo sinks who almost bumped into me.

"Hi," she said. "Are you the new one upstairs?"

My arrival had been heralded. "Yes. I just started this morning. Am I going in the right direction?"

She pointed to a door with a long blond wig hanging on it. There was another door with a short brown wig on it. It was beauty parlor sign language for Ladies' Room and Men's Room.

"My name is Fran," I said. "Thanks."

"Myrtle," she said. "Isn't that an awful name to hang on a kid?"

Myrtle flashed a Hollywood grin. Her teeth were either all capped or she had one of the greatest mouths ever given out. The rest of her looked like a twelve-year-old boy, wiry, without a curve. Her hair was done in red spikes and her bony legs were filmed in yellow Lycra. A huge orange sweatshirt hung from her shoulders and ended mid-thigh.

"I've gotta run," I said. "I've got to do what I have to do and get back."

"Catch you later," Myrtle said and showed her big whites again.

I was thinking that Looks was pretty busy for a Tuesday, and I wondered what the place would be like at the end of the week, when beauty parlors usually are buzzing. Maybe there would be a line for the john.

When I got back upstairs, Billy was already on the phone.

"You mean he's been playing with a sprain?" he said, and then started spouting numbers.

I noticed that there were three phone stations, and at one of them the phone wasn't ringing. There also was some equipment lined up against the wall that I didn't recognize. I worried that Billy would expect me to know how to use it. Dick's office had been bare bones: telephones, copy machine, and typewriter.

In the afternoon there was some downtime, when I listened to the tape that took the calls during lunch and made notes of the phone numbers and what the callers wanted.

At one point, when neither Billy nor I had a phone to an ear, I asked, "When do you get around to arranging the dates the people called for?"

"No problem," he said. "Most of them are steady customers."

"I didn't know that a dating service was such a big business."

Billy smiled. Even his smile reminded me of a cat. His upper lip rose in the middle. And then there were those dimples. "There are a lot of lonely people out there," he said.

I didn't ask any more questions, although I was getting a weird feeling about what kind of catalogues people were ordering from. One man had asked for a "Lover's Best" and a "Super Dilly" before I asked for the item numbers.

The phone on the empty desk in the corner rang at about four o'clock. Billy turned on the answering machine at the desk he'd been using and glided back to the corner and wrapped himself around the chair.

"Helloooah," he said in a mellow voice. He was smiling. He made kissing sounds and turned his back to me. "I can hardly wait," he purred.

Embarrassed, I was glad when my phone rang. Obviously, Billy didn't need a dating service.

He was still on the phone talking in that sexy way an hour later, at almost five o'clock. I knew from listening to the tape that the phones ran from nine to noon and one to five. I was ready to go home. I was stressed and tired.

At five I flipped on the answering machine and stood up. Billy looked over his shoulder, signaled me to wait, drooled a few more syrupy blurbs into the phone, and hung up.

"Before you go," he said in his normal voice, "will you type up this stuff and fax it to the number on the top?"

"I don't know how to use the fax," I said. "How long will it take?"

"Depends on how fast you type," he said, smiling. "The instructions for the fax are right on the machine. I've gotta go. Lock up, will you? And let yourself in tomorrow. I won't be here until ten." In one fluid continuous motion, he tossed a set of keys on the desk, grabbed his jacket and the papers that I had worked on all day, and was out the door.

The pile of stuff I was supposed to type looked huge at first, but then I noticed that there wasn't much on each piece of paper. I didn't have the faintest idea, though, how he wanted it organized or spaced or how much to put on a page.

Then I tried to figure out which one of the machines was the fax. Lucky for me, it was labeled. The instructions seemed simple enough but I couldn't figure out how to turn it on. I stopped looking for the switch and decided to get started with the typing.

Billy's papers were loaded with numbers and some names that I recognized as sports teams. Other names sounded like horses' names. Some of the capitalized words meant nothing to me.

I had problems: Which page should I put first? How do I turn on the fax? The surge of elation I had ridden on all afternoon was gone.

The day was about to be chalked up as a learning experience when I heard footsteps on the stairs. For a second I harbored the hope that Billy had come back to show me what to do. Just about the time I realized that the footfalls were lighter and quicker than Billy's, Myrtle popped her head in the door.

"The usual baptism of fire," she said.

"Huh?"

"Billy gave you a wad of things to type and then breezed out, right?"

"How . . . ?"

"I did this job for three months," she said. "Then I got the job washing heads and doing pedicures. The pay's not as good, but I get tips and I like beauty-parlor work. I'm studying hairdressing."

"Oh, Myrtle," I said, almost in tears. "I'd really appreciate it if you could show me how to set up these pages and work the fax."

"Sure," she said.

"You're a lifesaver. How can I repay you?"

"You actually could do something for me."

"Tell me."

"Let me work on your hair. You know, practice for a few weeks. You've got good hair, lots of it, manageable."

I hesitated, looking at her spiked red locks.

Myrtle read my mind. "No spikes, I promise," she said and shot me her light-up-the-room smile.

"OK, but I can't tonight. I have to go to a meeting."

"Tomorrow's fine. My class doesn't meet until Thursday."

Our little deal made, she started to sort out the papers.

"What is this stuff anyway?" I asked Myrtle, lifting the papers with the numbers.

"That's a big business called Probabilities. Billy is a genius at making odds."

"Making odds?"

"Yeah. Like who's going to win what."

"Oh. Is that legal?"

Myrtle laughed. "The way Billy does it it is. People subscribe to his service. You type it up, it goes to the number you fax it to, and they reformat it and send it out to the subscribers. So it really doesn't matter how you set up the pages or how much you put on each page. Just make sure that every number is right."

I learned more from Myrtle than I had from Billy, and I thanked providence for sending her upstairs. At the same time, I wondered why she was so generous with her time. It might have been because she wanted a guinea pig for her hairdressing studies, but probably not, I thought. At that time, though, she made the difference between my quitting the job or staying another day. I stopped trying to figure out her motives. Some of my joy was returning.

I started typing and after a few minutes Myrtle grabbed a few pages and went to another typewriter. We finished the typing and faxing in an hour. Myrtle's typing was much faster than mine.

"You saved my life," I said. "You can snatch me baldheaded if you want."

She laughed. "You don't have to worry. I'm getting pretty good at styling. It's just that every week you'll have another look."

"Maybe I'll find the real me," I said. I was looking forward to Myrtle's experiments.

"You want to go out for dinner?" Myrtle asked.

"I have to go home and take care of my dog before

I go to my meeting,'' I said, sorry to have to turn her down after she had put herself out on my behalf.

Myrtle looked so crestfallen that I felt like a rat, so I said, ''But if you don't mind potluck, I'll make you some supper. I won't be able to hang around very long, though.''

Then I got the flashy choppers.

We were just about to leave when a door slammed downstairs. We both stood still. The beauty parlor had been closed for an hour.

''Was anybody still there when you left?'' I whispered.

She whispered back. ''They were all getting ready to leave when I left. I thought they were all gone.''

''Maybe we should turn off the lights,'' I said, ''and lock the door.''

Myrtle looked pale. I didn't feel as if there was a lot of blood in my face either. ''Good idea,'' she rasped.

We doused the lights and locked up and then stood there listening. I didn't hear anything but my pounding pulse for several minutes.

''Maybe we should call the cops and tell them we think there's an intruder,'' I said softly.

Then I heard something. Someone moving. But in the dark it was hard to know where the movement was. I was ready to scream. I thought it was in the room with us. ''Oh God. What's that?'' I gasped. I was weak with fear.

''Someone at the back of the shop.''

Then there was a voice. I didn't know what it said, but the tone was rough. Then another voice.

''Two of them,'' I said. ''I'm calling the cops.''

''Wait,'' Myrtle said. ''I think one of them is Sammy.''

''Sammy?''

''Samuel Plata. He owns Looks.''

I exhaled. ''Maybe it's safe to turn on the lights, then.''

"Just a minute," Myrtle said, still whispering. "I want to be sure."

That's when we heard the loud bang.

"A shot. Jesus!" I lunged toward the phone and felt for the buttons. My fingers felt like stumps. I dialed 911.

Myrtle switched on the lights, grabbed the office keys, and unlocked a file cabinet in the corner. I was jabbering into the phone, telling the operator that there was a shot and noises downstairs at 423 State Street. The operator asked me where I was. I was about to tell her that I was upstairs when I stopped dead. Myrtle was holding a huge handgun. It looked like a forty-five.

"Don't point that at me!" She was waving it around and I had visions of a fist-size hole being blown in something. I hoped it wouldn't be me.

"Better send an ambulance, too. We've got a shooter," the operator said to someone on her end.

Then there were footsteps on the stairs. "Hurry," I told the operator. "There's someone coming up the stairs." I was blubbering.

"Stay on the line," she said. "Tell me what's happening."

I heard sirens. *Please hurry,* I prayed. *Oh, please.* I hoped whoever was on the stairs would hear the sirens, too, and beat it. Myrtle had turned the gun toward the door.

"Who's pointing a gun at you?" the voice on the phone said.

"She's not, now. She got the gun out of a file cabinet. She's pointing it at the door. The door's locked. Someone's outside." There I was, terrified, and the crazy thought crossed my mind that I sounded like a commentator whispering at a golf match.

"Billy, are you in there?" The voice came from outside the door. "Open up."

"It's Sammy," Myrtle said, letting him in.

He had white hair, even though he couldn't have been forty yet. His eyes were very green and he had a cleft in his chin. A nice chin. A good nose, straight and well-defined.

"What's happening?" Myrtle said. "We just called the cops."

"Good." He took the gun out of Myrtle's hands and put it on the desk. Then he looked at me with the phone at my ear. "You got the cops on the line?"

I nodded.

He grabbed the phone. "I've been robbed," he said. "I was just robbed. The guy took a shot at me."

I sank to the floor and leaned against the desk. Tears of relief came rolling out of my eyes. I pulled a hankie out of my purse and blotted my face. The hankie came away with black blotches on it. Mascara and tears.

Sammy finished talking to the cops and came over to me. "Who're you?" he asked, smiling.

"She's Fran," Myrtle answered. "This is her first day."

"That's enough to make her cry without having a robbery downstairs." He laughed. He didn't act like a man who had just been shot at.

"You got that right," Myrtle said. "Did you see the guy who robbed you?"

"Not too well. The lights were off. I think he came in the back."

"We heard a door slam," Myrtle said. "We were just getting ready to leave."

The sirens were out front and Sammy raced to the door. "I don't want them bashing in the door," he said. He shouted as he ran down the stairs, "Hold it. I'm coming."

The police had us go to the station, where they questioned Myrtle and me about what we heard. But we had to wait around for them, because first one officer asked us questions and then another. This was not a small robbery, apparently. I overheard one of the officers say a couple thousand was stolen.

While I was waiting for the cops to let me go, Sammy was talking to an officer across the room. They looked like they were having a friendly conversation, standing facing one another, holding plastic coffee cups. Sammy was about five eight with broad shoulders, and even through his shirt it was easy to see he had muscular arms. His chest tapered down to a small waist. No fat anywhere. I guessed that he spent time at the gym.

When the police were finally finished with Myrtle and me, it was eight o'clock, time for my meeting to start. I called the Community Services Center to tell Polly what had happened and that I wouldn't be able to get to the meeting until after nine. I figured that Horace already would have had time to make a mess on the floor and chew the legs off the kitchen chairs.

"You haven't eaten supper yet?" Polly asked. Eating was important to Polly.

"I'll grab something while I feed Horace."

"You're still at the precinct downtown?" she said. "It's OK if you skip a meeting."

I thought about it while silence hung on the line. "I am tired," I said. "I didn't sleep well last night."

"Enough stress," she said. "Go home. Sleep. I'll see you tomorrow night, OK?"

"That would be good," I said. Then I remembered the car that had followed her. "Have you seen any more of that car that trailed you yesterday?"

"I'm not sure, Fran. I think someone stayed behind me all the way from my house to the center. But I couldn't be certain."

"Was it maroon and sort of sporty with those slats in the back that look like venetian blinds?"

"I couldn't tell what color it was. It did look like a sports car, though. And I didn't see the back."

"If someone's following you, don't go home after the meeting. Go to the cops."

"Don't worry. I will. You take care of yourself, too."

"Tell the others I'm sorry to miss the meeting. I'll see them next week."

Suddenly my arms and legs felt like rags. I begged off the invitation to Myrtle and promised her a rain check as well as an hour of my time after work the next day.

When I got home, I was delighted that Horace had only been sleeping and waiting for me to arrive.

Horace and I ate toast and milk and went to bed.

Three

A couple of police cars were parked in front of Looks the next morning. The officers were poking around behind the building in the parking lot, where Myrtle told me I could park. Billy had neglected to tell me there was a lot back there.

An officer who looked like a sleepy walrus stopped me as I started up the stairs. "You work up there?" he asked.

"Yes."

"Got a key?"

"Yes."

He called another officer and two of them accompanied me upstairs.

I told my story again and they nosed around the place as if it hadn't been done the night before. I was beginning to feel like a criminal. Maybe it was the way they asked questions. It was as if they expected every answer I gave would be a lie.

When Billy got in at ten, wearing a fresh version of the outfit he'd worn the day before, the cops were still at it and the phones hadn't been turned on.

"What the hell's going on?" He was not intimidated by a blue uniform. His eyes, a yellowish brown, blazed from under his brows and he looked ready to pounce.

It took some time before he calmed down and found

out what the hell *was* going on. When he heard how much the robber got, he whistled. "Maybe I ought to open a beauty shop," he said. Billy was entrepreneurial.

It was almost eleven when the cops left, so we worked through lunch. I didn't tell him how helpful Myrtle had been or how I had nearly quit the night before.

When the phones slowed down in the afternoon, I started typing up the odds sheets. Billy looked at me and his cheeks got those cute little folds in them. He was impressed by my industry, I hoped, since I was putting in a lot of effort to please him.

When the phone rang on the third desk around four, I expected him to start his cooing routine. He started the conversation with the same sexy hello, but his tone changed. He was talking about the robbery downstairs.

"Which form?" Billy asked and then wrote something down. He hung up and rooted through a drawer, coming up with a piece of paper that look like a questionnaire.

"Tomorrow morning before you start on the phones," he said, "go downstairs and ask the people these questions."

I took the questionnaire. "What's this for?" I asked. Billy was leaving a lot of things unsaid, again.

He took a breath and then started speaking to me very slowly, as if I were the village idiot. "As you know, Sammy Plata was robbed last night."

"Of course I know that."

"His losses are covered by an insurance policy that pays him back for fire and theft."

"That sounds like what a prudent businessman would do."

"And I am a freelance investigator for the Sunset Insurance Company, which is the company that insures Sammy."

"And you want me to do part of this investigation?"

"No."

"Good."

"No. I want you to do all of it."

"But I don't have a license." Even Dick, scofflaw that he was, had an investigator's license. How he got it is another story. And the work that I did when he was drunk was strictly sub-rosa.

"You don't need one in New York if you do investigations for only one person."

I was about to ask him if Sunset was considered one person.

"Don't tell me you didn't do work like this for your husband," Billy said. He seemed to know more about me than I knew about him.

"Well, yes, I did, but only, only, uh, when he couldn't do it."

Billy smiled a knowing smile. "This is nothing, small potatoes. Sunset is just covering its ass so it can pay the claim. Go through the motions and fill out the forms. When they pay me for the work, you get a twenty-five dollar bonus."

For twenty-five extra dollars, I told myself, I could add another chore to my work week.

When five o'clock struck, Billy was out the door. But this time I wasn't bewildered and most of the typing was done.

He won't get an extra hour out of me tonight, I thought before I remembered my deal with Myrtle. Who knew how long that was going to take?

At a quarter after five I locked up and went downstairs to the beauty shop. When I walked in, Myrtle and Sammy were talking to one another quietly. They were both frowning, but they stopped talking and turned toward me and smiled when they heard me. Sammy had a nice smile, too.

Myrtle had set up a daunting array of rollers, tubes, bottles, brushes, and combs. She put one of those big bibs around my neck. Sammy started pacing at the back of the shop.

I jerked my head toward Sammy, and Myrtle shrugged.

"Let's wash you first," Myrtle said, leading me toward the back where the head-washing sinks were and where Sammy was still pacing. He was carrying a brown paper bag. I remembered the cops talking about the stolen money being in a paper bag and wondered how much he had in the bag that night. How many people knew what he carried his money in? It wouldn't be very smart for someone to carry cash to the bank every night at closing time. Most businesses tried to make it hard for thieves to know when to plan a heist.

When a police car pulled into the driveway, Sammy looked relieved. "Lock up, Myrt," he said and went out the back door.

"Does he leave with a bag of money every night?" I asked Myrtle, who was wrapping my head in a towel.

"Yeah. You know, we were telling him not long ago that somebody would catch on and rip him off. It makes me sick to think about some guy with a gun . . ."

Myrtle left me and ran to the back door, locked it, and ran to the front and did likewise. "We don't have to make it easy for them," she said.

I was getting little shivers up my back. I wanted to be out of the place before it got too much later. Daylight saving time was due one weekend soon; I could never remember when. After that, I thought, I'll get home before dark even if Billy thinks of more for me to do.

While Myrtle was experimenting with my hair, I tried out one of the insurance questions on her. Did Sammy have any financial problems?

"Are you kidding? This shop is a gold mine." Myrtle answered matter-of-factly, as she tossed my hair, pulling a wad of it to one side and checking out the result.

I told Myrtle I had to ask some questions for the insurance company and that I would be coming down in the morning to do the work.

"Don't be surprised if you get snotty answers from

the others," Myrtle said. "They like Sammy and wouldn't like the idea of somebody investigating him." Myrtle seemed a bit put off herself. She was taking it out on my hair.

"Ouch," I said.

"Sorry," she answered, toning down the vigor with which she was raking my head.

"I like Sammy, too, what I've seen of him. It's not personal."

"Yeah, I know; it's business. I'll warn them that you're coming if you want."

"That might help. Thanks. Billy says the insurance people have to ask the questions so they can pay the claim. He says they have to cover their backsides." I wasn't lying about what Billy had said, but I didn't really believe it.

Myrtle smiled. "I'll tell them that."

The way Myrtle was flipping my hair around gave me second thoughts about turning over my appearance to her. But then I tried to think about it as an adventure.

The cops passed by a couple of times while Myrtle was transforming me. She snipped and sprayed and pulled and combed and curled and when she was done, she whirled me around to face the mirror.

My dark auburn hair was sprayed with a lighter red, and it stood out several inches from my head. I have never been especially pretty, but when Myrtle was done, I looked a little glamorous. I smiled. "If I ever have a date, you'll have to do my hair this way. I could never do it myself."

Myrtle was pleased.

"I'm having company tonight," I said, remembering that Polly had said she would come. Last night Myrtle and I were going to have dinner at my place before the robbery changed our plans.

Myrtle was on the same wave length. "I won't be able to do that supper until next week," she said.

"Good. I'll get something ready ahead. We won't

have potluck.'' The idea of cooking a meal appealed to me. I used to like to cook until Dick started complaining about whatever I made. I didn't know it then, but it was his way of finding an excuse to whack me. For a long time, I thought I deserved those beatings, and not just for my cooking.

I had to give myself a nudge to keep from mucking around again in my rotten past. I had been working on putting it behind me, but it did have a way of bubbling up, like methane in a cesspool.

When I got home, the message light was blinking. Polly couldn't come because Natasha was having a terrible crisis; her boyfriend, Carlyle, had done some serious damage this time. My stomach churned, wondering what Natasha had been through.

Another message was from my former mother-in-law. She said nothing about the funeral but said she had called the Cheektowaga Police Department about Dick's death. She also wanted to know if I had any baby pictures of Dick. I decided I would call her after supper and tell her that I would check as soon as I got some time during the day to climb up into the crawl space that served as an attic in this little house.

There was one more message. Sergeant Hauser had heard about the robbery at Looks. He said in a light-hearted way, ''Can't you keep out of trouble, Fran?'' Then he asked me to call him at the precinct. He would be there until midnight. I decided to call him right away and get it over with.

He sounded pleased. ''How did you happen to be on State Street in Buffalo when the robbery happened?''

''I have a job near there,'' I said, trying to keep it sketchy.

''I thought you were going to take a trip,'' he said, in a reproachful way, I thought.

I had told him I was going away after Dick died. I

didn't tell him that I was trying to put him off, that I felt he was taking over, that I had lost one tyrant and was afraid of another one moving in on me.

"This job came up and I thought it would keep me busy," I said. I didn't want him to be my confessor. I felt almost sorry for him. Probably he was in love. The idea made me feel guilty. Like I had a responsibility for him. I had to talk to Polly about this. I was almost sure he had let Dick die, and I wondered whether the sergeant expected me to be grateful to him for that. But it made me feel rotten and a little bit guilty, as if I had done something or said something to encourage the sergeant to act that way.

I tried to sound friendly. I even said something that indicated that I thought of him as a friend. I hoped he got it.

"Well, now that you're a working girl, how about lunch on Saturday?"

"This will be my first weekend. I'm still trying to reorganize my life. I have to shop for . . . I have to do my shopping." I cut myself off. I was starting to jabber and I didn't owe him an explanation.

"Some other time?"

I didn't answer that. I told him I had to hang up and get some things done because I had to go to work in the morning.

I felt crappy after I hung up and tried to forget it by working myself into a frazzle. I was feeling anxious about Natasha, too. I fed Horace and made myself a rather elaborate meal of hamburger and onions and peppers, mashed potatoes, stringbeans, and a salad of lettuce, olives, tomatoes, and bacon bits. I had done the dishes and vacuumed the living-room rug by the time Polly called.

"How's Natasha?" I asked.

"In the hospital," she said.

"Oh, no." The lump in my throat was growing. I

could feel the gurney moving down the corridor, see the pale green of the emergency room, the bright overhead lights behind the heads of the doctors and nurses.

"He came back again," Polly said. "I told her to move out. But she wouldn't. She said she didn't want to give up her apartment just because he was a jerk." Polly was tearful. She went on with the story. "Natasha bought a gun today. He had beaten her Friday, and he was waiting for her when she got back from the meeting last night. He came back again tonight, and he took the gun away from her."

"He shot her?" Tears were running down my face.

"Yes. She shouldn't have got the gun unless she was prepared to use it. She told me she couldn't shoot him." I remembered the night in the car when I realized that I could shoot if I had to. I wished I had gone to the meeting on Tuesday. Maybe, if I had told them what happened. Maybe it would have helped Natasha. *Maybe. Maybe.*

"This stinks. It really stinks. Is she going to make it?" I was trying to get mad instead of feeling overwhelmed.

"Her condition is serious. When she first got to the hospital, they said it was critical. The bastard shot her in the chest. He just missed her heart."

"Can I go see her?"

"Not tonight. They've got her sedated. Maybe tomorrow."

"Tell her I love her and that I'm rooting for her, will you?"

"I've been telling her that all evening. And I'll tell her again," Polly said. "How are you doing? You've had your share of excitement this week, too."

I told Polly about the job, but what I really wanted to talk to her about was what to do about Hauser. Then I felt guilty about adding my load to what Polly was already handling, and I kept seeing blood pouring from a wound in Natasha's chest.

"What about you?" I said. "Is that car still following you?"

"Oh, that. Boy, it seems so long ago already and it was only last night."

"What happened?"

"I did see the car following me and went to the precinct instead of to my house. I didn't get the plate number. He drove away with a roar as soon as he saw me stop by the station house. I told the cops about it, and I haven't seen the car since."

"Got any idea who it was?"

"A husband who blames me for his wife taking hold of her life."

"This has happened to you before?"

"Not this, but things like this. My neighborhood precinct does keep an eye on me."

After I said good-bye to Polly I cleaned the bathroom.

The next time the phone rang, I turned on the answering machine. It was Marsha. But I'd had enough for one day. She just repeated the earlier message.

Horace whined at me at about ten. I hadn't petted him all evening. I stopped my antiseptic furor and hugged the dog. He wagged his tail happily and licked my ear. *Relationships with dogs are so uncomplicated,* I thought. *They get used to you and accept you the way you are.*

By eleven o'clock, I was worn out with housecleaning. Besides, there wasn't much dirt anywhere, so I looked over the insurance forms before I went to sleep. During the night I dreamed about Natasha working for the insurance company and telling me that I'd made the forms out all wrong.

Four

My hair looked like a nest the next morning, and it was so stiff I couldn't make it do anything. So much for glamour. I washed out the color and the spray and was again a plain-looking woman with auburn hair. The haircut, though, was something new for me. My hair fell in a straight line, even when I moved my head. Nice. I smiled at myself in the mirror.

When I got to Looks, I tossed my head a few times for Myrtle and the gang and told Myrtle how pleased I was. The other beauticians, Kathy, Dan, Beth, and Gene, gathered round and checked out the haircut and, for the most part, told Myrtle she had done a good job.

Kathy, the ace with the scissors, was mildly critical about the cut at the bottom in the back. And before I knew it, I was in a chair and she was touching it up while the others watched and nodded. I had stray hair scratching down my back for the rest of the day, but what a haircut!

Myrtle had the folks primed to answer the insurance questions before they started work. They took turns. I should have spoken to them one at a time. I got started all wrong.

"It stinks that the insurance company should question Sammy's integrity," Dan said. Dan had a girlish way of talking and moving. It was exaggerated, as if he were playing a part.

"Sammy has a good business," Gene said without being asked. Gene was about five ten with one of those bodies that looked good in clothes, and he put designer duds on it. He would have been strikingly handsome, with his curly brown hair and well-boned face, except for his lips, which were pencil-line thin and pinched when he spoke.

Obviously Myrtle had told them the first question. The others concurred with Gene's assessment of Sammy's business.

"He wouldn't need to fake a robbery, if that's what the insurance company thinks," Dan said, raising a limp wrist.

"It's not what anybody thinks," I said, suddenly feeling as if I had to defend Sunset. "They just don't want to pay out thousands of dollars without asking a few questions first."

"Thousands?" Kathy said. "I had no idea this place was doing so well."

"It all adds up, dear," Dan said. "Your haircuts alone bring in a fortune."

Kathy smiled. "Maybe I should ask for a raise."

"Back off, gang. The lady has a job to do. We can discuss our salaries later," Gene said, barely quivering his lips. He was in charge when Sammy wasn't there.

"Sammy is good to us," Dan said. "This has always been a marvelous place to work." He batted his eyes a few times and tossed his head. His bleached hair swung across his eyes fetchingly.

There was more nodding from the others.

"Did everybody know that Sammy carried the receipts to the bank every night in a paper bag?"

They looked at one another.

"What's that supposed to mean?" Beth said in a snotty way.

Not to be put off, I matched her for snotty. "Just what

it sounds like. Who knew he carried large sums of money around in a paper bag?"

Beth looked like she was going to haul off and sock me, but before she could make her move, Gene said, "We all knew he did that, but he was going to stop because we told him it wasn't a good idea."

They all spoke at once.

"That's right."

"Yeah, we did."

"He was. He told us that."

"Thanks," I said. All this support for Sammy left me feeling as if I were storming a fortress. "I have only a couple more questions."

"What a relief," Dan said, wiping his sweatless brow.

"Is Sammy having any financial trouble? A lot of debts or losses, other than here at Looks?"

"No," Kathy said, "he's always flush."

"If he ever needed money, his father would help him," Myrtle said.

She got a couple of swift looks for that remark. I made a mental note of it.

"You'll have to ask him," Gene said, frowning toward Myrtle.

"I intend to," I said. "What about women? Did he spend money on women?"

There was another round of those looks that people give one another when they're all conspiring to keep a secret.

"There isn't any reason he should," Gene said. "He's happily married and his wife is pregnant." I had to look twice to be sure he was talking. He would have made a great ventriloquist.

"Karla adores him," Kathy said, too quickly.

"Karla is his little wife," Dan said. "A perfect princess." He seemed ready to go on extolling the virtues of Sammy's wife, but Gene cut him down with a glance.

"Where's Sammy now," I asked.

"He's not coming in until later," Gene said. "You could talk to him then."

Before I left, they told me they all, except Myrtle, had been working at Looks for years, and they got along well. Myrtle had been doing part-time work on Saturdays for about a year and had started full time about a month before.

One big happy family, I thought. But I knew a thing or two about families and how the private reality was a far cry from the public image.

I stopped in the bathroom before I went upstairs. As I came out, Beth was waiting there, as if she wanted to use the john next. I blinked. I wondered if she was still miffed.

As she passed me, she said, "Sammy gambles."

"What?" I said.

She looked toward the others at the front of the shop. "Shh. Keep it down. Sammy's a gambler." She went into the bathroom and shut the door.

A dissenter in their midst. Funny, though I had the impression that they were protecting Sammy, I didn't get the feeling that they knew anything about the robbery.

Sammy never showed up that day, and Billy told me to make up the report without talking to him.

When I told Billy about what Beth had said, he waved one hand. "She used to go out with him," he said. "Don't pay attention to her."

Just before Billy scooted out at five to five, he dropped the insurance papers on my desk. "Deliver this to the Sunset offices on your way home, will you?" He had signed the insurance report as it was. I thought it was sloppy work. It bothered me not following up on the information we had.

As the fax machine transmitted the numbers that would make a bundle for the subscribers to Probabilities, I reviewed what I had heard that day about Sammy's idyllic life. What was he doing going out with Beth when he was happily married? Or did he go out with her before he was married? She said she'd been working at Looks for five years. Would Sammy have hired an old girlfriend? But wouldn't Karla see to it that an old girlfriend was fired? Did Karla know about Beth? She certainly could have been the reason the Looks crowd exchanged glances when I asked about other women in Sammy's life.

I wondered whether any relationships were really what they seemed. I thought about the women in my group trying to maintain an air of normalcy while they were getting socked around. I remembered all the makeup I used to slather on to cover my bruises. Someone must have suspected what was happening to me. But everybody else wants things to be normal, too. Included in that everybody else was my own mother. Even she took a long time to face the truth.

But I had come to some sort of understanding with her and about her.

There's a funny thing about those understandings that you make while you're trying to heal. Your state of mind is like a sweater that you keep knitting, and then you think it's finished and it doesn't fit you anymore. So you rip out parts of it and knit it up in a new way.

I was still arranging things in my mind as I drove to the Sunset offices, but all that introspection stopped when I caught sight of a maroon car in my rearview mirror. No, I told myself, there are plenty of maroon cars. But I changed my route. I backtracked. He stayed with me. The guy in the car was bald with a dark fringe and he was wearing round metal-rimmed glasses. I tried to act as if I was singing to music so that he wouldn't get the idea I was suspicious. I went completely around one block with him on my tail before I headed for the precinct. I got a few of the numbers on his plate, the ones that weren't mud-covered.

When I drove up to the precinct, he backed up like he was shot out of a rocket, made a quick U-turn and raced off. I went into the station, but I didn't report to the cops there. Instead, I used the pay phone there to call Polly and gave her the information. I figured the cops in her precinct needed less in the line of explanation. Although Polly hadn't said so, I had a feeling that she knew who it was.

Delia Winston, who assigned the Sunset investigations, was still in her office when I got there with the report. Delia remembered me from the days I'd worked with Dick. She was a claims adjuster then. The promotion agreed with her. Her wardrobe had definitely gone upscale. Her wool suit was right out of a *New York Times* ad and her hair was expensively frosted and done in one of those flips that no ordinary woman knows how to do.

With some ambivalence, I mentioned what I'd heard about Sammy's being a gambler. I wasn't at all sure that Billy cared one way or the other whether I told Delia, but he had dismissed the information as unimportant. And Billy was my employer, not Sunset. But then, again, insurance investigations required a certain integrity. As I said, ambivalent.

"Why wasn't that in your report?" Delia wanted to know.

My face got red, I'm sure. "I didn't hear about it until after the paperwork was finished," I lied. "And when I asked Billy about it, he told me that Beth was a spurned lover and that Sammy wasn't a problem gambler," I said, truthfully.

"Well, I'm glad you told me," she said.

"To tell you the truth, I have mixed feelings about telling you. Billy was . . ."

"Billy does as little as he has to do to get paid," Delia said. "I don't give him anything serious to do. I thought this would be easy since it's right downstairs from him."

"Did you know I was there that night?"

"I was starting to put two and two together. We've already talked to the cops. As I remember you from the days in your husband's office, your hunches aren't far off the mark." She laughed.

It was true. I'd worked a couple of hunches before and saved Sunset some money. Dick got the credit, but Delia knew the situation.

"So?" she said. "Is your intuition telling you anything about this?"

"Nothing that I can be sure of, but . . ."

"That's enough for me. I'll stall the payment. You keep your ears open. I won't tell Billy. I'll just pay him the hundred for this." She held up the envelope. "If you come up with anything, let me know. Directly."

Billy got a hundred for a sloppy report, and he was going to pass twenty-five on to me.

"But I work for Billy."

"Do you have any objection to making a little on the side?"

"No. It's just . . . Give me about a minute to get used to the idea," I said, smiling broadly. "Thanks."

"No. Thank *you*. Another thing you might like to know is that the cops aren't satisfied with the answers they're getting, either. Here." She shoved a file folder to me. "Keep it."

When I read the report I could see that the cops had some misgivings, too. It looked like they were investigating Sammy as well as trying to chase down a robber. I was wondering how Delia got the file; it even had handwritten notes in it, as if the cops hadn't gotten around to typing up their findings. I looked at Delia, ready to ask her where she had picked up the file, but she was stuffing things in her briefcase in a big hurry.

From what I read in the file, it seemed the cops' questions were similar to mine: How come Sammy came back to the beauty parlor with the money? Myrtle had told me that everyone was gone when she came upstairs to help me. And what were Sammy and the robber talking about before the shot was fired? And who slammed the door?

When I drove out of Sunset's parking lot and all the way home, I kept an eye on the rearview mirror. But the maroon car didn't show up.

The Monday after the robbery, when I was walking through Looks at lunchtime, Sammy complained about the insurance company not paying up. He was talking to Gene, but I was sure it was for my benefit.

I tried not to look guilty when I walked through. I wasn't the most popular visitor. I got icy little smiles from everyone except Myrtle, who shot her high-voltage grin my way.

That night, after I locked the office door, I turned around and found myself looking straight into Sammy's emerald eyes.

I jumped and he grinned. A bully, I thought. I managed to smile back at him, but I felt like slapping his face. "What do you want?" I said, with as much of an edge as I could manage.

"An explanation," he said. "How come Sunset isn't paying up? What did you tell them?"

He moved close to me, threatening me with his body, but I knew those tactics and I also figured that Sammy wasn't about to slap me around on account of an insurance claim for a couple of thousand. I stood my ground and said, "I'm sure you've pumped your employees already. My report to Sunset covered the questions I asked them and the questions the police asked me. Period. You've got no gripe with me. Now back off before I start screaming."

Sammy stood aside. "You don't have to get so huffy," he said. "It's just that I lost a lot of money that day and the insurance company is stalling on the payment. I thought maybe you knew something about it."

"What could I have told them that would make them stall? I only started working here the day of the robbery. I didn't even know your name till that night."

"I thought you had heard something from somebody. I don't know. People talk."

"What people?" I asked. I was thinking that the tongues of his employees were firmly secured in their faces, except for Beth, but maybe that's who he meant.

"Never mind," he said and turned and walked downstairs.

I walked down behind him. I thought I might try a different approach. "Is there anything you want me to add to the report? I suppose I could do that if you think it would make a difference."

He turned to face me again. Wow, those eyes were something. "Maybe," he said. "Let me think about it. And thanks. You're OK. Really. A sweet kid." His smile was enough to melt my knees. Magnetism. He could turn it on.

Five

At the meeting Tuesday night, we talked about Natasha. The weekend before, we, the women in the group, had moved all of her things out of her apartment and into storage so that she could go to a shelter. Even though her boyfriend was in jail, she thought he might send someone after her or that he might get sprung by some legal glitch.

When I had visited her at the hospital on Friday, she had an IV in her arm and a wire running to a monitor. But she was sitting up and looking almost like herself. "I really hate to give up that apartment, Frances," she said.

"It's better that he doesn't know where to find you," I said, knowing that I had stayed in my house against the same advice.

She nodded. "I was lucky he didn't kill me. Lucky that the bullet missed my heart."

"The nurses are calling it the magic bullet," I said. "It went through you and took all the right turns."

Natasha smiled. "It tiptoed."

At the meeting, we spent an hour talking about stability and how our abusers undercut us.

One of the regulars in the group, Diane, who had three kids who were getting beat up regularly along with their mother, told us at the meeting that her husband had entered group therapy. "He went to a meeting last Friday," she said proudly. "He says things are going to be different."

Polly cautioned her. "He's only gone once," she said. "Don't expect miracles."

"What made him go?" I asked.

The silence in the room was palpable as Diane squirmed in her chair. I was wishing I hadn't asked. Everybody knew at once that she was trying to salvage some hope out of something awful.

Diane finally broke the quiet with a sob.

"Was it one of the kids?" Polly asked gently.

"He broke Merilee's arm," she cried.

The rest of us erupted in outrage and indignation.

"Leave the son of a bitch."

"I'd like to cut off his nuts."

"The bully. Picking on a little kid."

We finally got the whole story from Diane. Her husband had been arrested, and the judge had mandated that he go to counseling. Diane hadn't even called the cops herself. Her mother had done it because she just happened to drop in while Merilee was screaming.

We spent another half hour trying to figure out how come Diane and the rest of us don't call in the police more often.

The meeting ran late, and at eleven it was time for the center to close. Polly suggested that we have an extra meeting, maybe a bundle-up picnic on Saturday.

A great idea, we all said, except for Diane, who wondered what her old man would do when he saw all four of them trooping out on him on a Saturday.

"Tell him to call his counselor," Polly said.

Diane agreed, tentatively.

Before we left, Polly cautioned us about watching for cars following us. She had been especially nervous over the weekend when we were taking things to the shelter for Natasha. Polly gave each of us the addresses of the police precincts in the city and instructions on what officers were to be notified if we were followed.

Polly told us that a woman who belonged to the group several years before had recently left her husband. He thought she was at the shelter, Polly supposed, and had started following first Polly and then me, thinking we would eventually lead him to the shelter. The cops had found the maroon car, but they still hadn't found the husband.

I had to stop at the office on my way home. Another insurance case had come up that night, and Billy had called me at home at suppertime. He wanted me to start on it in the morning, he said, and I didn't have to come to the office because he had found someone to do the morning phone work.

I was wondering whether Delia wanted me to do this case Billy's way. If nothing else, I wanted to know why she would give a case to Billy when she didn't like his work.

I was uneasy about stopping at the office so late and was considering waiting till morning and going in before Billy arrived. But it was on my way, and in the morning it wouldn't be.

I told myself about lightning not striking in the same place twice. "Cowards die many times before their deaths," I quoted from something I learned in elementary school.

I circled the block a few times before I stopped, just in case the deserted husband was on the prowl, and left the car with its signals blinking on the street in front of Looks. I almost hoped a patrol car would come along and stop to investigate.

The pale night-lights in Looks made the hair dryers look like a line of robots. The mirrors on the walls caught the lights of passing cars and sent them streaking across the walls and ceiling.

My mouth was dry, and I had to go to the bathroom.

But I would wet my pants before I would go to the back of Looks by myself at this time of night.

I stopped still when a movement caught my eye. One of the potted palms was waving. I pushed my face against the glass door and peered inside. A hair ball rolled across the shined floor.

Then I reasoned that the heat must have come on and the palm must be near it. My heart was racing and I was feeling weak. With good reason, I told myself. There was a man with a gun here just a week ago. I went into the foyer and turned on the upstairs lights. If there was anyone there, I wanted to be sure he had plenty of warning and time to hide or get away.

I stomped up the stairs, whistling, I thought, like a man. I stopped to see if anyone was making noises like scrambling to get away. There was still no sound except for me, and the whole exercise was starting to be funny.

But I continued banging around, moving chairs, dropping phone books, opening and closing drawers, and clearing my throat in a deep voice, hoping that anyone in the building would think there was a crowd upstairs. Finally I found the papers that Billy left for me. Not on my desk where he said they would be, but on the desk that he used when his lady friend called.

There was a creak.

I listened.

It must be one of those noises that old buildings make, I thought, trying to assure myself. *Please, let it be*, I prayed.

Then the hum of the fan on the heating system started up. In the corner of my eye, there was a flutter, and my mouth shaped the scream that was growing in my chest. I turned my head toward the movement and breathed again. A paper had been blown off the desk by the rush of air from the heating system.

It landed in a pile of papers, probably blown off earlier when the fan came on. I picked up the papers and stacked them on the desk with a phone on top of them.

After I turned off the lights and locked the office door, I stood in the hallway and looked down the stairs. The flight seemed longer and darker than usual. I didn't know whether I was getting dizzy or whether one of the bulbs in the overhead light at the foot of the stairs had blown.

Resuming the stomping, I headed down. My bladder was almost painfully full and I was contemplating going to the bathroom, just so I would feel more comfortable during the ride home. After all, I told myself, I had been in the building for five minutes already and nothing had happened to me. And my car was still blinking away out on the street.

I started to look for the key and was almost to Looks' door when I stopped short, my chin dropped, and my knees got so soft I felt as if I would collapse. There, right in front of me, the door from Looks into the foyer was hanging open.

A little yelp erupted from my throat and I ran out, expecting to be grabbed or hit by a bullet any second. It seemed to take minutes instead of seconds for me to fumble for my car keys, find the lock, turn the key, press the handle, open the door, slide into the car, close the door, lock the door.

The world was in slow motion. I couldn't move fast enough to stem the fright.

Someone *had* been there.

I was hot and sweaty and shivering at the same time. The planet was all out of sync, a condition I tried to correct by flooring the accelerator. My eyes darted to the rearview mirror constantly until I was on the expressway heading east.

What do I do? I thought, when my blood stopped pounding in my head. It was almost eleven-thirty. *Call Billy? Sammy? The cops?*

I tried another angle: Someone could have left the door unlatched and it blew open later. As I put distance between me and the city, I felt safer, pooh-poohed the danger, and chided myself for playing bogeyman. I probably should have closed the door and locked it myself.

When I got home, the first thing I did when I came out of the bathroom was look up Sammy's phone number, but there was no phone listed for Samuel Plata. I tried Billy's home phone, but got his answering machine. I was reluctant to call the police, because I worried that they would ask me a lot of questions and keep me up all night. I briefly considered calling Sergeant Hauser, but the thought made my scalp crawl. An anonymous phone call to the police was another option, but I was sure that they would be able to trace the call, and then I would be in trouble.

Finally, after I was ready for bed and had tried Billy's number several times, I bit the bullet and called the Buffalo cops. I told the officer who answered that I didn't think anything was wrong, but that I couldn't go to sleep without telling someone that the door to Looks had been open.

The officer took my name, address, and phone number, thanked me, and said, "Good night. Sweet dreams."

I laughed and thanked him.

It was still dark and I was being chased through a warehouse full of hair dryers and being pulled from a deep and troubled sleep by sounds of knocking and ringing. Horace was alternating barking and whining. I couldn't get my eyes to focus on the clock. Several blinks later it registered. It was two in the morning.

There was more knocking and ringing. I put on my robe and turned on the light in the hallway. I could see flashing lights through the slats in the living-room blinds. My neighbors must wonder whether I run an after-hours joint for cops, I thought. When I looked through the peephole in the door I saw two men in suits.

"Who are you?" I shouted through the door. As if

anybody else comes calling at two in the morning with a revolving red light on their car.

"Police," they said, holding up their badges.

"What's the matter?" I asked, letting them in and letting Horace give them the once over.

They introduced themselves as detectives O'Connor and Brockway. "You called the precinct about the door being open at Looks," said, O'Connor, a fiftyish, red-faced Irishman whose suit looked too big. "You know Samuel Plata?"

"He owns the beauty parlor."

"What time were you there?" Brockway asked. He had an oversize handlebar mustache that dominated his face and everything else about him.

"About eleven twenty-five."

"What were you doing there at that hour?"

"I had to pick up some papers," I said and told them about the call from Billy. "What's the matter, anyway?"

"Plata is dead."

"Dead?" My legs wobbled. "Sammy's dead?" I sat down. Horace licked my hand.

"The patrol unit went to check Looks after you called," O'Connor said.

"They found Mr. Plata at the back of the shop. Shot in the head," Brockway said.

When I could find the route out of the spin my mind was in, I asked, "Was it another robbery?" My throat felt tight and the words came out squeaky.

"You were there a week ago when Mr. Plata was robbed. You and a Myrtle Divenzio." O'Connor checked his notebook. "Also on a Tuesday." He eyed me as if I had some explaining to do.

I didn't want to be a smart-ass, but I felt like asking him if it was against the law to be someplace on a Tuesday. But I told him it was just a coincidence that I was there late two Tuesdays.

All the while he was giving me fish eyes. He was taller than the one with the mustache. He didn't sit down. If he had, he wouldn't have had to bother hiking up the pants to keep the creases sharp. In the first place, there was enough room in the pants for two sets of knees, and secondly there weren't any creases.

Brockway kept smiling at me from under mustache. I wondered if they were playing good-cop, bad cop. But I thought, *No, everybody knows that game.* Cops were more subtle these days.

"May I ask you something?" I said. The mustache nodded. "When did it happen?" I liked Brockway because he patted Horace when the dog went near him. He was sitting on the edge of the couch.

Brockway said: "It could have happened while you were there, or shortly before or after."

I got a sudden case of the shakes. I was thinking that when I went up the stairs to the office, the door to Looks was closed. There I was banging around and probably covering any noise the killer made opening the front door. But even with all the noise I made, I would have heard a shot. Myrtle and I heard the shot very clearly during the robbery.

"If the killer left that door open," I said, "Sammy was shot before I got there. I didn't hear a shot." It made me dizzy to think about the killer lurking down there and going out the door while I was imitating a crowd upstairs.

"And you left there at what time?" O'Connor said.

"I was on my way home at eleven thirty."

"And the door was closed when you arrived?"

"I thought so."

"How long were you there?"

"I couldn't have been there for more than five minutes. I wanted to get out of there fast."

"Why was that?" Brockway said, smiling.

"Because of the robbery. I was afraid the robber would come back. Nobody lives in that block. It's all offices and shops." I realized I sounded high-pitched, sort of frantic.

"Did you hear a car in the back lot or notice any lights in the back?"

"No. I heard one creak, I heard the furnace go on, and I saw the door hanging open as I was leaving."

"How long have you worked there?" Brockway wanted to know.

"A week. The day of the robbery was my first day." I was wondering whether the robbery had been an omen that I should have paid attention to.

"Was Mr. Lightfoot there tonight?"

"Not that I know of." I told them about Billy's hours, told them about the phone call from Billy at suppertime, and told them I hadn't been able to contact him since I got home.

They repeated their questions in different ways. Another night's sleep shot to hell, I thought, presuming that I'd have to go to the station and wait and talk and wait some more. I was sure I was their chief suspect. I promised myself that in the future I would be like the three monkeys who cover the various orifices on their heads.

I vowed never to volunteer. But the sickening thought occurred to me that if something like this came up again, I would probably bumble through in the same way.

Finally they were gone and I was back in bed with a glass of wine by three. But my eyes were wide open. I had tried to call Billy twice and left messages for him to call me whenever he got in. But I was sure he wasn't going to be at his place that night.

I called Myrtle's house, too, but the man who answered was not only furious but furious in Italian. I couldn't make myself understood. So I'd awakened him for nothing. I didn't know anything about Myrtle's living arrangements, but she looked young enough to be living with her folks.

I shivered every few minutes, thinking that the killer had been in the building while I was there. I tried to remember if there was anything, anything at all, that would have told me that someone was in the building with me. Then I remembered the potted palm waving. I would check to see if there was a heating duct by that palm. Then there was the creak. But what would have been creaking? Would I hear a creak from downstairs? *Maybe the creak was upstairs,* I let myself think, and got another chill. Nothing else came to mind, except the thing that made me call the cops. The door left ajar. *But wait. Suppose it wasn't left ajar. Suppose the killer had been getting ready to come out.* If I had been standing up I would have swooned.

And where does all this imagining get you? I asked myself. I put my mind in another track. *Sammy. Sammy dead. Another robbery? The cops don't know. If not a robbery, what? Someone hated him enough to kill him? Who? A jilted lover?* Then I thought of Beth. According to Billy, she used to go out with Sammy. She told me Sammy was a gambler. *What was it to her?*

And as if I didn't have enough questions to contend with, I began thinking about Dick. Dick lying on the street bleeding to death while the sergeant sat in his car. Had it been made clear to the other officers that the sergeant had been there when Dick was still alive? Wasn't it Hauser's duty to try to stop the bleeding?

And then out of the blue my thoughts drifted to another Dick. The Dick I fell in love with when we were young. When we made out in the car to Rod Stewart singing "Maggie May" or Meatloaf doing "Paradise By The Dashboard Light." A long time ago. And I had mourned the death of love long before Dick died.

All the thoughts started running together, becoming jumbled and nonsensical. The next thing I knew my alarm was ringing, I had an empty wine glass in bed with me and a red stain on the blankets, and Horace was snuggled up against me. He seemed to sense when I was sleeping too hard to know when he got up on the bed.

An opportunist, like most males, my mother would have said.

I got a sharp jab thinking about Mom. I missed her still. I looked skyward, where I wasn't sure anybody was, and said, "I'm doing the best I can."

Six

The news hadn't hit the streets yet; my morning paper, arced onto my front step with perfect aim by my paper boy, Wally Klune, was mute on the slaying, as were the radio stations.

I still hadn't been able to get Billy on the phone to tell him about Sammy, so I followed the instructions he had given me the last time I talked to him.

I left about eight and headed toward the ski area south of the city. My destination was a resort called Sitzmark, which Sunset insured for liability and where a ten-year-old boy had been hurt on a ski lift.

The boy's parents were threatening to sue Sitzmark for negligence, claiming that the emergency procedures were inadequate and the employees were unqualified to operate the machinery. The boy had broken his arm when he fell off the T-bar and another skier fell over him.

It was a thirty-five mile drive, a route with sparse traffic and postcard scenery.

Plenty of time to think.

Sammy intruded on my thoughts, and I imagined the shadow lurking behind the door that stood ajar. *Maybe if I had gotten to the office sooner . . . ? What? What could I have done?*

My thoughts moved to the group. We had had plenty

to talk about. Polly had told the group about how I got my job, and again she'd called it a lifeline.

A lifeline. I played with that idea and got the picture of a lifeline thrown over the side of a boat to me. I was in cold water. As I got hauled in, water kept rushing into my mouth. I couldn't let go or I'd drown. So I hung on, hoping that I'd get pulled up to the deck and get warm. *Yeah,* I thought, *that's about it. Hang on and try not to swallow too much.*

In the meantime, I was hustling, trying to do what Billy wanted and to anticipate what he might want, and putting my uneasiness about his ventures on hold. I had my doubts and suspicions about the dating service and the catalogue sales and half expected to be raided by the cops when I sent out the odds over the fax machine. Never mind that the whole scenario was strange, that an insurance company would trust a guy who made gambling odds and made a business out of people's loneliness and horniness. I figured that Billy was fast on his feet, and I was lucky to have a job.

The farther south I drove, the steeper the hills rose and the deeper and colder were the valleys. In Buffalo and Cheektowaga, the buds on the trees were swelling, while the trees were still stark and wintry-looking in the hills.

Snow still clung to the north facing slopes, and at the ski area the diehards were traversing them. While in Cheektowaga, the daffodils spiking up through the ground in my yard had me looking forward to the warmer weather, the skiers here were hanging on to what was left of winter. It had been a long time since I'd strapped the boards to my feet.

The Sitzmark ski area was nestled in the valley at the base of the slopes, which were dotted with skiers. From the parking lot I had to walk past a couple of the downhill courses to get to the building that housed the offices.

I found the manager in his office cupping his hands around his steaming mug and looking like someone who needed intravenous coffee. His graying blond hair was artfully draped over the winter-tanned skin on top of his head, and his lean face was definitely Nordic. Surely, I thought, a superannuated ski instructor.

He grunted, "Hello."

"I'm here about the boy who got hurt on the lift," I said.

"Get out!" He suddenly sprang toward me.

I backed out the door, my eyes glued to his hands. It was an old habit: Watch the hands. I was tempted to call the trip a wash. What did I need with a violent ski bum?

He slammed the door in my face. I stood there panting in frustration and trying to gain access to the part of my brain where reason lay.

I gritted my teeth and knocked on the door and started shouting: "I'm representing your insurance company. You can talk to me or you can talk to the next guy they send. Or maybe I just report you as an uncooperative policyholder . . . or worse." I didn't have the vaguest notion what the "or worse" might be or where in the world I got the idea to say it.

Apparently the thought of my doing something worse than reporting him worked. After opening the door, he apologized and offered me a cup of coffee.

"I'm under a lot of stress," he said, as if that excused his behavior.

I refused the coffee, and he went through his script about the accident. It sounded memorized. Then he took me out onto the slope and showed me where it had happened and introduced me to the teenager who had been running the lift when the accident occurred. The kid looked scared.

They ran through their version of the events, which sounded plausible, and I took notes. They even turned on the ski lift that the boy got hurt on, which was shut down that day because the hill it stood on had bare spots. Before I left, the manager asked me what I was going to put in my report.

"What you told me," I said. "I'm no hot dog." Since hot dogs are daredevils who test the limits of what can be done on skis, he understood me perfectly.

He broke into a big grin and thanked me.

He put his hand out and I shook it reluctantly. I didn't want to touch him.

His tantrum on top of the strain of the previous night started a string of memories that I couldn't tamp down. And when I got back to my car, I cried, remembering the ski vacation Dick and I had taken the first year we were married. We had bought new clothes and a ski package that included four days on the Colorado slopes.

I skied better than Dick, and he took a couple of monumental falls trying to do things he wasn't ready to do. The second night we were there, a whole group of us gathered around the fireplace in the lodge singing and drinking. Some of us danced. Not Dick. I danced with someone else. When we got back to the room, he started telling me I was flirting. I protested, and that was the first time he beat me. No matter what I said, it was wrong.

"I wasn't flirting."

Whack.

"Stop that. I was only dancing."

Whack.

"Dick, stop. You can't do this."

Whack, whack.

I had screamed, and he put his hand over my mouth and told me to shut up or he'd whack me harder.

I don't remember much about the rest of the vacation. I know that my life changed after that. It wasn't mine anymore.

I finally stopped crying, sitting there in my car in that snowy little valley, and said out loud, "Spilt milk."

It was almost eleven when I got to the office. The police had the place all taped up again, and I didn't know whether upstairs was off limits this time. I pulled into the parking lot and was surprised at the number of cars. The whole Looks crowd and some others had taken up the parking spots. I had to go almost to the end of the lot to find a space.

The papers that I had stacked neatly on the passenger seat had gotten shuffled around, and it took me a few minutes to straighten them out. I started wishing that I had a briefcase to put them in, but then wondered if I would look silly carrying a briefcase.

The police had the Looks staff downstairs sitting on the benches. The cops on the day shift acted as if they'd never heard of me. I didn't know whether to be disappointed or worried that when they figured it out they'd give me a hard time. This time, I didn't volunteer, and I was permitted to go upstairs.

When I got to the office, I saw a familiar face, and it wasn't Billy's. It was Minnie, one of the irregulars from the battered women's group. Minnie had been married for thirty years and her old man had been thumping on her for twenty-nine. Every once in a while she showed up at a meeting banged up and vowing to leave him. He always apologized and she always believed his promise to never lay a hand on her again. He kept the promise once. That time he *kicked* her senseless.

"Hi, Minnie," I said. "What's up?" I was thinking that she was there to see me.

"You two know one another?" Billy asked. Billy's face was greenish and his eyes had deep rings under them. I wondered whether the police had found him the night before or whether he was wearing the badges of a wonderful evening followed by a stressful morning.

"Yes," I said. "We belong to the same club."

Minnie smiled.

"Mrs. Hughes is *trying* to learn your job," Billy said.

I didn't like the emphasis on the word trying. He got up from where he was sitting next to Minnie at my desk and waved his arm at Minnie as if to say to me, "See what you can do. She's all yours."

"I started this morning," Minnie said to fill the silence.

"Oh, so you're the new person."

"What happened?" she asked. "Why are there so many police here?"

Billy had probably been avoiding the topic. *What the hell*, I thought, *I might as well get it over with*. I turned on the answering machines and blurted out my story about the open door and the cops coming to my house, ending with the many times I had tried to call Billy.

Minnie looked worried and Billy frowned. He mumbled something that was meant to be sympathetic, I thought. It sounded like "Tough night." Then he flipped the switch for the phones and they started ringing.

"Give her a hand," Billy said. He looked like he had aged ten years. Even his walk was heavy and lethargic when he crossed the room on his way to the corner phone.

It was obvious that Minnie wasn't catching on real fast. And since I sometimes thought uncharitable things about people, I wondered if Minnie's brain had been damaged by the pummeling she had taken over the years or whether she hadn't come into the world with a complete circuit board.

"How are you getting along?" I asked her, thinking she might put the finger on one problem that I could remedy.

She started telling me how confusing it was to take the phone calls, and how it upset her to have people hollering at her. I looked over at Billy and he rolled his bloodshot eyes.

I told her basically what Billy had told me the first day. But I told her slowly and carefully, not leaving anything out.

She whined a whole list of "but this" and "but that" and "what if." And I blew it.

"Do you want this job or not?" I said, not quietly.

"This doesn't require a college education. You don't even have to think. Just do as you're told."

"You sound just like Edgar," she said.

I was about to say something about how I understood why she got beaned by Edgar all the time. But I stopped myself before I became a bully. I remembered the civilizing things that Polly said and took a deep breath.

"Maybe everybody sounds like Edgar to you when they are telling you what to do." That was about as civilized as I could be at that minute.

Then I made up a couple of forms with blanks for the information she was supposed to get from people and made a bunch of copies.

"Here, Minnie. This is what you have to get from the people who want a date. If they don't give you this information or if they want to talk to you about anything else ... dah-dah-dah what do they get?" I held up three fingers.

Minnie laughed. "The three." she said.

"And if the people calling about the catalogue want to complain or want any information?"

"I tell them to call customer service."

"Great," I said.

She went back to work and took a couple of calls without any problem. Then she started wiggling in her chair and she wasn't filling in a form.

I held up three fingers.

She looked like she'd been caught committing a cardinal sin. I picked up an extension and listened. A man was talking to Minnie and using her name. I hazarded a guess that it was Edgar.

I butted in on her phone call. "Mrs. Hughes," I said in my best snotty tone, "personal calls are not permitted during business hours." I heard a click and Minnie smiled at me. "If he calls again, give him the three," I said.

Billy's shoulders were shaking. I guess he needed a laugh, but I wasn't feeling like an entertainer.

*   *   *

Finally it was lunchtime and Minnie went home. I started to give Billy more details about the night before, but his face screwed up as if he were in pain.

"I've known him a long time," he said, looking down at the floor and shaking his head. Finally he shrugged and sighed. "Shit sure does happen," he said.

"I assume you didn't go home," I said, trying to change the subject.

He straightened his back.

Before he could protest, I told him how many times I called him and left messages.

"Maybe I just left my machine on," he said.

"Maybe," I said. "But someone so keyed into the phone as you are would eventually check the messages. If you were there."

Billy rocked back in his chair. "I'm glad you're such a good judge of character, Fran," he said.

My warning signals went up. "Why is that?"

"Because Sunset wants us to check into Sammy's death. Nothing like a police investigation or anything, just a little about his life and his friends."

"Are they still worried about paying the claim on the robbery?" Trying to sound businesslike but thinking I had stepped into deep doo-doo.

Billy cleared his throat. "No. This is a bigger claim. A policy on his life."

"Sunset has that, too? Who's the beneficiary?" My circuits were definitely crackling.

"That's what I like about you, Fran. No horseshit. Go right to the point."

I thought it was a compliment, but I wasn't sure. I haven't always been admired for my bluntness. "So? Who?"

"His wife, of course."

"Of course," I said. "So Sunset wants to know whether it's OK to pay her. How much?"

"The policy was for a million bucks."

I whistled. "I can see why Sunset would want to check her out before they paid."

"Yeah," Billy grunted.

"But do they think she hired a hit man so she could collect a million dollars? Come on. The woman is pregnant."

Billy opened his palms and raised them in the air.

"Besides, weren't you a friend of Sammy's? Wouldn't you be able to do this without leaving the office?"

"Delia asked me to have you do it," he said. The expression on his face was hard to read, but it wasn't exactly warm and cuddly.

"Well," I said, "suppose she did hire a hit man and then I go around asking questions? What's to keep her from hiring the guy for another job?"

"Nobody kills insurance investigators," Billy said. "Look, I'd give you a hand on this, but I'm up to my ears with work. It's the beginning of the baseball season, they're still playing hockey, they're opening that new track, and . . ."

"OK," I said, thinking that he was omitting his evening entertainment on his list of things he had to do. "But if I call you, you have to check your answering machine. Suppose I get into trouble. I have to be able to get in touch with you."

He made a face, fidgeted, and finally wrote down a phone number for me. "Ask for Mr. Lightfoot," he said.

I couldn't help smiling. I thought I knew what was going on in his head. If I asked for Billy, his girlfriend might get jealous. "I'll sound very businesslike. I promise."

Later that afternoon, while I was typing up the odds sheets and taking the afternoon calls, Myrtle came up. Billy had left early.

Myrtle's eyes were red-rimmed. "I can't believe

this,'' she said. "You know those cops think one of us did it?''

"I thought I was their favorite suspect.''

"Why you?''

"I was here last night. The front door was open. I called the cops.''

"Did you see anybody? Did you hear anything?''

"The cops already asked me all that stuff. I didn't think anybody was dead. I thought there was another robber.''

Myrtle remembered why she had come up. "I won't be able to do your hair downstairs tonight,'' she said. "It's all roped off.'' Her eyes were tearing up again. "Can we go to your place?''

"Fine,'' I said, patting her on the arm. "I'll feed you that dinner I promised you last week.''

"Great,'' she said. She touched my hand and smiled weakly. "I'll be there at six. Is that OK?''

"You could skip the class this week. I think your teacher would understand.''

"I'll feel better if I keep busy.''

I nodded and Myrtle left. I was thinking that I could get started on the work for Sunset while Myrtle set my hair. That reminded me that I had to call Delia to find out how come a case like this would be assigned to Billy. I couldn't believe that she thought I was such a hotshot that she'd put me on the case. There were other investigators in the city.

"Because Billy has a friend here who outranks me is why,'' Delia said when I called. "The bozo made it plain that Billy was to continue to get some of the claims overflow. I hope he doesn't find out I told Billy to have you work on it.''

"I wondered what happened. Thanks for explaining. While I've got you on the line, though, can you give me a hint about what you need in the Plata murder?''

"I'd just like to know the things the cops don't put

in their reports. Like what his wife wears, what rumors are around, what kind of furniture is in the house, what kind of cars are in the driveway."

"Right." I said. "And about the ski accident. I'll get that report in to you tomorrow."

When five o'clock arrived and I turned off the phones, I still had the insurance forms to type up. I decided to take them home and finish them there. I really didn't feel like hanging around after five. As I went through the foyer, I saw that one officer was still in Looks. Everyone else was gone.

I stopped and tried the door, but it was locked. He heard me, though, and came to let me in.

"The bathroom is in the back. We don't have one upstairs," I said. I really wanted to ask him how long they were going to keep the place taped up and to see if he knew anything about the investigation so far.

He let me in and told me to give the taped area a wide berth. There was still blood on the floor and dusty marks on the walls and furniture, even the hair dryers. I kept on walking.

I expected the detectives, Mustache and Big Suit, to come back and ask me more questions, but I didn't think they would tell me anything. I wondered, too, whether Sergeant Hauser would know anything about the investigation into Sammy's death. *No, forget Hauser,* I told myself, *keep him out of your life.* Besides, I still thought that Hauser had some explaining to do about Dick's death. I wanted the Cheektowaga cops to take another look at the way Hauser acted that night, but I was nervous about going to one of his superior officers and making my complaint. Who knew who his friends were?

When I came out of the john, I remembered to check by the potted palm to see if there was a heating vent. The vent was about five feet away, so I couldn't be sure whether the heat had made the palm sway last night.

The officer was waiting by the front door.

"Closing up shop now?" I said.

"Yeah. I was just waiting for you so I could tape up the building for the night." He had sandy hair, deep blue eyes, and small white teeth that made him look like a little boy when he smiled, which he did a lot.

"Will we be able to get in tomorrow?"

"Probably. There's another team coming in here later tonight. They should be done in a few hours." There was something else fetching about this policeman: His eyes didn't run up and down me; they stayed on my face. Not that there were any curves to speak of for him to see, but that didn't stop a lot of guys.

"I'm Fran Tremaine Kirk," I said, and then added brazenly, "but I'll be dropping the Kirk soon."

"Hi, Fran," he said, extending his hand. "I'm Ted Zwiatek. I'm not married, either."

We both laughed and kept on shaking hands. I don't know how long we would have stayed there, but the moment was cut short when a police car drove up.

"My ride," he said.

"Nice to meet you," I said.

"What time do you have lunch? I could stop by on my rounds tomorrow."

"Great," I said. "Noon to one."

And then he was gone and I stood there feeling like I was glowing.

Seven

I was not yet used to the idea of so much light so late in the day. Daylight saving time had just begun, but it made me think it would be a good idea to get out and jog. Horace would like that, too.

When I got home I pulled on a sweat suit and went up the street to the field, where there was a track of sorts. I had about twenty minutes before Myrtle was due to arrive.

I hadn't run in months, and before that the running was sporadic. My life with Dick hadn't lent itself to regularity. And western New York's snows played havoc with a running schedule, too. A gym with an indoor track was what I needed, I told myself.

While I ran and puffed, I let myself think about my encounter with Ted Zwiatek. There was something there, if I let myself go with it. But I knew that the worst thing people with problems did was to repeat bad relationships.

Polly summed it up way back when the group started to meet. "You're dependent and have no sense of self-worth, and he solves his problems by blaming them on somebody else and beating up the culprit. A marriage made in heaven."

I was breathing like an old horse after I jogged. Horace was panting, too, but he seemed ready to run some more.

"We're going home, boy. I'm not in shape."

We were about three houses from home when Myrtle's old Ford pulled into the driveway. She was getting her equipment out of the car when she saw me coming down the street.

"Boy, are you virtuous," she said. "I haven't done any exercise in weeks."

"You don't look like you need it. You're all skin and bones." She had jeans on and didn't look as reedy as she did in her Lycra tights.

I helped her carry her gear inside, where my answering machine was blinking. I pushed the button to play the messages and headed for the fridge to start the salad.

"I'm watching you," a man's voice said. I stopped dead, with my hand on the refrigerator door. That's all. A flat, chilling voice.

"What?" I ran back to the machine. My fingers felt cold and stiff as I pushed the buttons to replay the message. I wanted to listen to it more carefully. Click, the machine picked up. Then there was nothing, or was there breathing? Then the empty voice, "I'm watching you." More air after that and then the click. Not a receiver hitting a hook. Just a click.

No matter how clinical I tried to be in listening and analyzing what I had heard, my stomach knotted up the way it used to when Dick was coming after me in one of his rages. I thought I was done with that feeling. I didn't want to feel that way again.

"I'm watching you."

"What the hell is that?" Myrtle said. "Some loony?"

"I don't know." I was trying to put it in perspective. "Who would call me up and tell me he's watching me?" The man whose wife had left him who had followed Polly and me in the maroon car? Someone who knew I was investigating the robbery? Or the ski accident? Or the murder?

"It could be a wrong number," Myrtle said.

"I suppose," I said, knowing that if a bird was going to drop a load on somebody's new hat, it would be mine.

Myrtle and I ate and talked about what she was going to do to my hair. We were putting off talking about Sammy, and I was trying not to think about the phone call. It wasn't until she was styling my hair with a curling iron that I told her that Sammy's wife would get a million dollars from the insurance company.

"She's sitting pretty," Myrtle said, a little bitterly, I thought. "But she doesn't need it. Looks is a great money-maker. All Karla has to do is take over the shop and she'll be set."

"Does Karla know anything about running a beauty salon?"

"That's how she met Sammy. She used to work at Looks. Everybody said she was a genius with the scissors. People used to come from all over to have her cut their hair."

"When did she stop working?"

"When she got pregnant."

"Did you know Sammy before you started working at Looks?"

"I've known Sammy forever. His mother and father still live next door to us."

Suddenly, I remembered trying to call Myrtle the night before, when the man who answered shouted at me in Italian. It had been less than twenty-four hours, but it seemed like ages. I told her about it.

"Do you have any idea what he was saying to me?"

"So you're the one who woke him up at two-thirty in the morning." Myrtle laughed. "I could translate, but you don't want to hear it."

"Who is he?"

"Papa. He speaks very little English. He can, but he won't."

"But you have no accent," I said.

"I was born here."

"So he's been in this country a long time?"

"Yes. But he lives with Italians, works with Italians, and watches Italian shows on TV."

"I guess you speak Italian, then. I think it would be nice to be able to speak more than one language."

"There's one problem with learning a language at home. You learn to speak the way your folks speak."

I laughed. "Of course you do. What's wrong with that?"

"My folks don't speak cultured Italian. So it's not so much of an asset."

I thought Myrtle was being snobbish, but she was only about twenty, an age when parents don't get credit for much of anything.

"When you were growing up, did you see Sammy a lot?"

"When I was real little, my mom and I used to go there for Sunday dinner. My father was always working on Sundays. Sammy lived with his folks then. Later, when he had his own apartment, he used to come for dinner on Sundays. It seemed like we were always there on Sundays. Mom used to say Uncle Joe and Aunt Carmelita spoiled me. They'll probably spoil Karla's brat."

Myrtle spat out her last comment. No love lost between Karla and Myrtle; that was obvious.

"When did Sammy open Looks?"

"Mmm about nine years ago. Uncle Joe gave him the money to start. For a long time, Looks wasn't very busy. But in the last few years it's gone big time."

"Why's that?"

"Because he paid attention to business instead of being a playboy. That's what Uncle Joe says."

"What do you know about Sammy and Beth?" I asked.

Myrtle gave me a slight frown. "What about them?"

"Billy told me that they went out together."

"They did. But that's been over a couple of years, since Karla and Sammy got married." Myrtle's face flickered through expressions like a baby on the verge of crying. "Beth was still thinking he'd go back with her, though."

"Would she be mad enough at him to kill him?"

"Beth? No. I mean, I doubt it."

Myrtle was now teasing my hair into a high, wild do that looked like it was defying gravity.

I wanted to test Beth's contention that Sammy was a gambler, but I couldn't very well tell Myrtle who had said it without getting Beth in trouble with the rest of the Looks staff.

"Did Sammy do much gambling? Or don't you know?"

Myrtle looked a bit indignant as if it was some nerve to think that there was something she wouldn't know about.

"Sammy *was* a gambler," Myrtle said. "But not anything big time. Just a few bucks here and there."

The hairdo was done and Myrtle was pleased. She had brought a camera with her this time and took pictures to show her instructor.

"So as far as you know, Sammy hasn't been seeing anyone else?"

"No one else. He's been a model husband since Karla got pregnant. Are all men like that?" Myrtle's eyes were getting watery.

The question caught me off guard. "I don't know," I said. And it was true, I really didn't know what most men were like or whether there was any particular trait that could be ascribed to most men. My experience with men had not been good so far in my life. But I was hoping to get to know some of the good ones.

"He treated Karla like she was some kind of queen after she got pregnant. Just because she was carrying around his baby." Myrtle threw the rollers into the box for emphasis.

The phone rang again, and I was afraid to answer it. I let the machine kick in, but when I realized it was Polly, I picked up. She wanted me to make a tuna fish and macaroni salad for the picnic on Saturday.

"We'll meet at the Ridge by the main gate at ten," she said. "And will you pick up Natasha? She'll be out of the hospital tomorrow, and she wants to come."

When I told her about Minnie getting a job at my office, Polly said, "I know. She told me you helped her a lot."

"Is that all she said? I thought she would have told you that I was impatient with her."

"Maybe you weren't as bad as you thought," Polly said. "Minnie didn't complain."

Just as Polly was about to hang up, I told her about the phone call from the man who said he was watching me.

"Shit," Polly said. "He's getting worse. I'll tell the cops. You watch yourself."

"You think it's the husband?"

"He's the first one I thought of."

"But why is he watching me?"

"I don't know, but I'm going to notify the unit that's working on this."

When I hung up, Myrtle was packing her equipment.

"You don't have to rush off," I said to Myrtle. "Do you want a glass of wine or a cup of cocoa?"

"If you give me wine and I'm in an accident, you could be arrested. I'm still under age."

"Do you want a glass of wine? I've red or white jug wine."

"I'd like some white. I get red home brew till it comes out my ears."

"Does your dad make good wine?" I said pouring some white for both of us.

"His buddies think so."

"Do Sammy's parents speak English?"

"Oh yes. They both went to school here. Sammy's mother is a schoolteacher."

"They must be very upset."

"Everybody in the neighborhood is going around crying." Myrtle's eyes looked a little wet.

"Does Sammy have any old enemies in the neighborhood?"

"Not enemies. Some of the guys made fun of him for running a beauty parlor. A bunch of Guidos."

"Guidos?"

Myrtle laughed. "They call themselves that. Macho-types. Fancy cars, hot boats, and knock-em-dead clothes. They work out so they have muscles showing out of their sleeveless leather jackets. They keep scorecards on how many girls they ball in a week."

"I guess, if I were Sammy, I wouldn't worry if that gang called me names. What do you know about Sammy's friends?"

"I told you. Everybody liked him. He couldn't walk down the street without somebody stopping him to talk."

"What about Billy? Were he and Sammy close?"

"I heard they used to be real close. Years ago. Used to date the same girls, went everywhere together . . . Vegas, Reno, the races, fishing. Of course, back then, Sammy had all the money. Billy didn't have a nickel."

"So who told you all this?"

Suddenly she stopped talking and got red in the face. "You're doing it again, aren't you? Getting me over here, pumping me."

"I guess I'm not very subtle."

"What did you think you'd find out? What do you think I could tell you? Who do you think killed him?"

Myrtle grabbed me by the shoulders and shook me. But somehow I didn't feel frightened by Myrtle's attack. Maybe because she was female, I don't know.

I disentangled myself from Myrtle and pushed her back gently.

"But I'm not just being nosy," I said. "I'm doing my job."

Myrtle's breathing slowed down, and she was getting her normal color back. "It was probably that robber," she said. "Or Beth, maybe."

"You said before you didn't think Beth did it."

"I know." Her voice rose again. "But I've been thinking. She and Sammy used to hang around Looks after hours."

"And?"

"Maybe she was jealous of all the attention Sammy gave Karla after she got pregnant."

"Was she there Tuesday?"

"We all left at the same time. But she could have come back. Sammy came back."

"What about Gene?" I thought of his handsome, immobile face with its slit for a mouth.

"Sammy and he have been buddies since high school."

"How long has he been working at Looks?"

"Since the beginning. I think it was just Gene, Sammy, and Karla at first."

"Is Gene married?"

"He was. For a few years, I think."

"Any children?"

Myrtle looked at me and frowned. "No, not Gene."

"You don't like him?"

It's not that. I was just thinking that for a long time I hated Looks. I wouldn't go near it." Myrtle frowned.

"Why?"

"My mother took me there when I was twelve, and

she had Karla cut my hair. It was down to my thighs. I could sit on it.''

"And you got mad at Karla and the people in the beauty parlor?" I didn't ask why she didn't get mad at her mother. I let the question hang in the air.

Myrtle looked surprised, but she didn't say anything.

I thought of all the times other people's problems seemed so plain to me, but my own were shrouded in denial. Probably still were. I was working on it.

Eight

The next morning was Thursday, and Delia Winston called me and told me to go see Karla Plata. "I've already talked to her," Delia said. "She expects you."

"There's no form to fill out on this one," I said.

"Just think of it as a fishing expedition. Give me some notes on what you see out there in the affluent suburbs. I haven't gotten anything from the police yet, either."

"How's she feeling? Is she up to conversation?"

"She might be happy to have someone to talk to. Let her talk."

I drove out to Sammy's place in Orchard Park, where developers built some fancy digs in the eighties. The Plata place was in a development called Parkland Heights, which was situated on a rise that had a great view of Buffalo and Lake Erie. The houses were built so that each one had a view and one house didn't block the view from another.

Field-stone pillars flanked the main entrance to the settlement, a collection of large houses with lawns where each blade of grass seemed to stand at attention. Sammy's was a big Colonial with a horseshoe driveway and Greek columns holding up the front portico.

There was a shiny deep blue Saab parked in front of the garage. I wrote down the make, model, and license-plate number.

The woman who answered the door was obviously not Karla. She was about sixty and wore a pink uniform, something like the kind waitresses used to wear in diners. She stepped back to let me in before I told her who I was.

"She'll be right out," she said and walked toward the back of the house, leaving me in the tiled entrance hall, which had a wide, curving staircase. On the left was the living room, and the dining room was on the right. The furniture was mostly what the copywriters called Queen Anne, with those cute little curved legs.

The house looked like something out of a store catalogue. Clean, shiny, and unlived in. I heard a hum that sounded like a washing machine. Other than that there were no sounds. The predominant odor was lemon-scented spray wax.

A very blond woman in a stylish black-wool maternity dress waddled into the hall from the back of the house. "I'm Karla Plata," she said. She was stiff, cool; the hand she held out for a whisper of a handshake was icy. Her eyes underneath the heavy makeup were red-rimmed and the whites were bloodshot.

"Fran Tremaine Kirk."

"Sammy mentioned you." She pointed to a chair in the living room. "Please sit down." She settled her bulk opposite me in a matching chair. There was a small table between us. It had a lace doily on it and a ceramic vase containing dried flowers.

"Sammy told me you asked questions about the robbery," she said.

"I wasn't just being nosy," I said, defensively. "Billy had me do the insurance report. Mr. Lightfoot."

"And Sunset still hasn't paid. Was that your doing?"

Snot-nose question, I thought, but I said, "I don't

know. They didn't tell me. I'm not the only source of their information.''

"And now?" she said, arching one perfect eyebrow.

She was getting under my skin, but I tried to practice an exercise that Polly gave me: Address the words and not the tone. "Now I have to find out whatever I can about you and tell the insurance company."

She stiffened and her lips quivered. "Where would you like to start?" she said. The words were cooperative, but her face was set.

I had the eerie feeling that she and her house were cut out of cardboard, that if I pushed anything too hard it would disintegrate.

"I'm sure the police have asked you more questions than you wanted to answer," I said, getting ready to ask a few myself.

"No. They haven't asked me anything yet. They're coming this afternoon. The Buffalo cops don't trust the Orchard Park cops to ask me anything." She smiled a tight sarcastic smile.

"Can you think of anyone who would want to kill Sammy?"

"I have the best motive. A million dollars is a pretty good motive. Isn't that what you're supposed to find out about?"

Beating around the bush wasn't Karla's style, apparently. "Well let me educate you," she said. "A million dollars invested in something safe would net me something like sixty to eighty thousand a year. I couldn't live here with that kind of income."

I was certainly getting educated. I didn't have the vaguest notion what living on sixty or eighty thousand dollars was like. But I was gaining a healthy respect for the beauty-salon business.

"Myrtle says you used to work at Looks."

"Myrtle," she said with a sneer, "is a little busybody. And I have no intention of going back to work at Looks."

Something about Looks made her angry and unhappy. Also something about Myrtle. Karla seemed more human, less icy.

"It seems like a nice place to work," I said. "One big happy family. They all liked Sammy."

"They all *act* as if they liked Sammy."

"Did any of them have a reason to kill Sammy?"

"Beth, the other woman, might have gotten tired of waiting for him to leave me."

"Oh, you knew."

"Everybody knew. Even you." She was definitely trying to get a rise out of me. Maybe she was the type that needed a dustup once in a while to prove to herself that she was still alive.

I decided I'd get a few licks of my own in. "Well, why didn't he leave you?" I asked sweetly.

She again smiled her nasty little smile. "Because he comes from a traditional Italian family. And they don't leave their wives. They sleep around, but they stay married."

I decided that as long as I was there, I'd push all the buttons. "Did Sammy tell you anything about the robbery? I told him I could add to the report if he thought of anything useful."

Karla's face twitched and she put her hand on her stomach, which seemed to be twitching, too. "Just that there was a lot of money in the bag that night."

"Why did he use the paper bag?"

"He thought it would look unimportant. But I guess he did it too long." Karla looked suddenly tired. "Would you like a cup of coffee?" she said. "I need a snack. My blood sugar gets low."

"Yes," I said. Actually, I needed a snack myself. I was hoping for a doughnut or something with the coffee.

"Come on into the back," Karla said, leading the way, walking with her feet apart the way some women do when their bellies get heavy.

The back of the house was another world: all modern,

lit with skylights and a big greenhouse window with what looked like an orange tree growing in it. I guessed it would be called a country kitchen, but no manure on boots ever found its way onto those floors.

"So how are you going to live?" I said. I figured, what the hell. She already didn't like me.

She didn't answer me right away. "Gene might buy Looks if he can get the financing."

"He's already talked to you about it?"

"Gene and I go way back," she said, as if that explained why someone would offer to buy the business before the owner's body was cold. "I don't think he's as good a businessman as Sammy." Her voice broke. It was the first crack in her composure.

"I'm sorry," I said.

She gave me a cup of coffee and put a couple of bags of gourmet cookies on the counter, which was on one side of the cooking island and where there were stools. I sat on one and put my purse on another.

"I don't know what I'll do. I could stay with Sammy's parents in the old neighborhood, of course," she added with a smile that said something like, "Can you see me in the old neighborhood?"

"This is a nice place," I said. "How long have you lived here?"

"Two years, almost." She was more relaxed. She sat on one of the other stools.

"You could invite Sammy's folks to live here," I said, getting involved in the problem-solving.

"I won't be living with them anywhere."

"Maybe if you fired a couple of people, you could go back to Looks. I heard you were one great haircutter."

She smiled. "I was pretty good. But Kathy is good, too." Her face clouded. "I'd have to fire Beth, of course," she said, warming to the idea. "And Myrtle."

"But Myrtle is really just a kid."

"Myrtle is a pain in the ass."

"I like her," I said.

"That's because you haven't known her since she was a little brat. She's like everybody else on the West Side. If you come from the neighborhood, you belong to them. Everything is their business."

"It's not all bad to have people looking out for you, is it?"

"It's not looking out for you; it's like they have something to say about what you do. They own you." She was frowning and beads of sweat formed on her upper lip, where there was not a trace of hair. "When I colored my hair the first time—Dan did it—everybody on the street told me I shouldn't have done it. 'Let it grow back,' they kept saying. I never did."

"But that's all it was. Just talk."

"If you weren't raised with it, you wouldn't understand." She raised one manicured hand and flipped it backward.

I tried to pursue another topic. "Is Looks a big money-maker? I mean, if Gene bought it, could he make enough money to pay off the financing?" That's not what I meant, but I couldn't bring myself to ask what I wanted to know. And I wasn't sure she'd tell me.

"Business has been very good in the last three to four years. Sammy got the right combination of people and hired a decorator to redo the shop. He even ran some flashy ads."

I decided to plunge in. "Did Sammy have any other business?"

"He did some betting. He owns the building where Looks is. I don't know how much Looks brought in." In other words, she was telling me the bottom line was that she didn't know what the bottom line was.

"Did Sammy have a lawyer? An accountant? Somebody who could clue you in?" I was wondering how much of this conversation was really the insurance company's business. I was thinking I had caught this woman at a weak moment and she was telling me more of her business than she would have at another time in her life.

"I'll have to go through the papers," she said. "I've been putting it off."

When my eyes lit on the clock on the kitchen wall, I realized I would have to hurry or I would miss Ted Zwiatek, who had said he would drop in at the office at lunchtime. I had eaten four or five gourmet cookies already, but I could make room for lunch with the cute cop. I felt a tiny lump in my throat.

"By the way," I asked, "where were you Tuesday night?"

Karla gasped and regained her composure. "At my mother's."

"Where's that?"

"Where else? The West Side."

"Call me if you think of anything else I should know. Sunset wants this information so they can decide whether to pay you."

I started to give Karla a piece of paper with the office number on it.

"I know the number," she said.

I wondered if it would be a good idea to have a regular business card. But I put that notion in the category with my carrying a briefcase and stored it under *R* for ridiculous.

I asked to use the phone, and I called Billy to tell him I was coming in, but that I would be going out for lunch. He told me not to worry, that Myrtle had come in to work the phones and type up the odds sheets.

"Looks is still closed, then?"

"Yeah, the cops aren't done there yet."

"What happened to Minnie?"

"She called this morning and said she couldn't work here anymore."

I thought about Minnie's husband, Edgar, and wondered what kind of shape Minnie was in. I worried that

I shouldn't have cut in on the phone call. Maybe he took it out on Minnie. Then I reminded myself of what Polly told us all the time: "Don't take on more guilt."

As I left, I asked Karla whether any plans had been made for the funeral.

Again she twisted her lips into that stingy smile. "It will be on the West Side, of course. Sammy's folks have made the arrangements."

Driving away from Parkland Heights, I remembered the icy stiffness of Karla when I arrived and the vulnerable, almost helpless, demeanor she wore when I left. I didn't get the feeling that she was a killer or that she was someone who would hire a hit man, but there was something important being left unsaid.

And underneath that blond chic was a dark-haired girl from the West Side. She was still trying to cover those roots.

Nine

Myrtle had everything under control when I got back to the office. Billy was talking on the corner phone, the one he usually cooed over. He waved at me when I came in. He was wearing a sweat shirt under his vest and a red handkerchief around his neck.

What I wanted to do was ask Myrtle more questions about the neighborhood, but she was busy with the phones and the typing. So I started writing up the information Delia had requested.

I described the house and the neighborhood and the way Karla was dressed. Then it came over me. Karla's child would never know its father. Sammy was dead.

Dick was dead. Too much dying going on.

I had to nudge myself to keep from sinking into the deep blues. *Do your work and stop mucking around in it.* I told myself.

When Billy got off the phone, I asked, "What have you heard about what happened to Sammy?"

"One of the cops told me Sammy got shot in the head with a small caliber gun at close range. Two shots."

I gulped. "Do they think it was a hit?"

"It looks like it," Billy said. "But . . ."

"But what?"

"I don't think a hit man would have used such a small caliber."

95

"Sure they do," Myrtle said. "Don't you remember Louie the Butcher?"

"Yeah, but that was unusual," Billy said.

Obviously, Myrtle and Billy were privy to some history that I knew nothing about.

"Louie the Butcher?" I said.

"He was shot in his store," Myrtle said.

"Did they find out who did it?" I said.

"No," Billy said. "But the story on the streets was that he was laundering money and keeping some that wasn't his."

"Was Sammy doing any laundry? Did he have friends like that?"

"Who knows?" Billy shrugged and was about to go back to his odds sheets. But he could see I wasn't done. "Anything else?" he said.

"I spoke to Delia Winston at Sunset before I went out to see Karla," I said.

"She told me. They like your reports," he said with a kind of half grin, but still big enough to show the dimples.

Anybody who made odds as well as Billy did, I thought, had to play his hand close to the vest. Apparently Delia told Billy more than she let on.

"How long is Myrtle going to be here?" I asked, deciding to change the subject and wondering what the status of my job was, whether I was going to have to come in in the morning and take the phone calls.

"We'll take it a day at a time. Myrtle will be here tomorrow. Maybe by Monday I'll find somebody for the mornings."

"Too bad about Minnie," I said.

"Maybe," Billy said.

"So I'll keep going on Sammy's case then?"

Billy nodded and waved and walked out the door. The spring was back in his stride. I didn't know whether he would be back or not. Myrtle stared after him and I finally caught on: Myrtle had a crush on Billy. That's why she had come up to help me that first day. Probably why she had offered to help. I wondered why she ever left the job. Maybe she got too jealous hearing him on the phone talking to his lady love.

Myrtle came out of her reverie and glanced my way. Since I was staring, I quickly asked her for the address and phone number of Sammy's folks. With Myrtle doing the office chores, I could gather a little more information for Sunset and call Delia in the morning and see what else she wanted.

Myrtle took advantage of a lull to start pumping me about Karla. What was she wearing? What was the house like?

I answered her questions until her phone rang. She hadn't asked me about anything Karla said, so I didn't have to lie.

I called Sammy's folks and spoke to Mrs. Plata, my second Mrs. Plata of the day, and made an appointment to see her around one-fifteen.

As I left, Myrtle said, "My house is on the right as you stand in front of the Platas' place. My mother will probably be looking out the window." She laughed.

I went downstairs, expecting to see Ted Zwiatek in Looks. I went back to the bathroom. There was one patrolman on duty, standing near the roped-off area. When I came out, I asked the cop where Ted Zwiatek was.

The cop, a pudgy carrot-top with freckles, smiled. "Are you Fran?"

"Yes," I said, a little uncomfortable. I didn't like to seem as if I was chasing him.

"I'm Roland, Ted's partner. He asked me to tell you that he couldn't get here until one."

"Oh." I felt disappointed. I hadn't realized how much I was looking forward to this little lunch. "Thanks for letting me know, Roland. Will you be here when he gets back?"

"Expect so."

"Will you tell him I had an appointment on the West

Side and couldn't wait. Maybe I'll catch him tomorrow.''

"He'll be sorry he missed you," Roland said. "Can he call you?''

I was suddenly flustered and insecure about giving out my phone number. After all, I didn't know Roland, and I hardly knew Ted. I gave him the office number that Billy used for personal calls and for talking to Sunset. "He can leave a message for me at this number," I said.

I walked down the street to a sandwich shop and treated myself to the lunch I thought I would have with Ted. It wasn't the same. Too bad, I thought, but maybe it was just as well. Maybe he was one of those guys who broke dates all the time. I tried to get him out of my mind. When I had finished the last olive on my plate, I had almost succeeded.

The West Side had been an Italian enclave for most of the century, and if someone took me blindfolded into the neighborhood and then took the blindfold off, I'd know where I was. In recent years, some of the streets were changing to reflect the new wave of settlers, mostly Latinos. Some of the shops that had sold sausage and mozzarella and pasta now sported signs advertising tacos, beans, rice, and plantains.

Many of the houses were brick, stone, or masonry, with matching fence posts and wrought-iron gates and fences. In every block Virgin Marys in stone occupied places of honor in the landscaping, and most of the front windows had several coverings: glass curtains over scalloped shades and over it all satin drapes and swags.

Decorative iron benches were on some of the front porches, a sure sign of spring. In a month, the gardens would start sprouting their mixture of flowers and vegetables. A trellis of beans with giant cannas next to it, or Roma tomatoes surrounded by marigolds.

I was driving down North Avenue, thinking about the way people there seemed to go about their business in a normal way while others who were outsiders invested the area with mystery, menace, and Mafia. I had never met a person from the West Side who claimed to know anything about organized crime, but stories cropped up now and then in the media about West Side men who supposedly had high rankings in the local crime family.

Those thoughts led me to the memory of the voice on the phone the night before, the man who said, "I'm watching you." I hoped that the call was a fluke and I wouldn't hear from him again. *But,* I thought, *I ought to call the phone company and see what I can do about calls like that.*

It crossed my mind that I could call Sergeant Hauser, but only briefly. I was still trying to decide what I could do about my suspicion that he deliberately let Dick die, that he played God and decided Dick didn't deserve to live. I wondered what kind of answers Marsha got when she called the precinct. I hadn't heard from her since she told me she was going to call. Someone else besides me must have had questions, and that someone must have put the bee in Marsha's bonnet.

Maybe, if I got to know Ted Zwiatek, I could talk to him about it. It wouldn't hurt to have a friend on the police force. Ted didn't seem as pushy as Hauser but who knew?

I had mixed emotions about Ted Zwiatek: fascination and fear. I was still relearning the personal side of my life. It made me sweat to imagine myself getting physical with someone. I had been in bed with but one man in my life. And alcohol had put out Dick's fires years before I divorced him. His impotence just stoked his rage. Instead of going to bed, he would pick a fight and hit me.

And there I was, single again and feeling almost like a virgin. But I'm sure that's not the expectation a man would have about me. So I was nervous.

It was almost one o'clock when I got to the Plata house. Children who had gone home for lunch were walking back to the school in the next block. There was a crossing guard at every corner and people were standing out front watching the children pass. I was regarded with suspicion by several of the neighbors as I got out of my car. A curtain moved in the Plata house as I walked up the concrete path, and out of the corner of my eye, I caught movement at the window of the house next door, Myrtle's house, Myrtle's mother, as predicted.

Mrs. Plata answered the door. She had a copious amount of white wavy hair, surely where Sammy got the genes for his. And the chin dimple, too. Her rounded body was draped with a black embroidered chiffon coatdress, and she wore high heels. She ushered me to the kitchen at the back of the house.

As we went by the living room, I saw a man sitting in a chair in front of the TV. Actually, I didn't see a man. I saw a large shirt-covered stomach sticking out between the wings of a chair, and legs, covered in pinstripes, protruding from the seat. I guessed it was Mr. Plata. The rooms were dimly lit except for the kitchen, and when I saw Mrs. Plata clearly, it was obvious that she had been crying. Her hazel eyes were rimmed with pink and her makeup was streaked.

"I'm sorry," I said. "I won't disturb you for long. I am working for the insurance company that has the policy on your son's life."

Mrs. Plata's head nodded up and down a few times.

"I went out to Parkland Heights to see your daughter-in-law this morning."

More nodding.

"I understand you're a teacher," I said, hoping to establish a little more rapport.

"Yes," she said, but she offered nothing more.

I looked around the kitchen and noticed a lot of boxes, bags, and dishes. They were out of place in that tidy house.

Mrs. Plata read my mind. "The neighbors have been sending food all day. The refrigerator is full."

"Good neighbors," I said and couldn't help comparing this homely outpouring with the elegant isolation that Karla lived in.

"Good neighbors, yes."

"Karla doesn't know what she is going to do." I don't know why I said that when I should have been asking her if she knew whether Sammy had any enemies.

"Nobody has to worry about Karla," she said, with a bitterness that twisted her face.

"Why not?"

"She has always been able to look after herself. Nobody could tell her what to do."

I was thinking about what Karla said about people trying to control her, thinking they owned her, telling her not to color her hair.

"You don't like her?"

"She married my son."

That, I thought, was the way a family stayed closely knit. That sense of obligation bound like cement. But Karla apparently didn't feel the same sense of duty. She chafed at the chains.

"Do you know of anybody who would want to kill Sammy?" I said, finally getting the nerve to ask what I came to ask.

"No. Nobody. He was killed by a stranger. Nobody who knew him."

"Any reason for anybody to want to do such a thing?"

"No."

"Did Sammy have any debts that you know of?"

Mrs. Plata's mouth clenched. "Of course not."

The doorbell rang and Mrs. Plata left me in the kitchen. On the table, along with the cakes and covered dishes were a couple of open photo albums. I walked over and looked at the faces smiling up from the black pages. Joe Plata, fifty pounds lighter, in a bathing suit next to his wife, whose hair was already gray, and holding the hand of Sammy, adorable even then. He looked to be about five or six. The writing under the picture said "Joe, Carmelita, and Samuel. Angola Beach."

There were other pictures showing Sammy about that age, at Christmas, Easter, and another in his First Communion white outfit, holding his catechism and standing in front of a backdrop that looked like the hills of Italy.

The other book showed the Platas in color sitting in their living room with Sammy, his hair already going white, and a little girl. Even though the girl still had her baby teeth, there was no mistaking that smile. Myrtle. I remembered Myrtle telling about all the Sunday dinners she'd had with the Platas while she was growing up.

There was a group picture in front of a Christmas tree of Myrtle with the Platas and another woman. Myrtle was sitting on the woman's lap. I presumed she was her mother. I flipped a page and there was more history mounted on black pages with those triangular corner pieces that hold the photos.

Mrs. Plata came back to the kitchen carrying a couple of casserole dishes. She saw me looking at the pictures and sighed.

My back was to the door I came in, and I heard a rustling in the hallway. Mrs. Plata looked past me and a peculiar expression passed over her face. It was part surprise and part disapproval. I didn't turn to look.

"Will Mr. Plata speak to me?" I asked. I was thinking he was standing in the hall listening anyway.

"No. He's too upset. Maybe next week."

By the next week the insurance report would be history. "Have the police come to ask you questions?" I asked.

"Yes. I told them the same thing," she said. She moved toward me and I understood that I was going to be ushered out. Mrs. Plata wasn't the kind of woman one argued with.

"Karla says you are making the funeral arrangements," I said as I got the bum's rush down the hall.

She paused then for a second. "Visiting hours are tomorrow. At Drago's. The funeral will be Saturday. It's private. Just family."

Sammy's mother stood by her front door watching me until I got in my car and drove away. If she hadn't done that, I might have walked around the neighborhood and asked some questions.

It occurred to me that nobody did anything in that neighborhood that was a secret. In my mind, I saw several neighbors at the Plata door as soon as my car had turned the corner and was out of sight.

Ten

I went back to the office and finished writing up what I had so far for Sunset. Then I worked alongside Myrtle until it was time to shut down the phones. She was quiet, for Myrtle, and we were both out of there a few minutes after five, Myrtle to her styling class and I to my house and my dog.

I was hoping to get in a short jog, just to build up my stamina, but the sky was doing one of those western New York cloud massings. We'd had a mild March, but it wasn't unusual to have snow in April if the temperature dropped. The sooner I got home, the better my chances were of getting in a run before the clouds let loose with whatever they were holding. So I tabled a trip to the mall.

I wasted no time doffing my work clothes and pulling on my sweatsuit. The answering machine was blinking, but I decided to wait until I got back to listen to the message. Horace was leaping around with anticipation. He loved to go for a run with me, but he didn't always stay by my side. He took side trips, chasing down rabbits or squirrels.

A large field abutted the end of the street my house was on. Joggers had worn paths through the high grass and had posted signs along the way showing the distances from point to point. There was a half-mile loop and a quarter-mile loop and a one-mile course through the woods at the far end of the field.

I did my warm-ups and felt strong, much better than the last time out. As I jogged toward the field, I was trying to decide whether to go for the mile or just take the half-mile loop and see how I felt.

As I approached the field, a car pulled up and almost stopped. I expected the driver to roll down a window and ask directions, but the car, a sporty silver model, crept along beside me. The windows were tinted so dark I couldn't see the driver. I didn't know one car from another, so I looked for words on the body that would identify it. But there were none. When I got to the field, I turned in and the car sped up and drove away.

I don't know why I didn't get the license number. Considering that an angry husband had been following Polly and me, and that someone told me on the phone that he was watching me, I was stupid not to pay attention. I guess I was doing my ostrich routine.

If that had happened when my ex-husband was still alive, I would have been afraid that he was after me again. I couldn't imagine that there was anybody else out there who was nurturing a burn like Dick Kirk's. But I was unnerved, and it made me think of the gun that Hauser had arranged for me to buy when Dick was making his unannounced visits after he had gotten himself rotten drunk. I promised myself that I would keep up on the target practice.

I started an easy lope around the quarter-mile track, just to see how I was doing. I was surprised at my speed, almost as good as my track-team days in high school, and I was not breathing too hard yet. I could see the road from the track and the silver car was gone. Since I couldn't see the driver, I reasoned, he could have been looking at something on the other side of the street. He might not have even known I was there. And, for that matter, the driver could have been a woman.

I headed for the track through the woods, feeling fast

and strong, and what passes for happy. Happy. I was still investigating what that word could mean. So were the other women in the group: Natasha, Minnie, Diane, all of us. Polly told us we had to give ourselves permission to be happy.

I was halfway around the track, at the farthest point into the woods, when I was reminded again that trouble doesn't wait until you're ready for it.

I saw the silver car through the thicket.

I stopped dead, trying to decide whether to go back the way I came or to continue. Either way was pretty isolated. Horace was not nearby.

The car was there because I was, that seemed clear. But where was the driver? I still couldn't see inside the car. I was looking and listening, but my heaving breath made it hard for me to catch any other sound.

The snap of a twig made me turn.

He was right behind me, lunging, hands out, trying to close the gap of a few steps between us, ready to grab at me. He was big and lanky and the son of a bitch was wearing a mask.

I leaped as if I was shot out of a rocket and stretched my stride full out. I heard the heavy footfalls behind me, and I reached for more speed. I was running and thinking of something I had heard about rabbits outrunning foxes because the fox was running for his dinner and the rabbit was running for his life. I was praying that I wouldn't fall. I could still hear the running steps behind me. I wondered if he had a gun or a bow and arrow.

A bow and arrow is quieter, I thought. He could shoot an arrow and be gone and no one would hear. I wondered when they'd find my body.

Tears that suddenly filled my eyes were blinding me and I was starting to gasp. I asked the heavens: *Where is the edge of the field? Where is the daylight?*

There. The field. I thought I was slowing down. I was numb with exhaustion. I didn't hear the feet anymore. Had he stopped to take aim? I was glad I had been able to outrun him this far. *If I live through this*, I vowed, *I will never let myself get out of shape again.*

I didn't stop until I got to the street, where several runners were warming up. When I looked back, no one was there.

I glanced at my watch and realized that I must have broken my old record for a mile. The rabbit runs for his life.

"Did you see anyone chasing me?" I gasped to the runners.

They looked at me, concerned, wide-eyed. Probably reacting to my face, which must have been telling quite a story.

"A man tried to grab me in the woods. He chased me. His car followed me and then parked in the woods." I blurted it all out.

"We've got to call the cops," one of the runners, a small woman whom I'd seen on my block, said.

"What did he look like?" "What did he do?"

I gasped out the rest of the story and then asked, "Has there been trouble here lately?"

"No. But we don't want any. Are you going to call the cops when you get home?" the woman from my block asked.

"I sure am," I said.

"Good," said another woman. "This field is too nice a place to run not to have it safe."

"Maybe they'll patrol it for a while and chase whoever it is away," the small woman said.

Although the man was gone, my story made them decide to stay out of the woods and run on the paths in the field.

Horace! I remembered suddenly that he hadn't been near me since I went into the woods. I looked around to see what had happened to my dog. I was envisioning the man in the woods hurting Horace because he couldn't catch me. I called, "Horace, come."

I called again. And again. I was about to ask the runners to help me find him. Then I saw him jumping up over the grass to see his way.

Oh, Horace.

I was so glad to see him. After he jumped all I saw was his tail moving closer to me. Then he jumped again. I hugged him and rubbed him all over when he got to me.

When my mind finally clicked back into gear, I knew that I had to do something about what was happening to me. The phone call was no fluke, I was sure now.

When I got home, I called the police. All of the officers had heard of me because of the many times I had called them before and after my divorce. After I told the desk officer what had happened at the running field, he asked me whether I had a new boyfriend. That made me boil.

"That's not fair," I said. "You're blaming the victim, here. The silver car was in the neighborhood just a few minutes ago. Silver with tinted windows. The guy in the woods was wearing a mask, for God's sake."

"OK. Hold on. I'll notify the patrol unit."

The line went dead. I noticed that the answering machine was still blinking. When the officer came back on the line, I went on to tell him that the other runners were upset by what I had told them. I also told him about the phone call and the husband who had been following Polly and me. And I stressed that the Buffalo cops had a unit that was looking for the deserted husband.

"Do you think the incidents are related?" he asked. He had settled down to a more professional approach.

"I don't know what to think." Then I told him that I had a new job that entailed doing some footwork for an insurance company before they paid the claims.

"Have you investigated anybody who would want to bother you?" he asked.

I told him that I had started with the robbery of Sammy Plata at Looks.

Before I could finish telling him about Sammy, he cut in. "Sammy Plata? The guy that was hit downtown?"

"Hit? Do you think it was a hit?"

"Just rumors, Mrs. Kirk."

"I'm not Mrs. Kirk. I'm Ms. Kirk."

"OK. What about Sammy Plata? Did you find out anything about him that would get you in trouble?"

"No. But in case I do, I want you to know that I'm asking questions about his death, now. The company insured his life, too."

The officer laughed. "Sounds like they need some new underwriters."

"It's a small operation," I said, glad that the officer couldn't see my reddening face.

"And they hired you to investigate a murder?"

I could almost hear the sneer in his voice. "Actually they hired my boss, William Lightfoot."

The cop cleared his throat. "I see," he said. The sneer had changed to merriment. "What else do you do for Mr. Lightfoot?"

"Answer phones, do clerical work. Why?"

"Oh, nothing," he said. "Maybe I was thinking of another Lightfoot."

"Could we get back to my problem?" I asked. I thought the cop had an attitude.

"Which is?"

"Which is that I got a nasty phone call and somebody tried to attack me in the woods."

"We can put a trace on your phone if you come to the precinct and do the paperwork. And we'll keep an eye out for that silver car. That's all we can do."

I sighed. I knew the cops meant well. They wanted to protect the citizens, but they couldn't go out and round up everybody in the neighborhood and question them. "Thanks," I said.

"And you be careful. You can get hurt poking around in murders," he said.

"I can?" I said, remembering Billy's assurances that nobody hurts insurance investigators.

I heard papers rustling and then the officer said: "Do you want us to let Sergeant Hauser know? He used to keep tabs on what was going on at your place."

"Yes. He was very helpful. But . . ." I was about to tell him that this wasn't a wife-beating matter any longer.

"He'll call you when he gets back. Meanwhile, keep your doors locked and call us if you see anything unusual."

I wondered if all the cops at the precinct had tapes in their heads that they ran: "Keep your doors locked and . . ." I'd heard the same line so many times.

"Thanks," I said, and hung up.

The blinking light caught my eye again and I played the message. It was Billy, calling to say that Looks was opening up again the next day and Myrtle wouldn't be taking the phone calls. I was to go to the office in the morning. He also said he had picked up a message for me at the office from Ted Zwiatek, who said he would drop by the office the next day.

I got a happy little buzz hearing from Ted. I was able to picture him just then: sandy hair with a lock falling into one deep blue eye, and that sweet baby smile. I felt about thirteen years old. I shook myself and told myself to cut it out.

Concentrate on what you have to do, I thought, trying to stuff my feelings about Ted and about the man in the woods.

I wondered who had made the decision to open Looks the next day. Karla might have told me if I called her, but I thought she'd had enough of me for one day. I looked up the phone number for Gene. I had heard his name but wasn't sure how to spell it. Bartolli sounded right, and I found a Gene Bartolli.

I was uncomfortable about calling him. He hadn't been acting friendly toward me. With customers his chatter was quite animated, so I guessed he wasn't cranky with everyone. I dialed.

"Gene here," a live voice, not a machine, said.

"Hi, Gene. This is Fran from Billy's office."

"What can I do for you?" Definitely chilly. I could almost see his tight lips not moving when he spoke.

"I just heard that Looks is opening up again tomorrow."

"Yes. The cops finally finished."

"I went to see Karla this morning . . ."

He interrupted. "How are things in Yuppie land?"

"Pretty bleak. When I was out there, she told me she had been talking to you about what to do with Looks. Are you going to buy it?"

"I can't afford it."

"So what's happening? Who's going to run it?"

"I am, at least until she comes back."

"She's decided to come back?" Who was lying and why, I wondered.

"That's what she says now. Who knows?"

"I noticed she was a bit moody."

"Moody? Try bitchy."

"You think she'd be hard to work for?"

"Let's say this," Gene said, much more relaxed. "If she comes back, within a month there'll be a whole new staff."

"Ooh! That bad, eh?"

"The woman's a terror. That's why Sammy had her stay home." He chuckled. "I think he married her to get her out of the shop."

"That's a novel reason for nuptials," I said, laughing along with him. "But I'm sure that getting rid of Karla wasn't the only reason for the success of the business."

"I think Sammy learned from his mistakes," Gene said. "I know I learned a lot just watching him. He's done a fantastic business, in the last few years especially. But if the princess takes over, she'll run it into the ground."

Gene was getting almost gabby, so I tried to turn the topic. "Did the cops grill you about Sammy?"

"Grill is the word. And they took our fingerprints. How does a person who lives alone establish an alibi for eleven o'clock at night?"

"I don't know." I didn't tell him about my being in the building the night of the murder.

"They were brutal."

"I wonder," I said, "whether the guy who took a shot at him the night of the robbery came back."

"Different guy. The bullet from the robbery was a forty-five. Sammy was killed with a twenty-two."

"How do you know?" I asked. "Are the cops giving out that information?"

"I have friends," Gene said. I could almost see the satisfied thin-lipped smile.

"Sounds like good friends to have," I said. "About now, I could use some friends like that. Billy has me pounding the streets for the insurance company again."

"Let me know what you need. I can try to find out for you."

"That's real nice of you, Gene. Real nice. I appreciate that. Do you know if the cops have any suspects?"

"We're all suspects. Which means, of course, that they haven't the vaguest idea who done it."

"If you hear anything about who's being questioned or what direction the investigation is going, I'd like to know," I said.

"You've got it, Fran."

Funny, I thought, when I hung up, *he's got friends who know what the cops are doing but the cops still gave him a hard time.*

I had no luck getting Beth or Dan on the phone, but Kathy picked up on the first ring, as if she'd been waiting for a call.

After the usual preliminaries, I asked her what she thought would happen to Looks.

"Either Karla will run it or Gene will run it. It doesn't matter to me. I can get along with either of them."

"You get along with Karla OK?"

"I do, but she gets to Gene. He gets ballistic."

"Why? Have they had fights?"

"Does a wild bear crap in the woods?" Kathy laughed. "They can't take more than five minutes with one another and be on good behavior."

"When was the last time they argued?"

"The last time Karla was in the shop. It's almost a joke. They've never gotten along. When Sammy and Gene started the shop, Sammy had just started going out with Karla, so Sammy hired her and sent her to hairdressing school. I think Gene resented her. You know how it happens when two guys are friends for a long time and a girl comes between them."

"When did you join the crew?"

"Karla introduced me. I met her at hairdressing school. We were both at the top of the class for haircutting. We used to compete."

"What about Gene? Is he married?"

"Not anymore. He and Dan live together."

"But they have different phone numbers and addresses," I said. And Gene had told me that he lived alone.

Kathy laughed. "They live on a corner and the house has numbers on both streets."

"Dan is . . ." I started to say.

"Gene doesn't flaunt it the way Dan does. But I think Gene gets a kick out of Dan throwing it in people's faces."

"Were Gene and Sammy ever a couple?" I said.

"I'd have to doubt that. Sammy, from what I've heard, has always been interested in girls, girls, and more girls. Gene didn't come out until a few years ago. That's when he got a divorce and moved in with Dan."

Kathy didn't seem to know much about the business

end of Looks. During the rest of the conversation, she gave me the impression that she was the type who was very interested in what she did and didn't get too curious about things that were not related to her own pursuits.

I had started a notebook with information about Sammy's murder and decided to bring it up to date. I wrote for about ten minutes before the picture of the man in the woods flashed before my eyes again.

I tried to think about what I saw in that brief instant before I ran. The mask. A black mask that covered his whole face. The rest of his clothing was black, too. I couldn't see a weapon of any kind. No. Both hands were reaching toward me. I shivered and tried to push it all back. I didn't want to think about what he had in mind. What he would have done if he had caught me. I wondered if it was me he was after or just any woman.

A crazy thought overtook me: I would have been glad to hear there was a rapist loose in the neighborhood, because then it might be that I wasn't being singled out. And I already knew I could outrun him.

Eleven

I didn't sleep well. The man in the mask kept chasing me and getting mixed in with other ogres to keep me moaning through the night. In the morning I looked as if I had spent the night on a toot.

I tried to hide the circles under my eyes with makeup. Since I intended to go to Sammy's wake before returning home, I had to dress appropriately. But the dress I'd chosen, a navy blue rayon, made me look as if I should be *in* the coffin instead of walking by it. A taupe and brown herringbone suit with a rust shirt looked a little better.

I called the paper boy, Wally Klune, and made arrangements for him to take care of Horace. Wally was grown up for his years; there always seemed to be a lot going on behind those amber, deep-set eyes.

That morning Looks was buzzing. Every chair was full and clients were hip-to-hip on the benches waiting their turn. Friday was always busy, but since Looks had been closed for two days, there was a lot of work to be done.

Myrtle breezed by, saying, "Sorry I couldn't fill in today."

I headed toward the back to the john where I passed Beth getting a load of towels. "It's even busier than the

115

usual manic Fridays,'' Beth said. ''The ghouls have come to pry.''

A woman with rollers in her hair came out of the bathroom. ''Beth,'' she said in a low voice, ''I heard a rumor that Sammy was executed, you know, mob style.''

''I didn't hear anything like that,'' Beth said. ''I really doubt that.''

The woman walked away unsatisfied. Beth turned to me and said, ''Just because Sammy came from the West Side, they think he was killed and his weenie was cut off and stuck in his mouth.''

I blinked and fought off the impulse to retch. Leaving a corpse like that was a new concept for me. Certainly, no newspaper ever reported such details about mob hits. I didn't want to appear as naive as I was, but I couldn't think of anything to say that would make me sound worldly. I said in a whisper, ''I haven't heard anything like that either.''

She turned to walk away. ''Another client waiting,'' she said. ''This one claims I take ten years off her face.''

''Beth,'' I called after her. ''When you get a minute this afternoon, I'd like to talk to you.''

She stopped. ''Are you still working for the insurance people?''

''Yes. Do you think you'll have a few minutes to talk to me? Anytime you're free will be fine.''

''Maybe in between appointments. Do you want me to come upstairs?''

''Would you mind? I won't keep you long.''

''OK. But I'm not promising. We are busy.''

When I came out of the john, Myrtle called me from the little room at the back where she made the coffee. Myrtle did all the jobs that anybody who was labeled a stylist wouldn't do: She swept, cleaned, shampooed, manicured, pedicured, and did the wax jobs that removed hair from lips and chins and thighs.

She was pouring coffee into cups on a tray when I entered the kitchen.

"Want coffee?" she asked.

"Thanks," I said. "But I can get it myself while you deliver those."

Myrtle grinned with that flashy mouth of hers. She was gone and back before I finished stirring in the coffee whitener.

"I saw you talking to Beth," Myrtle said.

"I couldn't really talk to her. I asked her to come upstairs in between customers."

"I know something you can ask her." Myrtle turned to the shelf where the cups and glasses were stacked. She pointed to two stemmed wine glasses. "These weren't here Tuesday night when I cleaned up."

"Why ask her about those glasses?"

"Maybe she met Sammy here that night. And . . ."

"And drank wine? Here?"

Myrtle made a little *O* shape with her mouth. "They used to meet here. Before."

"But I thought that was all over."

Myrtle shrugged. "Beth never wanted it to be over. That was no secret."

"Are you sure the glasses weren't somewhere else in the shop?"

Myrtle shook her head. Knowing Myrtle's fondness for poking her nose into things, I was inclined to believe her.

"Did you ask the others if they knew anything about the glasses?"

"No. But they don't poke around here much. I get the coffee. I was the first one here this morning and the last one out the night Sammy died, at least officially. The cops have been here since Tuesday."

"Does anyone else have a key?"

"Everybody's got a key."

"Then anybody could have been here drinking on Tuesday before Sammy and the killer were here. And if somebody brought the glasses here, they'd know where to put them when they were done with them.''

"Sammy is the only one who would have left glasses here. Nobody else would buy glasses like that and not take them home.''

"Why?"

"Look at the bottom.''

I got a hanky out of my purse and picked up one of the glasses. It was heavier than I expected it to be. I turned it over and saw the little label that was still stuck to its bottom. It said Waterford Crystal. I smiled at Myrtle. "Of course, it's possible the cops left the glasses here,'' I said.

Myrtle giggled.

"Were they in the cupboard just like that?" I asked.

"Yes.''

"All clean and put away?''

"Yes, why?''

"Do you think whoever was drinking with Sammy would kill him? I mean, would a couple of people drink, wash up, and then one kill the other?''

"All the more reason to ask Beth if she was here. Maybe she left and somebody else came.''

"Did you tell the cops about the glasses?''

"I just found them this morning.''

"Maybe we shouldn't leave them here. They may have fingerprints on them. Maybe we'd better give them to the cops.''

I wrapped the glasses in paper towels and put them in a paper bag, wondering whether the cops would think they were important. They had overlooked them, because they didn't know that they weren't there before Tuesday night.

I would call the precinct and talk to one of the detectives that came to my house that night. O'Connor or Brockway. Big Suit or Mustache. In the meantime, I'd store the glasses in the trunk of my car, where I had a box of rags that would make a safe place for them. It was when I was on the way back from the parking lot that it occurred to me that someone else might miss those glasses, and that someone might own a gun.

As I reentered the back door, I noticed the smudges where the cops had dusted for fingerprints. There was a chalk circle on the top of the door frame. In the middle of the circle was a hole. It was a large hole, bigger than a twenty-two would make, I thought. I wondered if it was the bullet from the night of the robbery.

I tried to remember the night of the robbery. That week and a half was an eon in my life. But too much had happened since. And that night I was trying to finish my first day of work. I didn't think then that every detail could be important.

On my way out, I stopped to talk to Dan, who was standing alone at the desk at the front of the shop.

"I'm still doing work for the insurance company, Dan. If you're not too sick of answering questions, could you tell me what you know about Karla and Sammy? Did they get along?"

Dan gave me one of his charming smiles. "But isn't it obvious? The girl is pregnant. They must have been getting along." He leered at me in a gross way.

"Do you think she'll come back and run the shop after the baby is born?"

Dan put his hand to his head. "Oh God. I hope not."

"Why?"

"Because Gene and Karla will do nothing but fight."

"Were you here after hours on Tuesday?"

"Of course not. I was home. Gene will tell you that."

Actually, Gene had told me that he lived alone. I figured that if I told Dan that, he and Gene would have a fight.

"Do you remember what you did Tuesday night? You and Gene."

"Well," Dan looked coy, "you are a nosy one."

I waited.

"We watched a program about the vanishing rhinoceroses, if you must know. I cooked a wonderful veal dish with spinach and pasta. And some friends came over for a few drinks about nine-thirty.''

"You already told the police this, I suppose. And they asked you for the names of the friends.''

"Aren't you the clever one.''

Dan's routine was getting old.

"Do you know anything about a couple of Waterford wine glasses that were left in the cupboard last Tuesday?''

"Waterford? Here? Next you'll be telling me you believe in fairies.''

I felt like telling Dan to cut it out. "You didn't know about them?''

"No. If I'd known they were there, I would have snitched them.''

One of the women who had been sitting on the bench came over to ask about what she should do with her hair, and that ended the conversation with Dan. Just in time, too. I was either going to throw up or hit him.

Shortly after I got upstairs and was about to turn the phones on, the smiling police officer of my fantasies came walking in the door. I hoped I didn't look too silly smiling back.

"I know you're busy, Fran,'' he said.

"It's time to turn on the phones,'' I said. I smiled again, blinking with anxiety. Billy was there, watching me, and I was batting my eyelids like a cartoon character. The meeting wasn't going the way I wanted it to go at all. "Can I give you my number at home?'' I said in desperation.

"Yes. Great. I'd like that. I'll call you.'' Ted Zwiatek sounded as nervous as I felt. I was relieved, sort of, that he wasn't suave.

"Good,'' I said and wrote my number for him.

He looked at the piece of paper and smiled before he

put it in his chest pocket. "I'll call you," he said again and patted the pocket.

As he left, I caught Billy's eye and must have turned a bright shade of pink. But Billy just said, "Seems like a nice guy."

"He does," I said.

I threw myself back into the other work that William Lightfoot had hired me to do. I had all but forgotten about Beth by the time she showed up.

"You want to talk to me now?" she said.

I turned off the phones and asked her whether she'd been at Looks after work on Tuesday. Billy moved a little farther away, turned his back to us, and tried to look as if he wasn't listening.

Beth looked at Billy and apparently was satisfied that he wasn't paying attention to her. "No. I haven't stayed late for a long time." Beth pursed her lips and got a wistful expression on her face.

"Do you know anything about a couple of crystal wine glasses that were left in the cabinet in the kitchen?"

"Crystal?"

"Waterford."

"I can guess who left them."

"Who?"

"Sammy. It's something he would do. The bastard. I bet he was here with somebody."

"Would he do that? I mean, with his wife pregnant?"

"She's no angel either."

"What do you mean?"

"Just that."

"Do you know for a fact that she went out with someone else?"

"No. But she must have. Wouldn't you? If your husband was like Sammy?"

I wasn't sure how reliable Beth's statements were, and Billy was definitely having a hard time maintaining his aloofness. I thanked Beth and told her to tell me if she thought of anything else I'd want to know.

No sooner had Beth left than my employer got his usual late afternoon call and went into the corner and slavered over the phone. Suddenly I realized that something was different about Billy. Not his clothes, he was back to his usual costume: bow tie, dressy shirt, jeans, and boots. But his hair. The pony tail was gone. He had a normal haircut, except for one long lock that curled over his shoulder. I almost asked him who cut his hair, but I couldn't do it. There was that off-putting quality about him that kept me from saying anything about the way he looked.

It occurred to me that it was Friday night, when the bars would be full of hopefuls and when steadies would go out and make out. The only plans I had made for the evening so far were to go to a wake and make phone calls about a murder.

I was thinking about how to put some fun in my life. There would be the picnic at the Ridge with the group the next day, but that wasn't the kind of fun I was thinking about now. The fun I was thinking about had to do with a smiling policeman.

As Billy made preparations for his exit, I asked him if he knew anybody who would want to kill Sammy.

"In the old days," Billy smiled, "there were plenty of people who might have wanted to snuff him."

"What was he like in the old days? Who would have wanted to kill him then?"

Billy took a step back from the door toward my desk. "He was wild. He had girls calling him, bookies calling him. He got into fistfights at bars. You name it, Sammy did it. Drugs, too."

"But no more?"

"No. He got interested in money." Billy was heading for the door again.

"One more question." I said, smiling.

"Shoot."

"When do you make the dates that people call for?"

Billy laughed. "I don't."

"What happens to them?"

"I take the sheets to the girls. They make the dates."

"What girls?"

Billy laughed again. "The ones that live in my house."

I wasn't sure I wanted to know any more, but I had started this. "You live with girls?"

"Women," he said, clearing his throat. "Actually, they're women."

I was getting a funny picture of Billy living in a brothel. "What kind of a house do you live in?" I ventured.

"Nothing like that. A regular house. The women go out with men. The men don't come to the house."

So it's not a brothel, the women go out, I thought. I was uncomfortable suddenly, and I let myself name one of my workaday activities: I had been pimping by phone. I don't know why it hadn't bothered me before this. The fact that I finally was bothered probably had something to do with the way the Cheektowaga cop had acted when I mentioned William Lightfoot.

Had I actually thought that I was just signing up dates? Billy was looking at me inquisitively, looking more like a cat than ever. I thought he was reading my mind.

"So?" he said. "Do you have a problem with this?"

"Maybe." I did, but I wasn't ready to quit.

"I thought you were working out pretty well," he said. "I am going to get someone else for the mornings. And I'm going to use those sheets you made out for Minnie to train the new girl, or person."

My face was hot. This was the longest conversation I'd had with Billy. Until then I had thought he was sort of mysterious. I wished he had stayed a mystery. I hoped I wouldn't start crying.

"Finish up and come home with me," he said. "You can meet the women."

Twelve

I followed Billy's car and kept an eye on the rear view mirror; it was getting to be automatic for me to be watchful. I felt like a deer in hunting season.

Billy led me to the arty section just north of downtown Buffalo, where galleries, craft shops, and antique stores were interspersed with gourmet delis, ethnic restaurants, and boutiques. On the side streets were the big old houses where the nouveau riche had put down their roots in the second half of the 1800s and the early 1900s.

Billy took the last available space in a driveway next to one of the older houses on Ashland Avenue, a Victorian complete with gingerbread. The paint job was recent. Spindles, railings, curlicues, and moldings were a bright blue, and the exterior walls wore a coat of gray.

I found a place to park about half a block away. Billy waited for me on the front walk. "Nice place," I said. "You live here with the women?"

"Yup," he said, sort of smugly, I thought.

I saw a face at a window that opened onto the front porch, a pretty face with a halo of red hair. The redhead met us at the door and gave Billy a hug and a quick kiss. She held out her hand into which Billy placed the dating slips that I had worked on.

"This is Fran," Billy said to the redhead.

125

"Hi, Fran, I'm Valerie." Then she called out, "Hey gang, Billy's got company. It's Fran."

Women converged on us from all sides, down the stairs, from every doorway. Easily fifteen of them. All pretty, and most of them younger than I. They all greeted Billy with hugs and kisses and me with smiles. It was like a sorority house. Some of the women were wearing rollers in their hair. One was holding out her fingers as if she'd just polished her nails. Several were wearing robes. They all seemed to have heard of me. I'd never been so famous.

Billy introduced me to the women, one by one, and told me where each one was from. Most of them were from the towns around Buffalo, like Hamburg, Lackawanna, Amherst, Williamsville. A couple of them had been brought up right in the city, including one from the West Side who looked a little older than the others. I couldn't keep that many names straight.

Valerie was looking through the sheets of paper and some of the women peered over her shoulders. "Here's a new one. That's for you, Lina. The rest are regulars." She handed out the sheets to the women standing around waiting. Then she said to Billy, "Dot and Jill are the only ones not busy tonight."

"Send out," Billy said. "Neither of them can cook."

A woman with rollers said, "Neither can you, Billy. You could have hung wallpaper with that spaghetti you made last week."

"You said you liked the stew I made," a small woman said defensively.

"I didn't say I liked it. I said it was edible."

"It's the same thing," she protested.

"Dogs eat shit," another woman said. "So shit is edible."

"Are you saying my stew was . . ."

Billy held up his hands and made a *T* as if he were calling time-out in a game. The women dispersed except for two, one of them the creator of the edible stew. She was Jill. The other one, Dot, had made the remark about Billy's spaghetti.

"What would you like for supper?" Dot asked me.

"I have to go to a wake," I said. "I wasn't expecting to eat here."

"Sammy's wake is the social event of the season," she said. She looked as if she were going to go on, but Billy frowned.

It was obvious that Billy gave the orders around the house.

"We'll let you go as soon as we eat," Jill said. "We won't make you do the dishes."

We sat at a long table in the huge kitchen at the back of the house, eating pizza and antipasto off paper plates. Billy got a phone call that kept him several minutes. I was wondering where his lady love was.

"Billy's real upset about Sammy," Dot said in a whisper after Billy went to the phone.

Jill shook her head. "In all the time I've lived here, I've never seen him like this."

We heard a noise and thought Billy was returning. They looked guilty.

"How long have you been living here?" I asked Jill.

"About a year. Since I started working on my master's."

"Master's?" I said.

"Yeah. In anthropology."

"What about you?" I said to Dot.

"English."

"English?"

"My master's will be in English."

"What is this, a graduate-school dorm?"

They laughed. "Almost," Dot said.

"Five of us are doing graduate work," Jill said.

Billy came back to the table and gave me a sly glance.

I had to admit that the women weren't exactly what I had expected. They seemed almost wholesome.

When Billy went to the phone again, I asked: "How many dates do you go on in a week?" The word "date" stuck in my throat, though.

Jill laughed. "Why? Isn't Billy paying you enough?"

I think I blushed. "No. I was just wondering. I get a lot of requests," I said. "Enough to keep you all pretty busy."

"We have substitutes, too," Dot said. "Valerie takes care of the sub list."

I wanted to ask them outright whether they were hookers.

"You could be on the sub list," Jill said.

I thought of this as an opening. "What kind of dates do these guys want?" I blurted out.

"They make it quite clear when you call them back." Jill laughed, a belly laugh.

"Some of them are kind of shy. But you get so you know," Dot said.

I got the picture.

"So. Do we put you on the list?" Jill asked. She was sure that I wanted to join their ranks.

"I couldn't . . ."

"They don't all want to go to bed," Dot said. She had apparently figured me out the way she figured out the shy ones on the phone.

"Oh!" I said, too obviously.

"No. Some of them want to do it in the car," Jill said, and rocked with laughter.

"Stop," Dot said to Jill. And then to me, "Really. We get a lot of requests for dinner dates. Like someone in town for a meeting who wants someone attractive and young on his arm."

I smiled. Billy walked in, having heard the tail end of the conversation again.

"Sure," he said. "You could send Fran out on one of the dinners. The next time you get one of the corporate calls."

"I don't know," I said. But what harm would a dinner be, I thought; it might even be fun.

"I'll tell Valerie. She'll call you," Dot said.

I shrugged, but I felt giddy, adventurous, and not a little bit silly.

They had ordered a lot of food, but we were doing it justice. Dot and Jill tucked away the pizza with pepperoni by themselves. I was working on the one with the anchovies with Billy. Billy ate his fill of pizza and then licked his fingers, adding to the cat image I had of him. I half expected him to keep on licking up his arm and then wet one finger and pull it over his ear.

While we ate, some of the women who had dates stopped in the kitchen before they left. Some had questions about what they were wearing. Do you think this is too tight? What about the color of this scarf? And each one tacked a slip of paper on a big bulletin board that hung on the back wall.

When Dot saw me staring at the bulletin board, she told me that the women left notes saying where they'd be and what time they expected to return home.

"That's a good idea," I said.

Billy and Jill and Dot exchanged looks and smiles, as if to say, "Isn't she a piece of work?"

I had belabored the obvious.

When I got up to leave it was almost seven-thirty. Dot and Jill told me to come back again on a weekend during the day when most everyone would be home.

"Come for a Sunday dinner," Billy said. "It's a big production."

"I will, soon, thanks," I said. The weekend ahead of me was already pretty well spoken for, though. I'd have to do my laundry and clean the house on Sunday and tomorrow was the picnic.

"Are you going to Sammy's wake?" I asked Billy.

"No," he said. "I'm going to the funeral tomorrow."

"Oh, Mrs. Plata told me it was going to be a private funeral."

"It is, I guess. I was, uh, invited."

"Who . . ."

"Sammy's father."

I almost spoke up and asked him how come he was invited to a funeral that was supposed to be just for family. *But*, I thought, *maybe I'm defining family all wrong*.

Thirteen

It started raining as I drove away from Billy's place. The dark and rain and my lousy windshield wipers had me straining to see the road. I was leaning forward with my face close to the glass.

There wasn't much traffic. Maybe that's why I noticed the car that was driving practically on my rear bumper. I sped up and then slowed down, but the car stayed behind me. The list of people that I imagined it could be was short. The guy in the woods, or the one who called and said he was watching me, or the husband of the woman from the group, or the killer. It was unlikely they were all the same person. Unless. Then my mind did one of those paranoid tricks. I asked myself whether Sammy was killed by mistake, whether the killer was after me that night. That thought almost paralyzed me, until I told myself how ridiculous the idea was.

Who would be following me? My ex was dead. He was the kind of person who would try to terrorize me like that.

How do I get away from this guy? I thought. I didn't know if my car had enough pickup to lose him, and besides, I didn't like the idea of speeding around in the rain and not being able to see. Trees and telephone poles are just as lethal as guns.

Would he pull up next to me and shoot me? Would

he take a potshot at me from behind? Even peering hard through the rearview mirror and turning around and looking back when I stopped at a traffic light, I couldn't make out the face of the driver. I turned onto Elmwood Avenue, where there were more lights and more people, but I still couldn't make out the face in the car. The car looked old, but not rusty like most of the cars in western New York get after a few winters of road salt. And I couldn't be sure what color it was in the rain. Dark, maybe maroon, or blue.

I was getting disoriented. Where was the precinct? My mind wasn't cooperating. But I got lucky. As I passed a small plaza I saw a police cruiser and jammed on my brakes and made a left in front of a pickup truck. The guy following me jammed on his brakes, and so did the driver of the pickup. I pulled into the plaza and drove right up next to the patrol car.

The officers didn't notice me; they were listening to their two-way radio. When I got out, the car was gone, but the pickup truck driver was behind me screaming rotten things at me.

I ducked into a big cut-rate drugstore and ran down one of the aisles. I picked up a bottle of baby aspirin and paid for it. On my way out, as per Polly's instructions, I called the precinct where they were keeping track of the deserted husband and told them about being followed. The cop on the other end of the line lost interest when I said the car was gone and I hadn't gotten the license number.

"As long as you're all right now. That's good," he said.

"Yeah," I said, and hung up and walked out into the lot.

The pickup driver was still hollering, and the cops were listening to him. He came over to me in a menacing sort of way, and I held up the bottle of aspirin and said, "Sorry. Sick baby."

His face melted. "That's OK, lady. Next time,

though, give a guy a little warning. Your baby doesn't need her old lady to be dead.''

The cops had already decided that they weren't needed and went back to doing the things cops do in between the times when they *are* needed.

"Take care of that kid, now," the pickup driver said.

"Yeah," I said. "Sorry I drove like a maniac." Meanwhile, I was searching for the car that followed me. After I pulled out of the plaza, I kept my eye on the rearview mirror, but whoever it was was gone, and I headed to the funeral parlor, gulping air all the way to try and tamp down the adrenaline rush. If I had run a mile just then, my time might have put me in the Olympics.

Drago's Funeral Home was on the West Side, a few blocks from the Plata house. Once I got used to the idea that nobody was following me any longer, I relaxed. I wondered who would be at the wake. I also was kicking around the idea of Billy being asked to Sammy's funeral. Obviously, Joe Plata thought Billy was close enough to Sammy to be invited to a family funeral. I hadn't noticed that Billy was so upset, yet both Dot and Jill thought he was acting like someone in deep grief. Every time I found out something about Billy, it seemed there were more puzzles instead of solutions.

When I arrived at the funeral parlor, it was almost eight o'clock and there was a crowd spilling out onto the sidewalk in front. People were hurrying away in the rain, waving good-byes. *Damn*, I said to myself, *am I too late?* I thought the visiting hours were from seven to nine.

I pulled my car into a spot that had just opened up and trotted through the raindrops. As I entered the carpeted foyer, I could see a few people still putting their coats on. I didn't recognize anyone. The official greeter, a portly black-clad septuagenarian with a nameplate on his lapel that said, Domenick Drago, asked me if I had come to see Mr. Plata.

"Yes," I said. "I'm sorry. I seem to be late. I thought you were open until nine."

"Ah, no, Miss. We close at eight. But please, you may go in for a few minutes and pay your respects. If you need anything, I will be in my office just over there. There are conveniences downstairs." His smile was an oily obsequious expression, but the glint in his dark gray eyes was cold steel.

He sort of herded me toward the coatrack. I had intended to keep my coat on and hurry in and hurry out, but I was getting the feeling that that was not de rigueur, and that no social lapses would be tolerated.

The smell of flowers was overpowering, just like every funeral home I'd ever been in. It made me remember that less than two weeks ago my ex-husband was lying in a bier on the south side of town. I hadn't gone to see him, but I still saw him in my nightmares.

Sammy was laid out in a black pinstripe suit and white-on-white shirt and gray tie. His hair, always a bright white halo around a tan face, looked even more like a halo in the cool light of the room. His hands were across his chest and on his left hand was a wedding ring. Entwined in his fingers was a Rosary. A large heart made of red roses lay across the bottom of the casket. It said "Husband." Between the coffin and the wall was another heart. This one, easily seven feet high and just as wide, was inscribed with the words "Beloved Son."

The walls were densely lined with flowers. I tried to find the ones from Looks, to which I had contributed, but it was a hopeless search in a forest of huge floral pieces.

I stood by the coffin for a respectful few minutes and then went to sign the guest book, which had been squeezed into a corner by the surge of blooms. Before I signed, I scanned the names, finding all the folks from Looks in one section. They must have visited together, I thought. Myrtle and her folks had been there as well as every Italian politician in the city and some that weren't Italian. Sammy had dimensions I would never plumb.

As I was signing the book, another visitor walked in the door. Since she had her coat on, I doubted that Mr. Drago had seen her. The visitor wore a very long, dark gray cashmere coat over a black wool dress. She was about five two and slim with a crown of curly jet-black hair. Her face, though neatly made up, was scarred with grief.

She had the habit of tossing her head, which at first glance seemed to be designed to get the hair out of her eyes, but she did it even when the hair wasn't hanging in her face. She hadn't noticed me standing in the back, so I stood still and watched, ready to cast my eyes downward should she look my way.

She stood next to the casket, looking down at Sammy and occasionally tossing her head, for several minutes before I realized that tears were falling from her eyes onto her coat and the floor. I almost started to cry myself when she reached over, touched Sammy's hand, and bent to kiss him lightly on the lips.

Probably I made a sound when I swallowed the tears, because she looked up then, and turned and ran out of the room.

I followed, but she was out the door before I could grab my coat. Outside it was raining harder than before. I looked into the night to see if I could catch sight of a receding figure, but she was gone.

I ran to my car, stepping in every puddle along the way. My head and feet were soaked. I drove around the block and through the streets near the funeral parlor, hoping to find the woman who came to say good-bye to Sammy. I didn't know what to say to her, but I had the feeling that she was important in Sammy's life, if not his death. I gave up after fifteen minutes. Whoever she was, she wasn't hanging around the streets.

As I passed the funeral parlor for about the third time, a car drove up behind me, very close. *Not again*, I prayed. It was too late and too dark and rainy to get any help. The car practically rode my bumper for half a block before its horn blew. As I strained to see the driver, the overhead in the car went on and there was Myrtle, smiling and waving.

I pulled over and she pulled in behind me, got out of her car, ran through the rain, and jumped into my car.

"I thought that was you. What are you doing hanging around here?"

I told Myrtle about the woman in the funeral parlor and how fast she disappeared.

"Did you get a good look at her?"

"Yes, she looked like someone I've seen before. But I don't remember where."

"How old was she?"

"Thirty-five, maybe."

"Another one of Sammy's old girlfriends, I bet." She laughed, too hard.

"Sounds like there's an army of those."

"Legions, Fran. Legions." She giggled.

I wondered whether she had been hitting her father's wine cellar. I also wondered if Myrtle, herself, ever had a crush on Sammy. Since she seemed to be fascinated by Billy, and since she lived right next door to the West Side Lothario, it wouldn't be far-fetched. "How many of his old girlfriends do you know about?"

"Oh, lots," Myrtle said, "but I'm sure that there are lots I don't know about. After all, I'm only twenty, and he's been at this since before I was born." She waved her arms around while she talked, and she kept on laughing, as if she were a little high.

"How old was Sammy?"

"Thirty-nine."

"Was he ever married before?"

"Of course not. He was having too much fun to get married. And his father could fix anything for him."

"You mean pay for abortions?"

"Among other things. Uncle Joe has a lot of connections."

"What about the rumor that Sammy was hit?"

Myrtle hummed. It sounded like the theme from "Jaws." Then she said, "That would start a lot of trouble. There'd be cars parked all over with bodies in the trunks."

If Myrtle had any more information, she wasn't going to give it to me. She was too flip and jolly.

"Where have you been this evening? Having a good time?" I asked.

She got a smug look and nodded. "You betcha, Frannie-wannie."

She was getting out of my car when I said, "Be careful driving."

"Don't worry. I've been careful all evening, and I'm not far from home."

As she drove away, I wondered what she'd been up to. Surely she'd been drinking—or worse. She'd never mentioned a boyfriend or what her social life was like. She had to be doing more with her time besides washing heads at Looks and going to hairstyling classes. I realized that although she had talked to me for hours, there was much about her I didn't know.

As I drove toward home, I remembered that I had to get gas so I wouldn't have to do it in the morning when I had to pick up Natasha. In order to save ten cents a gallon, I went about a mile out of my way to get filled up at a cut-rate self-service gas station near the airport. I was already wet so a little more rain wouldn't hurt.

While I was pumping my gas, I noticed a car parked in the lot by the diner next to the gas station.

A silver car.

I was sure it was the same silver car that followed me into the woods. The design was so distinct, and the windows were tinted.

When the pump stopped, I paid up and then took a

route in the shadows to a spot where I could see the silver car's license plate: 183 UVE. Inside the diner at the tables lined up along the windows, people were eating, smiling, talking, but there was no one I recognized.

Should I wait and see who comes out and gets in the car? I thought, but immediately nixed that idea. Horace had only had Wally Klune for company all day. And I wasn't up for a stakeout. I called the police station and Hauser answered.

"This is Fran Kirk."

"Yes, Fran. I've been trying to call you."

"I just want to tell you that the car that followed me into the woods yesterday is parked outside of the diner on Transit Road. The license number is 183 UVE."

"Are you sure it's the same car?"

"Yes. I don't know what kind of car it is, but it's the same shape, it's got tinted windows, and it's silver."

"Good work. We'll check it out. Hang on a second will you?"

While I was on hold, I pointed out the car to the gas station attendant and asked him if he knew what kind it was. He went out and walked around the car. I hoped the owner wouldn't come out and see him or me. I tried to blend in with the boxes of auto parts on the shelf. The attendant came back just as Hauser came back on the line.

"Are you all right, Fran? Where are you?"

"At the gas station next to the diner. I'm leaving now and going home."

"I'll wait for you at your house and make sure everything is OK."

"You don't have to do that. Whoever it is doesn't know I'm here."

"Just to be sure."

He hung up, and I got the uncomfortable feeling again that I had been getting about Hauser. I didn't want to hurt his feelings, but I didn't want him, either.

The attendant was waiting. "That car," he said, "is a classic. A 1957 Chevy. It's in beautiful shape."

"I guess there aren't too many of those around," I said.

He laughed. "Especially in silver."

I drove home and told the Hauser, who was waiting in a patrol car at my front door, what kind of car it was and asked him if he had checked the license number.

"The computer was down, Fran. I'll try again tomorrow."

"What were you trying to call me for?" I asked.

"About your call to the station. About your phone call and the man who ran after you in the woods."

"The officer who took my call took care of it. Or as much as he could do." I definitely wasn't going to tell him about the car that had followed me that evening.

"You know I'll go the extra mile for you, Fran."

He gave me a look that was straight out of an old Humphrey Bogart movie. I wanted to laugh. He was turning it on. He gave me the creeps.

"Thanks for your good thoughts," I said, stiffly and, I hoped, coldly. There was no point in being nice. It let him think that there was a chance.

Before he would leave, he looked around my yard and waited outside while I checked the inside of the house. When I told him several times that everything was fine, he left, and I breathed easier.

After I peeled off my wet stockings and wrapped my head in a towel, I checked my messages; there were a lot of them.

"Hi, Fran, Bret Hauser here. It's about noon."

"Hi. This is Ted. Call me. My number is 546-7884."

I halted the tape and played it over again to get the number right. Then I dialed his number and got his machine.

"Hi," I said to his machine, "I just got home. It's about nine o'clock. It was nice to hear from you." I smiled. Then I listened to the rest of the messages.

"This is Natasha, don't forget to pick me up in the morning for the picnic."

"This is Bret Hauser again. Call me later when you get home from work."

Funny, I thought, he gave me the impression that he'd been calling me this evening.

"Hi, Fran. I just called to chat." It was my ex mother-in-law. "I've called the precinct about what happened to Dick. I think I'm getting somewhere."

What did she mean? I thought.

"Hi. It's Ted again. I was hoping to get you before supper. Thought we could go eat together. I'll call you tomorrow."

"Damn," I said.

The next call was an open line for a few seconds. Then I heard a sound like someone breathing. A lump seemed to form in my chest, and my scalp tingled.

"Damn bastard," I said.

The breathing grew more rapid, louder, raspier. Then the line went dead.

"Stupid jerk," I said. I was angry and frightened. I felt besieged. I got the thirty-eight down from the box in the closet, where I had put it after Dick died. Hauser was right about one thing. The gun was some comfort.

I had planned to talk to Gene again, but it was too late by the time I fed Horace and got my clothes and the food ready for the picnic.

A glass of white wine in hand and Horace at my feet, I hit the remote button and turned on the TV. It had been days since I'd done my couch-potato routine. After the news, the local station gave the weather forecast and I cringed. Cold and possibly snow forecast for the next morning. Nice weather for a picnic! I got up and pulled out warmer clothes.

When I went to bed after the news, I took my notes on Sammy's death. I made a note to myself to do something about the crystal glasses that Myrtle had found in Looks. Ted, I thought, I'll turn them over to Ted. I added to my notes what I had heard from Billy and a description of the woman at the funeral parlor. Something was troubling me about the woman in the funeral parlor, and I went to sleep with her on my mind. She and the corpses of Sammy and Dick danced through my dreams.

Fourteen

Horace was licking my face and whining. I tried to open my eyes, but they were glued shut. There was a crust along my eyelids. Once before, when I was about thirteen, my eyelids had stuck together. That time, I had rubbed off all my eyelashes in my frantic attempt to open my eyes.

I got out of bed and groped my way to the bathroom, grabbed a towel, wet one end of it, and started dabbing. When I finally could pull the lids apart, I saw they were swollen and greenish clumps were matted in my eyelashes.

Horace was standing next to me, still whining. He had to go. When I opened the door to let him out, the whiteness of the landscape hit me like a bolt. One of western New York's April snows.

At eight o'clock Polly called. She thought we should cancel, but I had a suggestion.

"You want us to come to your place?" Polly said. "Are you sure? I mean, with Diane's kids?"

"There'll be enough grown-ups to keep the kids safe. And they can play outside if Diane dresses them warmly. Horace loves kids."

"I'll call them and see who's up for driving in the snow."

"The roads are probably slushy," I said. "I'll bet the snow will be gone before noon."

I straightened up, dusted the floors, made the bed, and cleaned the bathroom before Polly called back. One of the women at the shelter would drop off Natasha, she said, and the rest would descend on me at ten. I went around the house, picking up anything fragile and, in general, kid-proofing the place. A couple of the women had less than savory records, so I put the few valuable things that I had in the extra closet in my bedroom, the one with the lock. I locked up the gun, too.

Before ten, my eyes had resumed their normal shape and were no longer oozing, and I had made enough coffee to sink the *Titanic*.

"It's nice of you to have us," Natasha, the first to arrive, said in her velvet voice. She had an angry red scar on the side of her face and she walked slowly.

"Are you sure you're up for this?" I said.

"I need this meeting," Natasha said, her eyes growing liquid. "I have to do some serious reworking of my priorities."

I shook my head. I thought how close she came to dying.

"Yes," she said, holding her index finger and her thumb about a half-inch apart. "He came that far from killing me."

"I'm glad you're still with us," I said, and hugged her.

She wiped her eyes and said, "I made black-eyed peas."

"No pun intended?" I asked.

She guffawed and began to look like her old self. "Where are we putting the food?" she asked. She stopped by the gate that I had put in the doorway to the kitchen, eyeing Horace, who was on the other side of the gate, wagging his whole back end in greeting.

"Horace doesn't bite. I'll take the gate down."

Natasha stood like a stone as Horace sniffed her.

"Come here, Horace. I'm sorry, Natasha. He really is a gentle dog."

She didn't look convinced. I put Horace in the bedroom, but I knew he would start howling when he heard the crowd. I told Natasha that I would let him out later.

Diane and her kids burst into the house as if someone had opened a sluice gate. The children didn't even bother to take off their boots. They were all over the place before they were introduced. Even Merilee, with her arm in a sling, was keeping pace with her older sister and brother.

"Whoa," I said, somewhat harshly, "you kids get back here and take off the boots."

The kids and Diane were wide-eyed and did as they were told. It ran through my mind that they acted crazy whenever their father wasn't around. Maybe I couldn't blame them.

When the boots were off, I offered the kids some cookies, trying to soften the impression I'd made on them.

Polly and Minnie showed up together. Minnie had a lot of makeup on one eye. Brenda and Amy also drove together. Brenda and her husband often fell off the wagon. And when they drank, they fought, physically. He always won.

Amy was almost a newlywed, and she was eight-months pregnant. Her husband had been hitting her for seven months. Brenda and Amy had both been light-fingered at one time.

Polly said we could start the meeting, that no one else was coming. By then, Horace was out of the bedroom, Natasha had found a place in the corner of the couch where she felt safe from Horace, and the kids and Horace were rolling all over the floor. They were a little rough with the dog, but the dog obviously was in heaven, even after he got whacked once with Merilee's cast.

Minnie told us that she wanted to get a job and leave

Edgar. She told the group about what happened at Billy's, about Edgar calling her and my cutting in on the call and telling her not to take personal calls. But the way she told it it sounded as if she were dumping on me, not Edgar.

I thought of myself as someone who was getting better, who was more able to stand up for my rights, who was feeling more empowered. But sometimes, when I did something like telling Edgar to get off the phone or telling Diane's kids to take their boots off, I felt that the women resented me. Since they were what passed for family for me, I was hurt.

Polly spoke up gently and told Minnie that Edgar shouldn't have called her at work, that he was exercising control by doing that. "Maybe it was better for Fran to tell you about personal calls than to have the boss do it," Polly said.

Minnie looked at me and said, "Maybe you're right. At first, I was glad she did it. It made Edgar hang up. But then, when I got home . . ."

Polly launched one of her "significant" questions: "How many of you have gotten your opinions turned around a hundred and eighty degrees after you got beat up?"

That got everybody started. Amy said she started snubbing her mother after her mother tried to intervene.

"And you need your mother now," Diane said, sympathetically.

"But I've been so rotten to her." Amy was crying.

"She's still your mother," Polly said. "Call her."

"Tell her you're sorry," Minnie said.

"She'll be glad you called," Brenda said. "When I had a fight with my mom, she was real glad I called her."

My mind flashed back to a time my mother tried to say something to me about Dick. I knew what was coming and kept steering the conversation to other things. I even blamed her for not seeing what was happening.

How stupid I was. *Am I any smarter now?* I asked myself.

What happened to Natasha was grist for Polly on the ways we have to defend ourselves. Her message was that we should use weapons that we know we can handle and have a chance of winning with, like going to Family Court, calling the cops, leaving the house, telling people what is happening.

"Yeah," Brenda said. "Don't try karate when he's got a black belt." We knew Brenda was talking about her own situation. She had told us before how her husband had goaded her into slapping him, and then he'd hauled of and punched her and told her later that he had a right to defend himself.

The group broke for lunch at noon. The snow was almost gone and the sun was out. The kids ate and went out in the backyard with Horace. The food was good, and there was plenty of it. Plenty of smiles, too. We had found a new closeness, and we all knew it.

I was standing in the kitchen when Natasha came in from the living room. "Do you know there's a red car driving back and forth out front?" she said. "Do you know anybody with a red car?"

I followed her back to the living room and looked out the window. A few seconds later a red car cruised slowly by. The man driving had a beard and sunglasses. When I opened the front door, the car sped off.

"What was that all about?" Polly said.

"A car going back and forth, watching the house. He just drove off. Should I report it to the precinct that is watching out for that husband?"

"Oh, him." Polly said. "They've got him. I'm sorry. I meant to tell you all as soon as I arrived."

Brenda, who had heard, shouted, "Hear that, guys? The cops got the husband who was following Polly and Fran."

At that Polly gave us the rundown on the Eatons, Harold and Christine. Christine had left town with her two kids. She hadn't taken anything with her except a few items of clothing for herself and her children. Harold, thinking she had gone to a shelter, had followed Polly and then me, hoping we would lead him to her.

"When did they get him?" I asked Polly.

"I don't know. The detectives from the task force that deals with battered women called me yesterday."

"Damn." I was glad he had been caught, but that left me with somebody else following me, somebody who might have something worse in mind than locating his missing wife.

Polly and the others looked at me, waiting for an explanation.

"That means the guy last night wasn't Harold Eaton."

I told them all about the car following me before I went to Sammy's wake.

Polly said, "If you couldn't see the driver, why do you assume it was a man?"

Everyone had something to say about that.

Then I launched into the story of the man in the woods who followed me in the silver car. I ended up with an account of the weird phone calls I'd been getting.

The women listened like kids hearing Red Riding Hood for the first time. When they asked me who I thought might be doing these things, I ran down my list of possibilities.

"Do you think," Natasha said, "that the man in the car could be a friend of your ex? I worry that one of Carlyle's buddies might come after me because I had him put in jail."

"I hadn't thought of that," I said, "but by the time Dick died, he'd broken with most of his friends."

"What about his mother?" Minnie said.

"The guy in the woods was much bigger than Marsha,'' I said, laughing nervously. "I don't get the feeling from her that she would have me followed or hurt, though.''

"I think it's someone you know,'' Brenda said.

"Of course, it's someone she knows,'' Amy chimed in. "You have to make a list of all the people you see regularly,'' she said to me. "Then look at the list, hard, and concentrate. One name will pop right out at you if you have the right name on the list.'' Amy was big on extrasensory perception.

Natasha, though, had a more practical solution. She suggested that Brenda, who worked for the phone company, see what she could find out about the calls I was getting. Although Brenda wasn't supposed to do things like that, it was very easy for her to manage, and she had traced a couple of calls once before for a woman who used to come to the group.

"Can you really trace calls?'' Amy said. "Boy, I wish I had known that a month ago.''

"We do work like that in my department for the cops sometimes,'' Brenda said.

Brenda was starting to look like a resource person to me. It crossed my mind that I should leave some nice things out for her to lift and tuck in her purse, but then I scolded myself for being nasty and decided on a more direct tack. "If these calls are related to the cases I'm working on, I may be able to pay you for the information and charge it to the insurance company,'' I said.

"Great,'' she said, looking delighted.

"And this doesn't go any further than these walls,'' Polly said. "We don't go home and blab this to our significant others. It might get someone in trouble.''

"Like me,'' Brenda said.

"You know, Brenda,'' Natasha said, "I might want to use your services some time, too.''

We all looked at Natasha, who was nodding her head and looking defiant, and laughed.

"Bravo, Natasha,'' Polly said.

"Go get him," Minnie said, and started us laughing. It was definitely a case of the worm turning to hear Minnie say that.

Then Minnie wanted to know more about the murder at Looks, and that led the others to ask more questions about it and what I had to do to investigate.

We didn't talk about our beatings. We talked about Sammy's murder. Even Polly didn't steer us back to our own problems.

"Beth did it," Amy said. "I feel it."

"No, no. The wife." That was Minnie's opinion.

"Maybe some of us, besides Brenda, can help," Amy said. "What can we do?"

"I don't know," I said. "But when I think of something, I'll be glad to have help."

"Make sure you have our phone numbers next to your phone," Amy said. "Or maybe we should take turns staying with you until all this nasty stuff stops."

Although I appreciated Amy's concern, and knew that what she was feeling came from the goodness of her heart, the solution she came up with, taking turns staying with me, didn't sit right with me.

Polly saved me from turning down Amy's offer.

"It might be a good idea if each of you kept the phone numbers of the others handy so that when you need some support you have someone to call. Especially if you can't get me on the phone. But I think what we can do now to help Fran is clean up the mess we made of her place."

"No, it's all right," I said. "I can clean up tomorrow."

But they all started bundling up the food, washing dishes, cleaning off the cupboards, and sweeping up crumbs.

"I haven't seen any more of that car," Amy said.

"It's funny," I said to Polly. "Whoever it is must want to be noticed. If it is the same person, that is."

"I see what you're getting at," Polly said. "An ancient silver Chevy and a red Corvette."

"Is that what the red car was?" I asked.

"Maybe it's a Chevy dealer," Polly said. "You own a Chevy, don't you?"

"Yes. An old Caprice."

"Do you take it to a Chevy place for servicing?"

"Yes."

"Check out the yard next time you're there. See if the silver and red cars are in the lot."

"We can all keep an eye out for the cars," Amy said.

Meanwhile, Diane was collecting the kids and washing them. They had gotten muddy from rolling around in the melted snow with Horace. She told us she was afraid to take them home dirty.

We all pitched in and cleaned up the kids, who squirmed and giggled at all the attention. The atmosphere was friendly and warm. I was glad I'd invited them.

"The children were really good," I said to Diane, who seemed flustered before she could collect herself.

"See, kids. You can have a good time, and grownups will think it's all right," she said.

We all looked at one another in that heartbreaking way we do when we realize someone has just told another secret. I got the picture of the kids getting whacked around for laughing too loud.

"What a lovely day," Natasha crooned. "I even got to like your dog."

We laughed, and as they left, we hugged one another.

After they were gone, I called Hauser to check on the license-plate number of the silver car.

"I'm having trouble finding that in the computer," he said. "It may be an expired plate or something. Perhaps on Monday when the computer whizzes are in I can have them do some of their magic tricks to see if they can track it down."

I hung up and went through my list of expletives that I reserve for frustration.

Then I threw myself on the couch and closed my eyes. I was more tired than I should have been at four-thirty in the afternoon.

Even good stress makes you tired, I told myself.

Then I wondered if I was getting a cold and if the crusty eyes that morning were the first symptoms. I couldn't seem to get warm, a sure sign that I had a fever.

The next thing I knew, the phone was ringing and it was dark. My eyes were crusty again, and I was able to open them only partway. I didn't know where I was at first, and it was only after I realized which direction the ringing was coming from that I got oriented and woke up to the fact that I was in the living room on the couch.

The answering machine clicked in before I could get to the phone. I heard a deep muffled voice say, "Good evening, Mrs. Kirk. I know they're all gone and you're alone."

I had heard that voice before. He had told me he was watching me. I ran to the phone and picked it up. I yelled into the receiver, "You come here and you're a dead man." I heard a click. Then I collapsed onto the floor, wracked with sobs.

Fifteen

Sunday morning, I woke up with a headache and a runny nose, and I felt as if I'd been tumbling in a clothes dryer all night. I had every blanket in the house on the bed.

The medicine chest was my first stop: aspirin for my headache and the pains in my legs and arms and Tylenol to dry up my nose. I groaned as I padded around in my robe and slippers. Horace stayed near me; he was worried. He didn't look too peppy, either. Diane's kids had worn him out.

I was holding the coffee cup close to my face, steaming my sinuses, and thinking that I had been pushing myself, trying to do well at the job, trying to do what Sunset wanted, trying to become a stronger person, not to mention getting weird phone calls and being chased and followed. No wonder I had a cold. Stress. Too much stress. I probably shouldn't have invited the group over, I thought. But then I remembered how sweet they had been and wondered whether they'd changed or I had.

When the phone rang, I prayed: *Don't let it be that jerk; I can't take it now.*

It wasn't. It was Delia Winston from Sunset Insurance. Who gave her my number at home, I wondered, and why was she calling me on a Sunday?

"Sorry to bother you," she said, "but we have a bit of an emergency and I was hoping you could help us."

"What's up?" I wasn't in the mood for anybody's emergency.

"Your employer, William Lightfoot, has left town and left us, and you, too, probably, in the lurch."

"What?" She had my attention. All I could think was: There goes my job.

She told me that a woman had called her at home and told her that Billy was leaving town for an indefinite period. That was all. No reason, no instructions for anybody. Just good-bye.

"Nobody called me." I was disappointed in Billy and wondering what I would do. Now I didn't even have a former employer to get references from.

"We were hoping that you could continue working on the Sammy Plata case," Delia said.

"I guess I could," I said. "I'm still trying to digest this. Why did he leave? Why did he leave like this?"

"Billy? Who knows about Billy. He's good at what he does, but it's always on his terms." She sounded somewhat bitter. "But what about it? Can you help us out?"

"Yes, I think so. How do we work it out? Do I come to your office?"

"You can work out of your house if you want. We don't have space in the office. To start, I'll pay you a hundred a day, plus expenses."

"Expenses?" That was a new concept. Not one that I would have learned from Billy, probably. I was trying to remember whether Dick had ever charged for his expenses. Then it occurred to me that if he had, he probably wouldn't have told me about it. That would give him more loose change.

"Your phone, your car, hotels, plane fare, stuff like that."

"Oh," I said, thinking that it was big time. *An expense account. Wow. And a hundred a day. To start.*

"OK," I said. "This new arrangement begins when?"

"Right away," she said. "We're not happy with what we've heard so far. The police are working on the theory that it was another robbery. That the same guy came back for more money."

"But I heard that the gun that was fired during the robbery was not the same one that killed Sammy."

"Ah, you know that? Good."

"I won't be able to do much today," I said. "I woke up with a brutal cold. But I can make some phone calls."

"Phone calls count," Delia said. She sounded relieved. "I need somebody I can trust on this. You can work seven days a week on this if you want to. Later on, if you get your license, I'll get you on the hourly schedule. That's when you get the big bucks."

Seven hundred a week, plus expenses, is already pretty big bucks, I thought. "Do you want me to get anything out of the office? The forms, or anything?"

"No. We change the forms all the time, anyway. Just come in tomorrow and we'll fix you up with some ID."

I hung up and laughed like a maniac. My cold seemed to have vanished. I wished my mom was still around so I could tell her my incredible luck. I called Polly instead.

"Aren't you glad I suggested you call about that ad?" she said.

I hated I-told-you-so's, but I was glad she had pushed me. "Yes," I said, "yes, yes, yes."

And then she wanted to know about Billy. I hadn't told her much about him, not even the little bit that I knew. When I got a few minutes into it, she stopped me.

"I remember, now," she said. "He's always on the edge of the law, always thinking of new ways to do things that other people get arrested for."

"Sounds like Billy," I said. Then I told her about the dating service and taking calls from the would-be daters.

"Daters?" her voice was loud. "More like johns."

I protested. I knew what that made me. I told her they had all kinds of dates.

"It may be," Polly said, her voice simmering under the surface, "that sometimes some of the women go on dates during which there is no sexual activity. But the reason Mr. Lightfoot sets up the business that way is so that he isn't arranging for the selling of sex."

"The women are very nice." I didn't like to hear her talking so harshly about them.

"When did you meet them?" she said, her tone still disapproving.

For some reason, I didn't feel like backing down. "I went to the place where they all live."

"The whorehouse?" she bellowed.

"It's not a whorehouse. Men don't come to the house."

"Of course," she said, more subdued. "They wouldn't."

"Five of them are in graduate school," I said. I didn't like the idea of the women I'd met being labeled "No Good."

"What are they studying, animal husbandry?" Polly laughed at her own joke.

I laughed, too. "One is taking her master's in anthropology, I think another one is studying English. Really, Polly, they're very nice."

She finally relented and admitted that the women might "really be nice people, but be careful." And before she hung up she wished me good luck on the job with Sunset.

Some of the glow that I'd felt after talking to Delia was gone, and I was feeling the cold again. But if I was going to earn my hundred, I had to make some phone calls.

I got out the notes I'd made so far, and dug around in the cardboard box in my closet for the few notes I'd taken on the robbery. I laid it all out on the living room floor, hoping that some direction would become clear to me by looking at all the debris. Nothing happened.

I went back to the beginning. The day I arrived at 423 State Street, the day Sammy was robbed and Myrtle and I were upstairs. There was something fishy about that robbery, but what? Did Sammy know the robber? Is that why he was talking to him? Then why the shot? Was that just window dressing? The cops had found the bullet on the exterior wall of the building, as if someone had shot in the air after the action was over. It must have been staged.

And why would Sammy have to stage a robbery? His business was good; everybody said it was good.

Hmm. Most of the people who said that worked for him. Did they know something they didn't say? They did close ranks around Sammy as if they were trying to protect him.

And then there was Beth. When the others closed their ranks, she left a gap. What was she trying to tell me when she mentioned Sammy's gambling? Maybe Sammy was still gambling and owed money. People get shot for not paying their debts. And Beth said she wasn't at Looks the night Sammy was killed, but Myrtle seemed to think that Beth was there that night.

I was just about to dial, when I realized that I had to start keeping a log of what I did and what I spent money on. I rooted around in the boxes and found an old loose-leaf notebook that I'd had when I was a senior in high school. It had "Dick" written across the front, with little hearts and the words "love" sprinkled between the letters. What a jerk I was. It made me angry to look at it, but a tear swelled in my eye.

I threw out the yellowing dusty papers and saved the clean sheets, thinking that was a metaphor for the rest of my life. I smiled as I wrote the date and time and, "Call to Beth Marin re Sammy Plata case." I held it out and admired it as if it were a painting.

Then I slapped myself in the face and said out loud,

"Get real." I had to write down some questions to ask her, get my head working. I couldn't just think how great it was to be an insurance investigator and expect the work to do itself.

By the time I made some coffee, I was out of the clouds. Having a cold helped to dampen the illusions, too.

When Beth answered, I got right down to business and asked her about Sammy's gambling.

"I shouldn't have said that. I don't think he's been gambling much lately."

"Why did you say it, then?"

"It's complicated."

"Could you try to make it simple for me?"

"You know that Sammy and I used to date, right?"

"Yes."

"Well, about two years ago, he stopped seeing me. No explanation. He said I could continue to work at Looks if I wanted to, but that we wouldn't be going out anymore. I kept on at Looks, because I thought we would get back together."

I was wondering what this had to do with Sammy's gambling.

"I couldn't believe he was ditching me. I mean, we were hot together. Really hot." She sounded tearful. "One of the things we'd do is come up with crazy words while we were making it."

Do I want to hear this, I asked myself, *or put this in my report?*

"The next day, Sammy would look for the words in the racing form. You know what crazy names horses have."

"Yeah, I've heard."

"I tell you he won most of the time with those words. Then he would give me part of the winnings. We had such good times." More sniffling.

"So?" I said. "When does this get complicated?"

"Now," she said, as if she had straightened her body

and was getting ready to plunge into a cold lake. "Recently he had been very nice to me."

"How recently?"

"In the last few months. He even asked me to pick a couple of horses for him. But of course, it wasn't the same."

"Of course."

"The horses didn't win. But I had the feeling that he wanted to get back together. So I asked him."

She really started bawling then.

"And what did he say?" I asked when she quieted down.

"He got mad at me. Told me not to be pushy. That was the day he was robbed. After work. I stayed, thinking he and I would . . . but he told me to get out. Later I thought maybe he had lost a lot of money on the horses I gave him and he faked the robbery to pay his gambling debts."

"Do you know who took his bets?"

"He had a bookie on the West Side. One of his cronies from the neighborhood. Once in a while Billy took a bet for him."

"Billy? He was a bookie, too?"

"Billy takes bets, but not the way other people do it. Sammy used to say Billy's system was too indirect and that he never was sure where the money went."

I remembered what Polly said about Billy doing things that other people were put in jail for.

"Do you remember the name of Sammy's bookie?"

"Frank or Fred or something. I'm not sure."

I told Beth then about Billy skipping town and asked her if she had any idea why he would leave.

"I know he was seeing a girl from the West Coast. Maybe he went back with her."

"Do you know her name?"

"Jeannie. She came into the shop once to have her hair done. And what hair! Gorgeous. She was very pretty. Older than she looked, though."

I made a note to ask the women at Billy's house about Jeannie. Then I asked Beth if she had come back to the shop on the night Sammy was killed.

"You sound like the cops," she said. "But I already told you that I didn't. And I told you more than I told the cops. After the night Sammy got mad at me, I tried to get out of the shop early so that I wouldn't be alone with him. He scared me, you know, the day of the robbery, he got so mad."

When I hung up, I filled in the notes. I still didn't know where I was going. I wondered whether Billy's disappearance had anything to do with Sammy's murder.

Cold or no cold, I told myself, *I have to go see the women in Billy's house.*

Sixteen

When I got to Billy's house, the women were in a panic. They talked all at once.

"Fran, we didn't have your number."

"Are we glad to see you."

"What are we going to do?"

"Who's going to take the phone calls?"

By the time they stopped talking, I was getting the distinct impression that I was supposed to take over where Billy left off. They didn't seem so much distressed over Billy's disappearance as the fact that he wasn't there to do the things he had been doing for them.

"Can't you take the calls yourselves?" I asked.

They all looked at Valerie, who said, "It doesn't work. We tried it. Someone is always trying to steal someone else's date, or someone forgets to write down something important. Billy's system was the best. And, frankly, you were the best one he had."

I was flattered, sort of. But the word "pimp" kept popping up in my mind. I didn't think I'd heard the last of Billy, though, so I tried to think of some way to help them.

"One of you will have to take the calls tomorrow," I said. "I have a key to the office. Someone will have to meet me there at eight-thirty so I can show her what to do."

The response was not cooperative.

"Eight-thirty! Are you crazy?"

"I'd be walking in my sleep."

"Not me. I'm not even in REM sleep by then."

"Can't you call in a temporary?"

"We pay enough so that we shouldn't have to make such sacrifices."

"I'm out of here. No way do I open my eyes before ten."

"You'd have to dynamite the bed to get me up."

"That's what I heard one of your customers say."

"Valerie," I said, "can we go somewhere and talk about this?"

That did the trick. They stopped complaining, at least temporarily.

"You'll think of something," Dot said, patting my shoulder as she walked away.

In my talk with Valerie I found out that the women had been running the dating service before Billy hooked up with them (to coin a phrase), but that they had come to depend on the system that Billy worked out because the bills got paid and things got done. The picture that came to me of the house before Billy arrived on the scene was one of chaos.

Valerie also filled me in on the percentages and the fees that Billy worked out. Without too much mental exercise, I saw that Billy made out pretty well. I asked Valerie about the bills at the office and the house, how they got paid and who paid them. She didn't know from bills. "Bills? The bills were Billy's."

I was thinking that maybe Billy earned his percentages. These women seemed to like being treated like children, but I had no intention of taking over as housemother. Or madame.

Then I asked her where she thought Billy was.

"With that slut, Jeannie."

My eyes popped a little at that.

"I don't think she told one ounce of truth. And she

had Billy at heel," she said, adding that Jeannie had told the women she was from the West Coast but was vague about exactly where.

"Do you know anything about Billy taking bets on horses?"

"He used to take bets for the girls."

"Regularly?" More of Billy's far-flung enterprises.

"Yes. Why?"

"I'm trying to figure out who was taking bets for Sammy Plata."

"The guy from Looks? I thought he was born-again and had no more vices."

"What did you know about Sammy?"

"The girls who have been around for a while knew him when he was still a sinner." Valerie laughed. "He used to be a regular at the clubs. He'd hang around the jazz places until dawn."

"Did you ever go out with him?"

"Sure. He was good looking, easy with money, fun to be with."

"So when did he stop the night-owl routine?"

"I heard it was when he got married. A couple of years ago. Isn't his wife pregnant?"

"Yes. Any of the other women know Sammy?"

"Marie's known him and Billy since high school."

"And what about Billy? Does anybody else know anything about Billy?"

"We all talked ourselves blue this morning, trying to figure out where he would go, and nobody knows anything. What a rat."

"When did you discover that his things were missing?"

"This morning. There was a phone call for him and he didn't pick up."

"I'd like to look through his apartment," I said. "Maybe he left something. Some clue to his new address."

Valerie laughed. "We went over that place like vultures," she said. "Come on. Take a look."

Valerie led the way up the stairs to the rooms at the front of the house that had been Billy's, telling me about how thoroughly she and the others had searched Billy's rooms, and how completely he had been moved out. "The place was cleaned out, like he was never there."

"That doesn't sound like Billy," I said. "Maybe somebody helped him."

Valerie shook her head and shrugged.

"Maybe it was going on for some time. Maybe someone has been moving his stuff out little by little."

"That's possible," she said. "We didn't go into his rooms very often."

Billy's front room had a big leaded bay window with stained-glass designs across the top. The furniture was old and simple, like the stuff that you'd expect to see in a doctor's office in the thirties, mostly oak veneer. Glass-front bookcases, desk, tables, chairs. All plain.

In his bedroom there was one window that looked out over the driveway and had a fire escape. The bed had no headboard; it was on one of those Sears-Roebuck frames that roll around if you move in your sleep.

I looked in the closet, in the drawers, under the bed. Valerie was right. There wasn't a trace of him. The bed even looked unslept-in. The sheets had been taken off and the mattress wasn't wrinkled or caved in at any spot. The pillows were bare, too, and stacked on the dresser.

"It looks like somebody just cleaned the place," Valerie said. "And the cleaning lady comes on Monday."

I was starting to feel tired. "Maybe I'll talk to Marie and then go home," I said. "I've got a cold."

"I thought you looked a little gray," Valerie said. "It's going around."

Marie was a small, dark-haired beauty who ran to fat. "I never liked Sammy," she said. Her voice was soft and husky. "He was a wise guy."

"You don't look old enough to have been in school with Billy and Sammy." I meant it, but she took it as flattery.

"I'm getting too old for this business," she said.

"How are you at bookkeeping?"

"I took business courses in high school," she said.

"Do you want to take the phone calls at the office?" I thought Marie could be the answer to the phone problem.

"You heard what we said before. The other girls wouldn't want one of us to take the calls."

"But you wouldn't go out on dates anymore. You'd have to stick to the phone work only."

"But what about my regulars?"

I didn't want to deal with Marie's regulars. I didn't want to hear about them. "You'd have to give them to somebody else."

"I couldn't do that."

There went my good idea. "OK. I'll look for somebody else." Marie, I presumed, wasn't sure she was too old for the business yet. "What else do you know about Sammy?"

Marie got up and closed the door to the room, a small room that looked like it might have been intended to be a library but now had a TV and a load of videotapes on the shelves. I didn't look at the titles too hard, but I did see the name Debbie on a couple of them.

"His father knows a lot of people. He's powerful. No one would want to cross him. You know."

"Oh," I said, remembering what Sammy's mother said about the police not bothering Mr. Plata with questions. "What about Sammy's mother and his other relatives?"

"His mother's a teacher. His aunts and uncles live in Chicago. He was the only child. Spoiled. He always had nice clothes. And a car. He even had a car when he was in high school. The girls used to fall all over him." Marie shrugged.

"What about after high school?"

"The same thing. But he started working with his father."

"Doing what?"

"Collecting."

"Collecting what?"

"Whatever. Rents, bets. Delivering messages. All the young guys do that stuff."

"What about bookies? Do you know who his bookie was?"

"Of course." Marie laughed. "Frank, the Bean."

"The Bean?"

More laughter. "He farts all the time."

Nothing like an appropriate nickname. "Do you know where he lives? Where he hangs out?"

"He spends his time at Cafe Roma. They have pool tables in the back. The Bean loves pool. You know that ceremony that some Italian families have the first time they cut a baby's fingernails? They put a lot of money in the little fingers and then they cut. That's so the kid will grow up rich. In the neighborhood, they used to say that when they cut Frankie's fingernails, someone put a cue stick in his hand."

"So if I want to talk to him, I go to the Cafe Roma and go to the back where the pool tables are?"

"Are you crazy? They'd haul you out of there in a basket."

"I have to talk to him." The room had heated up and I was starting to sweat. "Could we open the door? It's hot in here."

Marie got up and opened the door and looked outside before she sat back down. *Who is she worried about?* I wondered.

"Let me see what I can do." Marie rested her chin on her hand and drummed her fingers against her cheek. "Give me your phone number. I'll have the Bean call you."

I thought how nice it would be to have a card with

my name and phone number on it. Instead, on a small piece of paper, I wrote my home number and the number I called when I got the job with Billy. I didn't want Frank the Bean calling the dating service.

"Do you see Frank the Bean often?" I asked her, trying to figure out her connection with a pool hall denizen who had gas.

"No. But I see people who see him. You gotta know that once a West Sider, always a West Sider. It's like a family."

"So I've heard," I said.

Then I asked her why she thought Billy had left town.

"I heard something about that," she said, "from one of my regulars."

"Who?"

"I can't give his name. He's married."

"What did you hear?"

"After Sammy got shot, my friend told me that Billy would have to look for somebody else to protect him."

"Protect him from what?" I heard my voice go up an octave.

"I guess the clubhouse guys were trying to move in on him. You know, the odds he made."

"How did Sammy protect him?"

"Sammy didn't, but his father did."

"Is that why Billy was invited to the funeral? Was he close to the Platas?"

"He was a good friend of Sammy's. Mr. Plata didn't like Billy, but he was good to him because of Sammy. That's all changed."

Since I didn't understand how Billy did what he did, and cared even less why he did it, I had to take Marie's word for this. "Why would someone want to move in on Probabilities?"

"Control. It's all control."

"I've heard that before," I said, thinking of the reason I used to get beat up by Dick. If I smiled at a guy, he'd whack me when we got home.

"If they got the odds before other people, they could move the cash around to where it would do the most good," Marie explained, showing an understanding of a subject that one would not immediately associate with her line of work.

"And Billy wouldn't do this?"

"No. He played straight with those odds."

My former employer went up one small notch in my esteem. And I wondered whether protecting Billy got Sammy killed. If it did, I'd have to be careful about the questions I asked.

I began to wish I hadn't given my phone numbers to Marie. God only knew what kind of guy Frank the Bean was.

Then I remembered the woman in the funeral parlor and told Marie about her, the way she cried and kissed Sammy.

Marie frowned and then blinked. "Sounds like about fifty women I know. Probably an old girlfriend."

I had thought for a second that she knew who the woman was. "Do you know any old girlfriend who would be so heartbroken that she might kill him?"

"That sounds like about fifty women I know, too."

"And he sounds like a man who could have a lot of enemies."

"You won't find anybody who'll admit they hated him," Marie said bitterly.

"Except you."

Marie smiled. "Some people have more to be afraid of."

"What's that supposed to mean?"

But Marie was done with her revelations.

When I left the house and climbed back into my car, my cold reasserted itself. It was starting to rattle around in my chest.

I made a few notes about the conversations at the house and noted the time and the mileage. I had to get used to keeping records.

I kept an eye on the rearview mirror because the last time I'd left that house I'd had a tail on me. After a mile or two, I was satisfied that I had no company, and I turned my attention to making an abbreviated list of chores for the evening so that I could dive into bed and sleep off the miseries.

Seventeen

I was shivering and aching all over by the time I got home. My eyes must not have been working right because I pulled into the garage in such an odd way that I couldn't close the overhead door. After several attempts to straighten the car out, I gave up and left it with one back fender wedged against the front corner of the garage and one fender sticking out into the driveway.

I fell onto the couch moaning. The aspirin I craved seemed too far away. I didn't even take off my coat. The light on the answering machine was blinking, but I ignored it and fell asleep. Even Horace's paws on my arm didn't keep me awake.

It was almost dark when Horace's barking jolted me wide-eyed. I couldn't remember where I was, but I was afraid. It took me a few seconds to remember that Dick wasn't around anymore. A few seconds more and I was remembering the guy who chased me. A scratching noise accompanied Horace's barks, and the noise was coming from the door to the garage. Horace was barking at something on the other side of the door. My memory clicked into gear again and I cursed myself for leaving the garage open. I didn't know whether to grab for the phone or run for the gun.

I was about to take the phone option when I heard a voice calling, "Fran." A man's voice. "Fran." Again.

I stood up and tiptoed to the door and peeked out. Ted Zwiatek stood in my garage, smiling.

The fear went away, but my heart did not stop pounding. As I opened the door, I tried to straighten my clothes and my hair, but it was hopeless. My coat looked like a dog's bed and I was sure that my face was a bloated red mass from the irritated sinuses and membranes.

I opened the door and smiled weakly and said something about having a cold. Horace leaped up against Ted's legs as if I'd never taught him to stay down.

Ted took one look at me and stopped smiling. He patted Horace briefly and unbuttoned my coat and pulled it down over my drooping shoulders and dangling arms. Then he led me to my bedroom, took off my shoes, and tucked me into bed.

"You stay there while I get you some soup," he said.

"Aspirin," I rasped.

"In the bathroom medicine chest?"

I nodded and pulled the quilt tightly around me. It was as if my mother had come back in the guise of a Polish policeman. Of course, my mother was Polish, so it was logical. Logical to someone whose mind was not firing on all cylinders.

Somehow, Ted not only found his way around my house as if he lived there, but he managed to make a pot of soup, the first bowl of which he fed me. The second bowl he brought in I managed to eat by myself.

"You're looking a little better," he said. "The aspirin must be working. Maybe the fever is down a little. It was a hundred and four."

I couldn't remember having the thermometer in my mouth. "What time is it?" I asked.

"Almost ten," he said. "This is not what I had in mind for our first date." He smiled wide. "But your dog and I had a nice chat."

"Creativity," I mumbled. "I was awake all night trying to think of something different."

He laughed. "I guess you're waking up. What's your dog's name? I keep calling him Rex, and he keeps looking at me in a funny way."

"Horace," I thought I said.

"Horse?" he said and roared with laughter.

"No, Ho-race. H-O-R-A-C-E."

"I think I like Horse better. Here, Horse."

Horace came running.

"Well it's closer than Rex," I said.

As I returned to the world of the living, I remembered where I had put the bookmark in my life and some of the things I still had to do that evening.

While Ted took my car keys and unwedged my car, I called Myrtle and asked her to take over the next morning. I wasn't going to say anything about Billy being gone because I thought she might not be interested if there was no chance of seeing him. But she already knew. Don't ask me how. I was beginning to think that the West Side was like Africa, where some drummer broadcast the news for everyone.

But since Looks was closed on Monday, Myrtle consented to take over the phones for the day. I was thinking about asking Natasha to take over on a permanent basis, but I wanted to explain it all to her beforehand, maybe take her to the house and have her meet the women. Natasha had a very matter-of-fact attitude toward life, and I knew she thought that prostitution ought to be made legal. She might, I thought, even like the setup that Billy had devised.

Natasha hadn't gone back to her old job for fear that Carlyle or his friends might come after her there. It wasn't that she liked the job, but it was a job. Until she was sure that there was no more danger from Carlyle, she had to avoid places he knew about.

The call to Natasha would wait until tomorrow,

though. Ted was there, and I was getting a kick out of the way he was bustling around my house.

Over glasses of sherry, I started to tell Ted about what I had found out about Sammy. When I got to the part where I went to the Plata house, Ted began to get uncomfortable.

"You don't want to mess with Joe Plata," he said. "Promise me, Fran, that you won't do anything dangerous."

I hadn't even gotten to the part about giving Marie my phone numbers so I could make an appointment to see Frank the Bean. Nor had I told him about the man with the silver car who chased me. So I changed course and told him about the glasses that I had been meaning to drop off at the Buffalo precinct.

"You haven't been holding these back, have you? That's tampering with . . ."

"Evidence," I said. "I just found out about the glasses on Friday." I told him about Myrtle finding the glasses and her assurances that they hadn't been there before Sammy died. "There might be some prints on them," I said. "Other than Myrtle's."

"Yours?"

"Give me a little credit," I said, huffily.

Ted smiled at me sweetly and a bit condescendingly, I thought. Then I gave myself a lecture about being a piss pot to a guy who just brought me back from death's door.

"They're in the trunk," I said, handing him the car keys again.

He stopped in the kitchen before he came back to the bedroom with the glasses, now sealed in a couple of my plastic bags. "Fancy glasses," he said.

"Yeah, that's why Myrtle thinks that Sammy bought them. Nobody else has the money to throw around on fancy glasses to leave in the back of a beauty shop."

"So who was drinking out of them?" he said.

"Probably Sammy and a woman he couldn't take home. Beth is the prime suspect."

"Who are the other women who work there?"

"Just Kathy and Myrtle. But it doesn't have to be someone from the shop."

"What do you know about Kathy?" Ted asked.

"She gives good haircuts. She lives in Hamburg with her daughter. Her daughter is seven."

"And Myrtle?"

"A West Sider. Lives next door to Sammy. Has known Sammy all her life. But she's a little young for Sammy."

"They're never too young," Ted said with a nasty glint in his eyes.

"What do you know about it? You have some inside information on cradle robbing?"

"Yes. As a matter of fact, I have my eye on a two-year-old blond in my neighborhood. When she gets old enough, I plan on asking her out."

I laughed. "What do you think you'll look like in sixteen years?" I was feeling almost well, so I got up and led the way into the living room. It didn't seem quite right to be feeling so good while entertaining a man in my bedroom. Especially since I had no intention of doing anything that is usually done by consenting adults in bedrooms.

Ted answered my question. "Oh, I'll have a potbelly that I got by eating my mother's cooking and drinking beers with the guys."

"Mother's cooking," I said, remembering my mother's. She used to starve my fevers, and then she would feed my colds. "I could use some solid food. Would you help me eat a pizza? Sorrentino's delivers until midnight."

"Sold," he said. "But I'll buy."

"No way. You've earned it."

"I don't like women to buy my dinner."

"Pretend I cooked it. Then it will be all right."

The sarcasm wasn't lost on him. His scorecard was racking up points.

While Ted and I downed the pizza, I found out that he lived within a half mile of my house and that his family had been in Cheektowaga since before the little houses like mine were built. I knew his house. A big farmhouse on a huge lot near the airport.

I told him a little about my life, giving only the barest outline of my years with Dick.

It wasn't until after Ted left that I listened to my messages. One was from Marsha, inviting me to have lunch with her some time during the week. I felt sorry for Marsha, but I was still mad at her, too, and I wasn't even sure it was anger that I wanted to work through. I made an obscene gesture at the phone and then wondered why she hadn't mentioned anything more about how Dick died. Maybe that's why she wanted to have lunch. Maybe there was something she wanted to talk over.

The next message was from Valerie, who wanted to know what was happening with the Monday calls. It was late, but not too late to call the house on Ashland, where sleep had a different schedule from that of the rest of the world. When I dialed the house, Dot answered.

"I'm studying," she told me. "I'll be up all night."

"I got a message from Valerie," I said. "She wanted to know about the dating service calls. Tell her we're covered for tomorrow and that we'll take it a day at a time."

"We're all nervous about this," she said. "We hope you can get someone soon."

To hear her talk, *this* had become my problem instead of theirs. I felt like telling her to go pound salt, but I showed remarkable restraint and said, "I can't promise anything."

She sighed. "Well, back to the books."

"Did you have a date last night?" I asked.

"Yes," she said. "It was Saturday. Everybody was out."

"And while you all were gone, Billy moved out?"

"No. At least, I don't think so. There was a light in his apartment when I came in. I thought he was there all evening."

"When did you see him last?"

"When he came home from the funeral. I guess there was some kind of meal after the funeral. Billy came back with Marie about five."

"Marie? Marie went to the funeral, too?"

Dot laughed. "She's an old friend of the family."

"What's funny about being a friend of the family?"

"She's not really a friend of the whole family. She's not Mrs. Plata's friend."

"Oh," I said, finally figuring it out and realizing that there was a whole lot more I could learn from Marie.

"And then Billy went to his apartment?" I said. "And you didn't see him again?"

"No. I went to get ready for my date. And when I came down to post my note in the kitchen, Billy wasn't anywhere around. But that wasn't unusual."

"Who saw him last? Do you know?"

"We were trying to figure that out this afternoon after you left. We're not sure who saw him last, but it was about six-thirty when some of the girls saw him downstairs in the kitchen making a sandwich. He took the sandwich upstairs and that was that."

When I hung up, I listened to the third message.

"Fran," a man said. "Marie said you want to talk to me. This is the Bean. I have to go out of town. Come Tuesday."

I suppose he meant come to the Cafe Roma. And he didn't say what time. I'd go just before lunch, I thought, before the Bean's intestines gave notice that digestion had started.

I was almost asleep before I realized that there had been no call from the guy who had been bothering me. I had nearly forgotten him. But not quite.

Eighteen

Monday morning I woke up at nine o'clock. I felt guilty about sleeping so late, but the sleep had done wonders for my health. On a scale of one to ten, my cold had slipped from an eight (debilitating) down to about a three and a half (annoying).

I called Myrtle, who I figured was already at her desk by the time I woke up. Myrtle sounded stuffed up.

"Are you all right? Do you have a cold?" I said.

"No. It's not a cold. Allergies, I think. When are you coming in?"

"I have some phone calls to make."

"You could make them from here."

"Do you need me for anything?"

"No, I just wanted to talk to you, that's all. So much weird stuff happening."

Looks was closed and she was probably alone in the building. I was guessing that she felt uneasy. "I'll be in as soon as I can," I said. "I'll try to get there before eleven. OK?"

"OK."

That seemed to satisfy her, and it would give me a little time to make calls that I didn't necessarily want Myrtle to hear. Myrtle had a way of commenting on everything, and I wanted to work out the office problem myself.

After I had showered and eaten my breakfast—instant oatmeal instead of Cheerios as a concession to my cold—I called Natasha and gave her the rundown on the phone work in the office, the catalogue sales and the dating service. I told her I didn't know how long the arrangement would last.

"Do you know Polly talked to me about your job?" she said.

"Polly was perturbed about it when I talked to her."

"It bothers her," Natasha said. I loved listening to Natasha. She enunciated every word, and her voice was musical and deep.

"How do you feel about it?"

"Me? You know it doesn't bother me in the slightest what these ladies want to do to earn money. They sell a service for which there is obviously a market."

"So do you want to do it for a while? Until I can figure out the finances, I can pay you by the day at the same rate that Billy paid me. The office is only about ten or twelve blocks from the shelter," I said, offering her further inducement.

"When I go into the street, do you know I wear a disguise?"

I noticed that she hadn't answered me. I didn't make a point of it, I just went along in the conversational direction that she had taken. "Ah," I said. "What's your disguise? I used to wear a gray wig and a dumpy old coat in the months right after the divorce."

"Do you still have the coat and wig in case I want to vary my look?"

"I think I do. I'll dig it out for you. But what kind of disguise do you wear?"

"A man's coat and a fedora. Carlyle wouldn't give a man in a fedora a second glance. Isn't this shit that we go through?" she said.

"Yes," I said. "Shit."

"When do I start?"

"This afternoon, if you want." I knew she'd get around to it eventually. "Myrtle's there. She can break you in."

I explained to her about Myrtle, which somehow I hadn't done before, and gave her the address.

"What about Myrtle? Does she have a big mouth? Will she blab about my living at a shelter? How much do I tell her?" Natasha was getting the jitters.

"I think you can trust her not to blow your cover, especially if you tell her your story. She's nosy, but helpful."

"You know, I have not once told the story to anyone all the way through. I've told it in bits and pieces."

"Don't forget to get the work done," I said with mock sternness.

"Yes'm, boss lady."

"Partner," I said. "None of this boss lady stuff."

"Anyway, thanks for thinking of me. I have a bad case of cabin fever."

"Later."

"Cat chow."

That was Natasha's way of making fun of the people who affect the Italian greeting *ciao*.

Next I called Delia and told her about my first day as an investigator for Sunset. I told her about the way Billy made his exit and when the women at the house saw him last.

"Do you have any idea what time the message for you was left?" I asked.

"Not really. Just that the overnight answering service took it."

"It would be handy to know when calls came in, wouldn't it?" I said, remembering that my answering machine had some functions that I had never programmed.

"What good would it do?"

"It could give us an idea of how far away he went. Not positively, of course, but possibly."

"Hmm. Never mind about Billy. He doesn't matter now. He's gone and good riddance. I won't have to put up with his half-assedness."

"I was wondering whether something happened at the funeral that persuaded him to take off. Sammy and Billy knew one another for a long time, even if they weren't bosom buddies anymore."

"Different types," Delia said. "Sammy was outgoing, flamboyant, dramatic. Billy is opportunistic, secretive, sneaky."

I caught that bitterness in her voice again. There had been something between her and Billy at one time; I would bet on it. Since she was my new employer, I held back on asking her anything that might make her uncomfortable, but I did have this penchant for blurting things out. It was only a matter of time. "Is it OK if I come to your place this afternoon? I'm trying to pick up the pieces at the office, too."

"You're not going to try to run the odds business?"

"No," I said. "I'm trying to cover the dating service phones."

"Dating service? What dating service?"

Oh, oh. "I've got a friend taking that over. Don't worry. It won't interfere with my work."

She seemed to be at a loss for words. I could almost hear the wheels grinding as she tried to make sense of this new piece of data. Finally, she said, "Oh, no. I'm not worried about you, Fran. I know you'll keep good records. You always did."

I thought back to the hectic unhappy days when I was working with Dick and struggling to keep the office running. And in the midst of all that, I had impressed this woman. "Thanks," I said. "You don't know how hard it was. Thanks for that."

"You're welcome. I'll see you later. If you can get here at noon, I'll buy your lunch."

"I'd like a rain check on that lunch. I won't be able to get there that early."

When I got to the office, a harried-looking Myrtle was mired in a stack of papers. I couldn't tell whether they were dating slips, catalogue orders, or old odds sheets. At second glance, I saw that they were all in Billy's writing, and I surmised that Billy had gone through the office before his hasty departure.

Myrtle, her faced creased with worry, continued with the phone and the slips.

I stacked the papers. Then I started to go through the file drawers to see if I could find a clue as to Billy's whereabouts.

I started with the Probabilities drawers. But somebody, Billy or someone looking for Billy, had already been through the files, if in their post-rifling state they could any longer be called files. Naturally, I wondered what Myrtle had looked through in the hours she'd been here alone. I wouldn't figure Myrtle for someone who would take the files apart, though. Just nosing through them was more her style. Besides, she had probably committed most of the stuff to memory when she worked for Billy.

But I waited until she went to the bathroom to continue my search.

Loose papers filled every drawer. The papers in each drawer were stacked almost neatly, but nothing was in folders. The folders I found in one of the bottom drawers, which I thought had been empty before. The rearrangement made no sense to me. But I hadn't been privy to the filing system of Probabilities.

It was then that I realized that the Probabilities phone that Billy used all day long was not ringing. I stopped the inventory and dialed Probabilities.

The number had been changed. It was now an eight-hundred number. I jotted it down. I'd call it later and leave a message. I should have known he would take that business with him. I wondered how long ago he had put in the request for an eight-hundred number. Maybe Brenda could find out.

The dating service files looked untouched and the drawer that was Billy's private drawer was locked. It looked like someone had tried to jimmy it. When I looked again at the desk that Myrtle was working at and saw the bent scissors, I figured that Myrtle's curiosity had been aroused again.

I heard the noises in the plumbing system and calculated that I had another minute or two to search without Myrtle looking over my shoulder.

Then I remembered that the gun was gone. I had been through all the file drawers I could open, and it wasn't there. I wasn't worried about that being the murder weapon, because it looked more like a forty-five than a twenty-two. And I knew it wasn't the gun the robber used because Billy's gun was in the office when the shot was fired downstairs. But I wondered whether Billy had the gun or someone else took it.

It looked like someone had been through the catalogue sales drawers, too, but I couldn't tell whether anything was missing. I stopped checking through those files when I heard Myrtle coming up the stairs.

When the clock blinked twelve, Myrtle tossed her head, sighed, and flipped on the answering machine. I was standing behind her and I saw her try to sneak the scissors into the drawer. There was something odd about Myrtle that morning. Maybe she's mourning the loss of Billy, I thought.

"What gives?" I said. "Did you go through the files?"

"No. No. Honest, Fran. This is the way I found it. I thought maybe Billy . . ."

"Left a forwarding address?" I said. "I was hoping to find one, too. Give me those scissors."

I poked around with the blades, trying to find the way the drawer was locked, but to no avail. "Maybe I'll call a locksmith," I said.

"Good idea," Myrtle said. Her head jerked to one side, as if she were developing a tic.

Just then we heard someone down in the hall, and thinking it was Natasha, I went out the door to greet her. But it was a Federal Express delivery woman with a package for me.

Myrtle hovered as I opened it. "Maybe it's from Billy," she said.

"Maybe we get some explanation," I said.

The package contained a couple of pieces of bubble packing taped together. When I cut the tape to get at the papers inside, a key fell out. The papers inside were blank.

"Maybe you don't have to call a locksmith," Myrtle said.

Natasha chose that moment for her arrival. A good thing, too, because I wanted to get a first look at that drawer alone.

She made her entrance wearing her man's coat and fedora. It was a good disguise.

"Can I help you, sir?" Myrtle said.

I laughed, and Natasha took off her hat. Myrtle realized her mistake immediately and her smile wiped the lines from her face.

Myrtle and Natasha hit it off right away. Within minutes, Myrtle was showing Natasha the ropes, and Natasha was telling Myrtle all about her recent brush with death. Myrtle was agape.

I checked the refrigerator to see if there were any sandwiches and whether they were fit for consumption. The fridge was cleaned out except for a six-pack minus one of diet Dr Pepper.

"Anyone for lunch?" I said.

"I've eaten," Natasha said.

"I'm not hungry," skinny Myrtle said.

"I'm going to get a sandwich. Are you sure you don't want anything?"

They shook their heads, and I left for the sandwich shop. My stomach was starting to complain. I ordered a big hero, with everything on it and a Classic Coke. Just to be on the safe side, I ordered another hero. If the other two got hungry seeing me eat, I didn't want to share my sandwich. Hungry is hungry. I had a cold to feed.

When I returned, Natasha and Myrtle looked at me and laughed at the size of the bag I was carrying.

"I got some extra." I said. "In case you guys were hungry."

I took my sandwich to the desk in the corner where Billy used to talk on the phone in the afternoon. I left the other hero in front of Natasha and Myrtle. A few minutes after I opened the wrapping and the odor of the sandwich drifted through the room, Natasha and Myrtle were attacking the other hero.

"There's diet soda in the fridge," I said.

I still hadn't opened the file drawer with the key Billy sent. At least I thought Billy had sent it. Other possibilities ran through my mind. Maybe there was a bomb in the drawer. Parts of Billy's body. The gun that was used to kill Sammy. Maybe I should have the package dusted for prints. Maybe I should give Myrtle the key and let her open the drawer. Maybe I should call a cop.

Then the cop I thought about calling was Ted. I was trying to remember what he told me about his schedule this week, but the memory was lost—somewhere in the delirium of the night before.

At one o'clock, Myrtle turned the phones on and Natasha and she went to work. I finished my lunch and started rooting through Billy's desk. The drawers were by far the sloppiest places in the office; not what I expected, because his clothes were always neat, though eccentric.

I sifted through candy wrappers, bits of food, paper clips, bobby pins, balls of string, plastic cups, old directories, lists on all kinds of paper scraps, a metric conversion table, a yo-yo, a nail file, a piece of lace, a small screwdriver, a case for eyeglasses, bottle caps, a black sock, but no clue to Billy's new address.

Finally, I took the key and opened the file drawer. Myrtle watched me, the phone on her ear. The drawer was empty except for a file that said "Fran" on the front. It contained a list of the bookkeeping information for the office, for the catalog sales, and for the dating service. How much to pay whom and when. The rent was to be paid to Joseph Plata, the list said. But Karla had told me that Sammy owned the building. I'd have to ask someone about that. I dialed Karla's number but got no answer. No answering machine either.

Myrtle was still watching me, so I waved the file at her. "Bookkeeping stuff," I said. "But no forwarding address."

Myrtle shrugged; the lines were back on her face.

Since I had a few minutes before I had to get on my way over to the Sunset offices, I took a wastepaper basket over to Billy's desk and began to clean out the debris. Bits of food would invite creatures, my Polish mother always told me. And I was my mother's daughter when it came to tidiness.

I pulled out all the drawers and emptied the crumbs, vowing to wash out the drawers later. I watched the debris fall into the can, one drawer after another.

After the third book of matches from Harry's Bar in Las Vegas fell past my eyes, I stopped and pawed through the garbage again.

If Amy, from the battered women's group, had been there, she would have held the matchbooks in her hand and tried to divine something from them. I opened the matchbooks to see if anything had been jotted down inside.

There were a lot of numbers in Billy's handwriting inside the matchbooks, but only one set of numbers looked like it might be for a phone. I tucked the matchbooks in my purse and checked out the rest of the garbage again, finally satisfying myself that it was meant for the trash can.

Nineteen

When I got to Sunset, Delia was still eating her
lunch. Behind her desk.

"Want some?" she said, pointing to a hero sandwich like the one I'd eaten earlier.

"No, thanks, I ate at the office."

"Are you going to run the office?"

"Everything's tentative."

"I know the feeling," she said, wiping the dressing
off her fingers. She reached into her desk and pulled out
a form. "Fill this out and take it up to the second floor,
and they'll take your picture."

The form asked for the usual information: height,
weight, color of hair and eyes. And across the top it said
Agent of Sunset Insurance Companies. "Companies?"
I said. "When did it become companies?"

"There was a merger about a year and a half ago."

"Who gobbled up whom?"

"Beats me. I only know I kept my job, the guy ahead
of me lost his, and I moved up."

I bet you know more than that, I thought. "Lucky
you," I said.

I left Delia to her lunch, filled out the form, and had
my picture taken. When I returned to Delia's office, I
had a laminated card that looked official. Delia handed
me some other forms, which I would need to turn in to

get paid, and then she started to grill me about what I'd found out.

I gave her almost everything I knew. I didn't tell her about the matchbook that might or might not help me find Billy. I wasn't even sure that Billy's new address was important in the search for what happened to Sammy. Besides, I felt that Delia hadn't told me everything about Billy. She sounded bitter when she talked about him. Too bitter. There must have been something personal.

"So when did you and Billy break up?" As soon as the words were out of my mouth, I was calling myself stupid and wondering whether she'd fire me.

Delia's face went through a range of colors before settling on a slight pink. "How did you know?"

"I didn't."

"You're good," she said, shaking her head. "Too good." She leaned back in her chair. Delia looked as if she was tuning up for a long recitation. "I don't know why I tried to keep it a secret anyway. Yes, I do. At first it was a secret because I hired him, and I don't like mixing business with pleasure. Afterward it was a secret because he dumped me and started seeing someone else."

"Jeannie?"

Delia laughed. "That dog? That kind of competition I could handle. No. Not Jeannie. But it took me a long time to find out who."

"Not Jeannie? But everybody says he's wrapped around her little finger."

"All an act. Jeannie's the go-between. She plays the part of the girlfriend, but she's not. His love affair is definitely a dangerous liaison."

"So? Who?"

Delia let me dangle. Then she dropped her bombshell. "Karla."

"Jesus!" I said. "And you've been sitting on this

information? This changes everything I've been working on.''

"Calm down.''

"Calm down? I've been poking my nose around on the West Side, getting funny phone calls, being followed, and I don't have a piece of crucial information that could put me in danger?''

"What danger? Don't overdo it, Fran.''

It was my turn to turn colors. But I managed to stop up my mouth and put my brain into gear. When I thought I could speak in a normal register, I said, "Doesn't this make Karla an even more tempting suspect?''

"It would if she had been anywhere near the beauty shop that night. But she wasn't.'' Delia put a finger up to one eye.

Delia must have spent big bucks to have Billy tailed. Or else she spent her spare time watching him.

"Don't tell me she was with Billy,'' I said.

Delia nodded. "At Karla's mother's place, as usual.''

"But . . .''

"The old lady's as deaf as a stump.''

"But Karla's so pregnant!''

"Maybe it's not Sammy's,'' she said.

"But if it's Billy's, do you think she'd try to pass it off as Sammy's? That would never work.''

"Why not? It happens all the time.''

My head was oversudsing. I was losing track of what happened where and who did what. I had had a mental list of people I wanted to see and questions I wanted to ask, but now it was all changed.

"How much of this am I supposed to keep quiet about?'' I asked.

Delia thought about it. "Keep your ears open. I'm sure it will come out. Just don't jump the gun, so to speak.''

"So to speak.''

"I am sure that neither Billy nor Karla killed

Sammy," she said. "I'm also pretty sure that neither of them hired anyone to kill Sammy."

"Pretty sure?"

"I don't think they're that kind of people. They're just sneaking jackrabbits when it comes to sex."

What a stupid position to be in, I thought. Delia probably picked me to do the investigation because she thought she could push me around and I'd be dumb enough to do what she told me. My self-esteem was plummeting, as it was wont to do whenever I was in a pinch. I did what I always do when I'm confused; I pretended to agree.

"OK," I said. "What direction do you see the investigation taking now?"

"I think the answer is on the West Side. Some kind of monkey business. Money laundering, real estate deals."

"How far do you want me digging around in stuff that could get me killed?" I was feeling pretty snotty.

Delia looked at me. She was cool. I was flustered. I felt like quitting, but I was hoping she wouldn't fire me.

"Right," she said. "It could be dangerous."

Then it hit me. "Wait a minute. You said you were almost sure that Karla didn't hire a hit man. And in order to pay the claim, all you really need to know for sure is that Karla didn't put a contract on Sammy."

Delia smiled. "That's all."

"That's all," I repeated. And I felt I was right back at the beginning. Maybe, if I knew who killed Sammy, I could be sure that Karla didn't hire him. And basically, that's what Sunset wanted to know. But it was still looking dangerous.

And if Delia found out about Billy and Karla, others could find out, too. Would someone want to kill Billy or Karla because of their affair? Sammy's father or mother? Is that why Billy disappeared?

But all that wasn't getting me any closer to the solution I was hired for.

"What have you got from the cops?" I asked.

She handed me a copy of the medical report. "You can keep that," she said. "Two bullets behind the ear, complete with powder burns. No other bruises or scratches."

"It says he was curled up. Maybe he wasn't standing when he was shot."

"Sounds like a hit to me," Delia said. "They had him kneeling and shot him."

I checked the report again, looking for something about the direction of the bullets. "It says the bullets went straight. If he were kneeling, maybe a short person killed him."

Delia shrugged. "Possible. And the second bullet must have been fired right after the first. The wounds are only a half-inch apart.

"Or the second one was delivered after he fell. The angle is a little different." I kept searching the report. "They haven't found the weapon."

Delia was wiggling in her chair, and I guessed that she had other things to do. "Fill out that pay form and I'll get you paid for yesterday," she said.

I picked up the money and on the way out I stopped at a pay phone. It would be a good time to try out the phone credit card that I had applied for months before and never used. A woman lined up behind me while I was reading the instructions on the back of the card. Maybe Delia was having me followed, too. I decided I'd wait until I had more privacy before calling the matchbook number, which I thought was probably a number in Vegas.

Before Delia had let her cat out of the bag, I knew what I wanted to say to Billy—if I got hold of him. But what now?

I stopped at the office before I went on to the West Side, where I wanted to visit Mrs. Plata again. I also wanted to take a look at the Cafe Roma and its environs before I went there to see Frank the Bean the next day.

Myrtle and Natasha flashed big smiles at me. Although nobody flashed a smile quite like Myrtle.

"She's doing great," Myrtle said. "I don't think she needs me anymore. Do you mind if I go home? I want to do my hair."

"Don't you get it done free downstairs?" Natasha said.

"Naw, I like to do it my way."

"You've done nice things to Fran's hair," Natasha said.

Myrtle bowed. "Why thank you."

"What could you do with mine? Have you worked on nappy hair?"

Natasha's hair at the roots was coming in curly. I surmised that she had missed a visit to her old beauty parlor because she was afraid that Carlyle or one of his friends would look for her there.

Myrtle stepped right over to Natasha's head and started to move the hair around. "I've got an idea," Myrtle said.

"Good," Natasha said.

When the phone rang, I answered. I didn't want to interrupt Myrtle's inspiration. It wasn't until about five or six calls later that Myrtle had finished working a bit of magic on Natasha's head. She had pinned a few curls up on top, snipped a few hairs at the front and the side, and transformed Natasha's make-do hairdo into a stylish coif.

Myrtle left and, naturally, Natasha had to go down to Looks to check herself out in the big mirrors. I looked up the Nevada area code and called the number in the matchbook.

"Hello." A woman's voice. I thought it sounded familiar but couldn't place it.

"I'd like to speak to Mr. Lightfoot," I said.

"Who's calling please?"

Who the hell was that? "Karla. Is that you?"

"Who is this?" Alarm in her voice.

"Fran Tremaine Kirk. From Billy's office in Buffalo. Is that you, Karla?"

Silence.

"I know about you and Billy."

"How . . . ?"

"What's going on, Fran?" It was Billy. He had been listening, and he was irritated.

"I was going to ask you the same thing."

We shouted things at one another about what was whose business for several minutes. It was the most emotional conversation I had had with my former employer.

He cursed mightily when I told him what Delia had told me, cursed himself for leaving the matchbook in the drawer, and swore me to secrecy about where he and Karla were.

"But what about Delia? She might tell someone. And if she had you tailed, that's someone else who knows," I said.

"But you didn't give her this phone number, did you?"

"No."

"Good. Tear up the matchbook. Erase the number from your mind."

"I just have to ask you one question." Stupid thing for me to ask, as if he'd tell me the truth. "Did you or Karla hire a hit on Sammy?"

"No. No need for that. Sammy knew. Besides, we had more to fear from him than he had from us." The tension had gone out of his voice.

"When did Sammy find out?"

"Karla told him a week ago. But he already suspected."

"When did you decide to leave town?"

"We were planning to leave soon anyway, but at the funeral, Joe informed us that we should leave pronto."

"So, Joe Plata knew, too."

"There's not much that Joe doesn't know. But he doesn't have this phone number, yet."

"Where's Jeannie?"

"She's out here."

"Who is she anyway? How come she's so obliging?" I asked.

"She's my cousin. She's great at making odds on tennis, golf, car racing, and stuff that I can't keep up with."

Another multi-purpose person among Billy's troops. "Did she know Sammy?"

"Yes, but she didn't kill him either."

"Have you got any theories on who did it?"

I could almost hear Billy making odds on whether it would be a good idea to talk to me about this. "Karla and I talked about this," he said.

"Yes," Karla said. She was still on the line. "Sammy told me on the night of the robbery that he had told the police that twenty-five hundred had been stolen. But he told me that he had ten thousand in the paper bag that night and that he had an idea who robbed him."

"How come so much?" I said, and then remembered that Delia had mentioned money laundering.

"He wouldn't tell me," Karla said. "I was surprised he told me as much as he did. We weren't getting along."

I was dying to ask her whose baby she was carrying. "Were you planning on getting a divorce?"

"Yes, but you know his family. They kept trying to keep it together. 'Do whatever you want, but don't get a divorce,' old Joe told me."

"So how come he told you at the funeral to get lost?"

"By then," Karla said, "he knew that the baby wasn't Sammy's. He just wanted me out of there."

"Oh," I said, remembering Karla's dislike of the West Side and its traditions. "I guess you don't miss Buffalo."

"The armpit of the East? No. I don't miss it."

If Buffalo was an armpit, I thought, then Vegas could be likened to another part of the anatomy that only a proctologist could love.

"Sammy didn't give you a hint about who might have robbed him, did he?"

Karla didn't say anything for what seemed like a couple of minutes. I could imagine her and Billy making faces at one another, mouthing words that I couldn't hear, maybe writing things down on bits of paper.

Finally Billy said, "Listen Fran. You don't want to get mixed up in this."

"I'm already mixed up in this," I said, rather loudly.

"You could just close up the office and walk away," he said.

"It's tempting, believe me. But the women at your house are at their wits' ends."

"That's not a long trip," Billy said. I guessed that he was smiling that raised-lip, dimpled, feline smile.

"I think they'd scalp you if you showed your face in town. I'm trying to arrange something to keep them in business."

"Have you listened to the answering machine for Probabilities?" Billy asked.

"Yes," I said. "I was going to leave a message for you on that number, but now I don't have to. How did you happen to leave that number in the desk drawer?"

"I just got the number Saturday evening, while I was getting ready to leave. It's an apartment of a friend of Jeannie's. We won't be staying here long anyway."

"What about the cops? Won't they want to talk to you?"

"I'm square with them. I settled with them before I left."

"Do they know where you are?"

"Yes. I had to tell them or they'd have an all-points out on me."

I wondered whether any of the cops were in so thick

with Joe Plata that they'd keep him informed of Billy's whereabouts.

"How many people knew about you and Karla?"

"Besides Joe and Carmelita, just Sammy. I doubt if Delia knows much. She probably told you everything she knew. And now you know more than she does."

"Are you still on the line, Karla?" I asked. "I'd really like to know if you've got any other information about the robbery."

"Poor Sammy," Karla said. "He had the world by the garbanzos for so long and then, bang. Nothing."

"It's possible the robber didn't kill him," I said.

"What do you mean?" she said.

"Different gun. Different type of gun altogether." I thought that Karla would be persuaded to tell me what she knew about the robbery if she got the idea that the robber wasn't a killer.

"Look," she said, "I don't want to hear about the West Side anymore. I'm sick of the goons, the secrets, the rituals."

"One more thing, Karla, and then I won't bother you anymore. You're still the beneficiary of Sammy's insurance policy. How will that go over with the Platas?"

Karla sighed. "That's my settlement. I signed over everything else to Joe before I left. House, Looks, the building on State Street, everything."

"Are you moved out of the house, then?"

"I have to make one more trip to get things out of the house. Joe's getting a truck for me."

"He seems to be treating you pretty well under the circumstances."

"You don't know anything about circumstances," she said, suddenly angry.

"Sorry," I said. "What did I say to provoke you?"

Billy spoke up again. "Karla has put up with a lot. You don't know."

"No, I don't. But I'm sorry, anyway, Karla. Will you let me know so I can see you when you come back?"

"I don't know. I'll only be there a day. I have to give the movers instructions."

"Then Joe will know where you are."

"He's all right. We had it out. The whole story. He understands."

"Oh," I said, "the whole story. Is it something I should know?"

"No." Karla sounded tired. "I'll call you to let you know when I'm coming. It'll be in a day or two."

"Thanks," I said. "Take care of yourselves. I'll keep you posted. I'll let you know when Sunset is going to cut the check."

When I hung up, I was determined to see Joe Plata, the man who made the sun rise on the West Side.

Twenty

I must have stood on the front steps of the Plata house ringing the bell for five minutes. If Mrs. Plata were there, she would answer right away, I figured. But if Joe were home alone, he might not answer at all.

Who'll win the battle of wills, I thought. *Will he get sick of hearing the bell? Will he worry about his neighbors seeing me on his front steps? Is he really home or not?*

I was just about to turn and leave when I heard the click of the lock. When the door opened, I recognized the potbelly, which I had seen in the chair the first day I visited the house. That was all I saw at first, because the light slanted into the foyer and left his face in the dark.

"Mr. Plata?" I said.

When he grunted, I said, "I'm Fran Tremaine Kirk. I . . ."

"I know who you are. What do you want?" I was still standing on the front steps, and he wasn't backing away to let me in. But my vision adjusted to the light in the foyer and the eyes that shot from the gloom were the emerald color that he had passed on to his son.

I knew what I wanted to ask him, so I fired away.

Front steps or not. "I'm working for Sunset Insurance Company. They have a policy on your son's life. His wife is the beneficiary."

"I know that. What's your business?"

"Did Sammy have any gambling debts?"

He laughed. Not a friendly laugh. "You're trying to link the robbery with the killing, aren't you? I told the cops and I'm telling you, they're not connected."

"But did Sammy have any debts?"

Joe narrowed his eyes. I heard a voice coming from inside. A voice filled with pain. "Stay here," he said, leaving me on the front steps. I was getting a chill, both physically and mentally.

What was that voice inside? Was it the television? Was someone being tortured by Joe Plata's henchmen? Was my imagination running in overdrive?

When he came back, he invited me into the foyer. Now I wasn't so sure I wanted to come in from the cold. But there was no more noise from inside.

I thanked him and then reminded him of what I had asked.

"Sammy didn't owe any money," he said. "But we all have debts."

I thought for a fleeting instant that the old man's face would crack and the tears would run.

"I know about Billy and Karla," I said, and watched to see what Joe Plata would do.

Under his cheekbones the muscles flexed, indicating that he was clenching his teeth. "It won't be long before everybody who wants to know will know."

I got a little bold and pushed. "I hear you're a powerful man in this town."

"Don't believe everything you hear," he said, narrowing his eyes and looking at me, I thought, as if he were wondering whether to have me iced. "And repeat even less." What he didn't say was "if you know what's good for you," but the implication was clear. He was getting ready to terminate the interview. The potbelly moved forward an inch or two, invading the space in which I felt comfortable.

"One more thing," I said, and told him about the woman in the funeral parlor.

Several expressions flitted across his face, but none that I could identify. Recognition, perhaps.

"Who was she?" I asked.

He shrugged. "Ask Dom," he said.

Oh, Mr. Drago. I remembered the funeral director's name was Domenick Drago.

Joe was stepping toward me, and I backed toward the door. My mind was racing, trying to cover the subjects I wanted while I covered the ground that he wanted.

"The office," I said. "Can I rent Billy's office?"

He stopped, and stood still, looking into my eyes with that intense green gaze that I had seen in only one other face. "You can have it at the same rate, same conditions that Billy had it."

Sometimes I amaze myself with my gall. "There's one condition I'd like changed," I said. "I'd like a bathroom on the second floor."

I thought Joe was going to slap me. Any aggressive move toward me I interpreted as one that preceded a slap. Old wounds, old scars. His eyebrows went up in indignation. Then he laughed, hard, and patted me on the shoulder and kept on laughing. He was obviously enjoying himself. "Good-bye," he said, and I was out on the front steps again.

Once in my car, the heat in my face ebbed as I gritted my teeth. *Some men really get my goat*, I thought. *And Joe Plata is one of them.* I kept my composure enough to remember to log in the time and the mileage, but I couldn't focus on what I'd seen and heard. I'd have to cool down to do that.

As I pulled away from the curb, I saw a woman walking in my direction, and I knew immediately who she was. I jammed on the brakes, put the car in park, and got out and headed toward her. She saw me and turned and took off faster than I've seen anybody run on spiked heels. She was fast and I was coming off a nasty cold. I didn't get my legs in gear fast enough to make the pursuit worthwhile. As it was, I was suddenly being tugged on from behind.

When I stopped and turned, there was Myrtle, all out of breath. "Hi. What are you doing in the neighborhood?" she said. She was wearing black lipstick that made her teeth look like piano keys.

"Let me go," I said. "I've got to catch that woman."

Myrtle let go. "What woman?" she said.

Sure enough, the woman was gone. "Did you see her? She was coming down the block."

"No," Myrtle said. "Why did you want to catch her?"

"She was the woman from the funeral parlor."

"Oh," Myrtle said. "I wonder who she could be."

"I thought you knew everybody," I said, irritated. "Who would be walking down this street?"

"I don't know everybody who walks down this street," Myrtle said defensively.

Did she know who it was? I tried to read her face, but she smiled and the brilliance washed away my doubt.

"Did Uncle Joe tell you anything that would help you?" Myrtle said, revealing that she had been watching.

"Only that I can rent the office on the same terms that Billy had."

"Does he know where Billy went?" she asked.

"Probably."

"Where?"

"Beats me."

"What about Karla? Where is she?"

"At her mother's?" I pretended to guess.

"No. Nobody's seen Karla since the funeral."

"Interesting," I said, hoping that Myrtle didn't see through me.

I got back in my car, after refusing Myrtle's invitation to have a cup of coffee with her, and cruised around the block for ten minutes, but I didn't see the woman again. There was something about her, something that I should connect, some nagging little hint, a maddening, tantalizing something.

My cold symptoms were returning. I dug around in the glove compartment, looking for a pill, any pill that might stave off the relapse. I found an aspirin and took it without water. By the time I had swallowed it, my mouth was infused with that salty, bitter, grainy taste.

It was time for me to go back to the office and check on Natasha and then head home for some chicken soup. Maybe I would come up with some answers if I slept on it. In any case, sleep seemed like a good idea.

But that wasn't to be. In my absence from the office, Natasha had had a call from Valerie, and after a long chitchat, they were fast friends.

Natasha wanted me to drive her over to meet Valerie. I consented, grudgingly. I didn't have much energy left.

"Valerie said I should check out Billy's rooms to see if I want to move into them," Natasha said.

"What about Carlyle and his friends?" I asked, alarmed at this sudden change in the state of affairs.

"Carlyle never hit me when other people were around."

"Some nights, though, almost everybody is out." I wondered whether Natasha was rushing into this.

Natasha's face clouded and then she got an impious look on her face. "Yeah, but I'll bet if the cops are called to that place, they get there fast."

"That's a distinct possibility," I said, telling myself that I could not control other people and that just because I had offered the job to Natasha didn't make me responsible for every subsequent event.

When we got to the house, the welcoming committee was waiting. It was like the night that I first visited, except this time there was no Billy to shut down the bickering.

Natasha filled the gap. "Whoa," she said in a voice unlike her usual velvet. "We can talk in a few minutes."

It worked. A contented quiet settled on the crowd.

"Meanwhile," Natasha continued, "here are the slips for tonight. Marie and Jill, where are you? You've got to call right away."

Valerie smiled as she passed the slips from Natasha to the women.

As Natasha and Valerie went up the stairs to Billy's old place, they were chatting away like long-lost sisters.

I took the opportunity to corner Marie again to tell her about seeing Joe Plata and about the Bean calling me.

Marie had her hair in rollers and was pasting on long fake fingernails when I found her in the kitchen sitting behind a soup-stained placemat and a bowl with three peas floating in about a tablespoon of red liquid.

After I thanked her for having the Bean call me, I asked, "Going out tonight? Who's the lucky guy?"

"One of the regulars," she said.

I decided to go for the big one. After all, Dot had practically told me who Marie's main man was. "Speaking of regulars, I saw Joe Plata today."

She dropped a fingernail into the bowl next to the peas and tried to keep her face from giving away any more.

"It's not important," I said. "It doesn't affect the investigation at all."

She put her head down as she fished for the fingernail and then dried it on a paper towel.

"I'd like to find out who the woman in the funeral

parlor was. I saw her today. Right on the street where Joe lives.''

Marie kept fiddling with the fingernail. "I hope I can get the damn thing to stick now that it's been in the minestrone,'' she said.

I was dying to ask Marie what she knew about Billy and Karla, but I thought maybe I'd take Joe Plata's advice and keep my mouth shut for the time being. It was possible that Marie knew all about it as soon as Joe found out. "The woman on the street,'' I said. "Got any idea who she could be?''

Marie pursed her pretty red lips and batted her lashes. "I told you, Fran, Sammy had a lot of girlfriends.''

"No one special? Someone who carried the torch for a long time?''

"You're sure it wasn't Beth?'' she said.

"I'm sure. This woman was smaller, with better taste in clothes, expensive clothes.''

Marie frowned. "Why don't you come over tomorrow. After you talk to the Bean. Maybe I can find out something for you.''

By the time I left, Natasha had decided to move out of the shelter and start a new life with the women from Billy's Dating Service. I wondered whether I had done the right thing in involving Natasha. I worried about what Polly would think. I worried about Natasha's safety.

It took me the entire half hour from the time I dropped Natasha at the shelter until I pulled into my driveway in Cheektowaga to shed the load I'd put on myself. Natasha was a grown-up, I told myself. And I couldn't take responsibility for anybody but myself. But I wanted to call Polly and talk to her. Polly would ream me out, I knew, but I didn't have anybody else to talk to about it.

Then I thought about Ted and wondered how much I could talk to him about. He did seem like a caring person. He was so solicitous about my cold. But how would he react to the mention of Billy's Dating Service? I decided that if I spoke to anybody, it would have to be Polly.

There were messages from both Ted and Polly on my machine. Just two messages, no breathers or men watching me, no irate ex-husband with a buzz on. Ted wanted to come over and Polly wanted me to call her. That's like normal life, I thought, just calls from friends.

Twenty-one

There was a lot of tension on the line when Polly and I talked, but I said what I had to say.

After a long silence, Polly said, grudgingly, I thought, "I just wish it had evolved differently."

"Maybe it won't be as bad as you think, Polly. You haven't met the dating-service women."

"Hmm, no, I haven't. Maybe that's what I should do."

Polly had agreed too readily. Something was up.

"Do you want me to give you the address and phone number? I got the impression that Natasha would be moving in very soon."

"She doesn't like the shelter," Polly said. "There are a lot of children running the halls, children crying at night. It's noisy and smelly. And you know Natasha. She's neat. Like you. And by the way, what about you?"

"Me?" Polly had shifted gears. "Me. Well, I didn't have a mystery caller today, and I haven't made much headway on Sammy's case."

"Oh God, I almost forgot to tell you. Brenda's been working on your phone calls. She told me she started yesterday and has the numbers for you."

"Great!" I said, "Do I call her at work or at home?"

"Try her at home. Maybe she and Buddy are sober

tonight. If they're in their cups, you'll have to wait to call her at work tomorrow.''

''Thanks.''

''Don't thank me. Thank Brenda. I think she's sticking her neck out to do this, but she's excited and proud to be doing it.'' Polly was sounding motherly.

''Of course, I'll thank her. I might even be able to pay her.'' I hoped I sounded grown up without sounding snotty.

''Right on,'' Polly said.

I laughed. Right on? I hadn't heard that in years.

I dialed Brenda as soon as I hung up. When a man with a slur in his speech answered the phone, I thought that it was lights out for Brenda this evening. But when Brenda came to the phone, she sounded fine.

''I was hoping you would call,'' she said. ''Someone already had a trace on the numbers that call your house.''

''What? What do you mean? Who?''

''The order is signed by my supervisor, just like the traces that come in from police departments. I can find out who requested it, but I have to wait for the right time. Anyway, since the trace is already on, I've got the numbers of everybody who called your place in the last week.''

''But who else is getting this information?''

''I'll know that when I find out who requested it.''

''Not only do I have anonymous phone calls, I've got some agency tracing my phone activity.'' My mind was running over the possibilities, none of which seemed plausible. I remembered the cop from Cheektowaga who had told me I could trace calls to my number if I signed the papers requesting it. But I hadn't signed those papers. I'd just have to wait to see what Brenda found out.

''I can give you the time of these calls and the numbers where they originated and the names of the parties that the numbers are listed to.''

''Wow, what service,'' I said.

I remembered that I'd had a breather on the line Friday and a man who called Saturday after the group had left. My heart was fluttering with excitement. I might really catch the bastard.

After Brenda gave me the list, I was disappointed to learn that the man who was watching me had called from a pay phone. Ditto the man who had called Saturday, a different pay phone, but not too far from the first, and both in Cheektowaga.

I also got a call from a number listed under Marco Polo; probably the number Frank the Bean called from.

I hit pay dirt with one call. It had come from Minnie's number on Friday.

"Minnie didn't leave a message for me Friday," I said. "Everybody else did, and I had one anonymous heavy breather on the line."

Neither of us said anything for a few seconds. And then we both said, "Edgar."

"That would figure," I said. "I cut in on his phone call that day Minnie worked in the office."

"Well, at least you know something."

"Can you continue this, Brenda, without getting into trouble?"

"Actually, it's not that hard, but I do have to be careful. And it's sort of fun."

"There's something else I'm curious about."

"What?"

"How long does it take to get an eight hundred number?"

"That depends," she said.

"Well, how fast can somebody get one?"

"A good customer can get one almost immediately."

"Ah," I said, thinking that Joe Plata might impress someone as a good customer. And Joe did want Billy out of town. "Thanks."

Brenda promised to copy the record of the people who called my phone, and I thanked Brenda again, as per my instructions from Polly. Brenda sounded pleased and she certainly wasn't drunk, but it was still early.

I was pretty sure that the man who called from the phone booths was not Edgar. Edgar was just mad and trying to be a bully. The other guy was more sinister. Even if I hadn't had the remnants of a cold, I would have shivered.

I called the Cheektowaga Police to see how Hauser made out with the computer mavens who were supposed to get the information on the silver car.

"He's not here," an officer said. "He called in sick today."

"Do you expect him tomorrow?"

"Mmm, no, he's off tomorrow."

"Thanks. I'll try him later in the week."

I didn't know whether to start all over again with another one of the cops there or bite the bullet and ask Ted to see if he could track down the owner of the silver car.

I was just about to dial Ted's number when Myrtle called to see when she could work on my hair that week.

"Can I get back to you on this?" I said. "I don't know how the week's going to shape up yet."

Myrtle and I chatted awhile about Natasha moving into the Ashland Avenue house and I told her I was going to see Frank the Bean and asked Myrtle what she knew about him.

"Frank's a bookie, a pool shark, and he has gas. That's it. Why do you want to go see him?"

"Sammy did gamble. And Frank takes a lot of bets, I'm told."

"Before long you'll know everybody on the West Side," Myrtle said, laughing.

"I'd like to know who the woman at the funeral parlor was. The one I saw on your block today," I said. "I wonder who she is."

"Maybe one of Sammy's old girlfriends."

"That's what Marie said."

"But I don't know his old girlfriends. I wasn't even born when he started having girlfriends."

"Maybe Mr. Bean will know who she is."

"The Bean knows betting and pool. He doesn't go out with women."

"What about Marie?" I said. "Does the Bean go out with Marie?"

"You mean a paying customer? I wouldn't know about that. Those things *are* secrets in the neighborhood. But everybody says that the Bean doesn't have girlfriends."

"Does he have boyfriends?"

Myrtle laughed again. I could see the big grin in my mind's eye. "Anything like that would be even more of a secret. And speaking of secrets, have you found Billy?"

I wasn't about to give away Billy's secret, but I didn't know how much Myrtle had managed to find out. "Billy called me," I lied. "He just wanted to make sure I'd gotten the package with the key in it."

"Where is he?"

"I don't know."

"Probabilities is hooked up to an eight-hundred number," she said.

She'd called Probabilities, too. "Yes, I know," I said.

"Do you have a number for Natasha?" Myrtle said. She'd had enough on the subject of Billy, I supposed. "I was wondering whether she would let me experiment on her hair for my course. It would be great to have such different hairs to work on. My instructor would flip."

"You'll have to talk to her in the morning," I said. "I can't give out the shelter number."

I looked at the clock when Myrtle hung up and decided that my social life would have to wait. The cold or flu or whatever I had was making me tired, I still hadn't eaten, and I needed time to think about the loose ends.

Horace needed a walk, but I did the lazy exercise routine: I let him out in the backyard. He would run around checking all the places that the birds and squirrels had landed during the day.

When I checked my cupboard for something easy and quick to fix, I found a can of beans. I laughed as I opened them, thinking that I would be able to duel with the Bean—gas for gas.

I rounded out the meal with bread and butter and tea and applesauce. Quick and easy. While I ate, I looked over my notes and added to them.

Edgar, I thought. Would he be likely to do anything more dangerous than call me and breathe heavily?

Horace was barking persistently. It sounded like one of those let-me-in-I've-had-enough-of-squirrels barks.

When I opened the door, I expected Horace to come running in, but he was at the back of the yard by the fence. I could just make him out in the gloom.

"Horace, come."

It was hard to see what he was doing, but he didn't come.

"Come on Horace."

It looked like he lurched toward me and then stopped.

"What's the matter, Horace?" I walked toward him, wondering if he had gotten caught in something. But I couldn't imagine what it could be.

A hand came across my mouth and a voice said in my ear, "Don't make a sound or you and your mutt get it." His other arm wrapped around my chest and he lifted me partly off the ground. He was big. The voice was gravelly, like the one on the phone.

He had been watching me.

I tried to turn my head, but his grip on my head was firm and I caught only a glance. All I saw was the face mask, like the one on the guy in the woods.

Horace started barking louder, more frenzied, as the masked intruder dragged me back toward the door. I hoped he wouldn't shoot the dog. I was sure it was the end. I was waiting for my life to rerun on fast-forward.

In my desperation, I struggled and managed to bite the hand over my mouth.

As the hand came away, I screamed. Horace barked louder.

The hand came back and socked me. "Shut up or you'll wish your husband were back to beat you instead of me."

That stopped me. This guy knew Dick. Or knew about Dick.

I could taste salt. Blood from the blow on my mouth or the tears, I didn't know which. He was pushing me through the kitchen. I tried to remember where my thirty-eight was.

"What do you want?" I said.

"Ha."

He pushed me toward the bedroom and I got the picture. I could still hear Horace barking, but I knew my neighbors were not the kind to react quickly to noises in the dark. My mind was racing. What could I do? Then I remembered the rape counselor who had spoken to the battered women's group.

She had told us that going to the bathroom, urinating or defecating had been known to deter a rapist.

Could I do such a thing? There I was, about to be raped and worrying about dirtying the bedclothes or being perceived as a dirty person.

But I was so frightened that I didn't know whether I had to go to the bathroom or not. I tried to calm myself, tried to make myself talk to this monster who had pushed his way into my house. Maybe talking to him would help.

He pushed me down on the bed and jumped on top of me, pulling first at my blouse and then at my slacks. Buttons snapped off. I heard fabric ripping.

My left arm was hanging off the edge of the bed and

I was trying to remember whether there was anything in the night table that I could use as a weapon, and wondering whether I could open the drawer without his noticing.

"Why are you doing this?" I said. No. that wasn't the right thing to say. "Do I know you? Is that why you're wearing a mask?"

The man turned my head toward him and I could see the glint of his eyes. They were gray. Then he kissed me. Shoved his tongue through the slit in the woolen mask into my mouth.

I tried not to retch. Then I thought, *Why not retch?* Somehow the idea of throwing up was less onerous than that of messing my drawers.

My hand slid along the rug beside the bed and hit something. I felt it. It was a big rawhide bone that Horace had been working on.

I managed one mildly effective retch, which made him draw back.

He was startled and wiped at the mask, which was spotted with york. I thought he gagged.

He looked at me again, through the slits in the mask, furious now. As he lifted his arm to whack me, the doorbell rang. I yelled, and brought up the chunk of rawhide and mashed it alongside his head.

He stood up, dazed, held his face, and ran from the room. "I'll be back," he said.

He was gone.

I reached for the thirty-eight, suddenly remembering that it was in the table by the bed. I went through the kitchen, where the door was still ajar. I grabbed a flashlight from the kitchen drawer and went out into the backyard and shouted for whoever was at the front door to come around to the back.

I yelled, "Help, help, help."

I saw a face appear at the next-door window. Then suddenly from the side of the house, Ted, Horace, and Wally Klune, the paperboy, appeared.

"I heard Horace barking and I let him loose," Wally said. "He was tied to the back fence. Then I went around to the front to ring the bell."

Ted took one look at me and said, "What happened to you?"

I saw his nostrils twitch. I smelled like vomit. So far, Ted and I hadn't had auspicious beginnings.

"A man was here. He pushed me into the house. He was going to attack me. Then the doorbell rang and he ran."

"I saw a car pull away," Ted said.

"Did you get the plate number?"

Ted said nothing.

"I did, Mrs. Kirk," Wally said.

Ted looked sheepish. "Good work, fella. Let's have it."

As soon as Ted was satisfied that I was OK, he got on the phone with the license number. I didn't know whether the cops wanted me to clean up or not. I smelled like a baby who had spit up. But there might be some evidence on me.

"Do I have to wait, Mrs. Kirk?" Wally asked. "I'm doing my collections."

"Oh, your collections. Just a minute, I'll get your money."

I told Wally to remember what had happened and that the cops would catch up with him later. "And thanks for untying Horace and thanks for saving me."

"That guy Ted drove up just as I rang the bell. We both saved you."

"But you got the license number," I said patting him on the shoulder briefly and then backing off as he re-coiled. I forgot how I smelled. "And even if Ted hadn't come along, you would have scared the guy away."

Wally grinned and showed his braces.

"If anybody from the newspaper asks me what happened, that's what I'm going to tell them."

More silver shone from Wally's mouth. "Do you think they'll put my name in the paper?"

"They might. I'll keep my fingers crossed, OK?"

"OK," he said. He patted Horace one more time before he left, and said to the dog, "Maybe you and me will be in the paper, Horace."

It was a long night. The forensic squad picked away at me and the bedclothes with tweezers for about an hour before they would let me get cleaned up. Then they made me put all my clothing in evidence bags. They took the sheets, too.

I began to wonder why they were being so careful. After all, the attack was foiled and we did get the guy's license number.

Ted had left while the Cheektowaga police questioned me and when he returned he was wearing a big smile.

"They got him," he said.

Waves of relief, almost like an intense happiness, rolled through me. I got chills, and then started to giggle hysterically.

"I'm sorry," I said. More giggles. "I'm so relieved. So happy. He said he would be back. And now they caught him. Tee hee hee hee."

It must have been five minutes before I stopped. I was about to ask who it was. But I knew who it was. I remembered how the guy smelled, remembered his size, saw his eyes through the mask, remembered the voice. Why hadn't I remembered these things before?

I didn't tell the cops I knew. After all, he was one of their own. That was why they were questioning me so carefully, why they were so thorough gathering everything that could be evidence.

"He mentioned my ex-husband," I said. "He told me that I would wish Dick were back beating me instead of him if I didn't do what he said. He must be someone who knows me or who knew my ex-husband."

I figured I knew who had put the trace on my phone,

too, and who it was who had chased me in the woods and why I never got the information on the license number. I also had a strong conviction that if any other cop had been there while Dick was bleeding on the street that Dick would still be alive.

Much later, my phone rang and a detective answered it. When he hung up, he said, "Sergeant Hauser wants you to know how sorry he is."

I felt like cursing him, telling the detective that I didn't care whether the shitbag apologized until eternity. I was sick to death of people who tried to take control of other people's lives, to take what they wanted.

I said only, "He can't take back the moment. Tell him that."

Twenty-two

The doorbell woke me the next morning, and I opened the door to a sleepy looking freckled kid with braces.

"It's in the paper, Mrs. Kirk. They took my picture last night and look, it's here."

It must have been a slow day at the *Buffalo News*, because the whole front of the community news page was plastered with pictures of not only Wally, but Horace, Hauser, my house, and Ted. Everybody but me. And that was OK with me. I was definitely getting enough publicity. All the wrong kind.

Along with the pictures was a long rambling story. *Where on earth were the editors last night?* Every piece of information that the reporter could find was listed dutifully in her story, along with all the old stuff about Dick and how he died.

But what I hated most of all was that she called me spunky. *Spunky!* Like some little nerd who talks back. God! I hated that. The only thing good about the story was it was too long and boring for anybody to read to the end, where she called me spunky.

"I guess you wouldn't have to go to school today," I said to Wally. "I mean, the cops kept you up so late. That ought to be an excused absence."

"Are you kidding? I've got to go to school today. To

show the kids the story and my picture. And you know what? My mom said the TV station called, too.''

I groaned inwardly. I hated the idea of dampening Wally's enthusiasm for the media. But I made up my mind that I would not be answering my phone.

The phone! I remembered poor Brenda. The phone would be ringing off the hook and Brenda would be trying to record all the calls.

I said good-bye to Wally and tried to get Brenda, but she must have been en route to work. So I called Polly. Of course, I had to give Polly the whole story before I asked her if she could get the message to Brenda.

Polly told me that I ought to try to live a less-stressful life.

''I'd like that,'' I said, thinking that it might even be possible now that Hauser was in jail and Edgar was soon to be confronted. The way I envisioned putting Edgar in his place was to sic Ted on him, preferably in uniform. However, I hadn't mentioned that to Ted yet.

I called Natasha at the office to tell her when I'd get there. I was already overdue by a half hour. Natasha didn't mention anything about the story in the paper, so I figured she hadn't seen it.

''The phones are very busy, Frances. Take your time. I'll be here,'' Natasha said, and hung up on me. I couldn't complain about her conscientiousness.

I spent about twenty minutes scrubbing again the floors and the places where Hauser had been the night before, as if washing up would erase the fact. It was the corollary to washing someone's mouth out with soap after a nasty word had been emitted. But all the scrubbing didn't erase the memory. It was still vivid.

While I was getting ready to go to work, the phone rang three times. I listened as a Channel Four reporter told my machine that he wanted the story for the six-o'clock news. The next call was from Marsha.

''Fran, I can't tell you how glad I am that they caught that terrible policeman. When he came to the house . . .''

I picked up. "Sergeant Hauser was at your house? What was he doing there?"

"He told me not to make trouble." Marsha started to weep. "He said terrible things about Dick."

Pot calling the kettle, I thought. "But why was he at your place?"

"After I called the precinct and asked about what had happened to Dick, the sergeant called me and told me he would explain everything to me. I wouldn't have let him come over if I had known what kind of man he was."

"Maybe you'd better call the precinct again and put in a complaint about the sergeant."

Marsha demurred at first, but after I gave her the name of the cop that was at my house the night before and told her some of the other things Hauser had done, she said she would make the call.

The phone rang once more before I left for the office. It was a radio reporter. I didn't pick up.

The media were not only besieging me by phone, however, as I found out when the garage door slid up. My usual view in the rearview mirror of the houses across the street was obscured by the vans of Channel Two and Channel Seven. Thank heaven for the automatic door opener. All I had to do was back out and push the button and drive away.

They pointed cameras at me and then jumped back in their vans and followed me. I could imagine the voice-overs that they were doing while they pursued me. I was hoping for some calamity to occur somewhere, some wildly dramatic news event to happen so that they would lose interest in me. But I had second thoughts about that. A calamity would hurt somebody else.

I drove right to the mall, where I knew my way around and hoped I could lose them. I led them up and down the aisles of cars, behind the trucks at the rear of the stores, and then played my ace. I had once had to make a pickup at the furniture store and knew that I could drive in one door and out on the other side of the building. As I hoped, they waited outside when I drove into the doorway by the loading dock.

The clerk inside was happy to open the other door, for a small fee, and I was on my way. I wondered if there would be reporters waiting for me at the office, and wished I had my old gray wig and dumpy coat with me.

Instead of risking another confrontation with the media, I pulled off the expressway and called Natasha again.

"Don't hang up," I said. "I need to know whether there are reporters hanging around there."

"Reporters? What have you been up to now?"

"A man tried to rape me last night. My paper boy saved me."

"Are you all right? I won't ask you questions now, but you must tell the whole story, every detail, at the meeting tonight." I could hear the phones ringing, but Natasha wasn't worrying about phones now; she was all concerned for my welfare.

"Yes. But could you look to see if there are media people hanging around?"

"Just a minute. I'll look."

Natasha was back quickly, the phones no longer ringing. She had turned on the answering tape. "I see one car out front that could be reporters. And when I went downstairs, Gene told me that there was somebody in the back earlier. Oh, by the way, Looks had to close today. They have a serious plumbing problem. The gentleman at the deli is letting me use his bathroom."

"Damn, what am I going to do?"

"That's simple. Don't come in. I can manage without you. That is, I can manage without you until later tonight. I would like some help moving after the meeting."

"You've got it," I said, "and thanks. I'll head over to the West Side to talk to Frank the Bean."

"Oh, yes, the man with the unfortunate intestinal problem. Myrtle told me about him." Natasha laughed her smooth, deep laugh.

"I plan to see him before lunch," I said.

Natasha laughed again. "A good plan," she said. "I'll see you later."

Cafe Roma had a sign in the window that said "Closed. Open at 5 P.M." I knocked and knocked, but no one answered. I went through the alley and around to the back, figuring that there must be a rear entrance. The alley was stacked with beer crates; there was barely room to squeeze through. I heard a loud yowl, and was face to face with a huge cat, who obviously thought I was intruding on his territory. He did not look like he was in the mood to be talked to or to have his head rubbed.

I put my hands in front of my face, in case he was thinking about jumping me. But as soon as I moved my hands, he was gone like a streak. I plowed on through the junk in the alley. Even with my cold, I could tell it didn't smell too great, either. Some of the drunks couldn't find the way to the bathroom.

The back door to Cafe Roma was propped open with a tire. Inside the place was dark. The rectangle of light from outdoors fell on a grimy tile floor that might have once been white.

"Frank," I called. "It's Fran Kirk. Are you in there?"

I thought I heard someone say something. I wasn't sure it was an invitation to enter, but I stepped inside anyway. I didn't go far, because I couldn't see.

I called again. This time louder. "Yo, Frank. You said I should come today."

Just as my eyes began to pick out shapes in the gloom, a door opened at the far side of the room, letting in more light that silhouetted a large body in the doorway.

"Come in here," the man said.

I couldn't make out his face, but his head was huge and he had a lot of hair. He was about six feet tall, wide-shouldered, short of neck, and probably weighed almost three hundred pounds.

"Frank?" I said.

"He's in here," the man said pointing to the room behind him.

I wanted to turn around and leave. I didn't want to advance any further into that alien environment. The man started to walk toward me and I backed toward the door I came in. In another second, I would have been off and running.

But the voice that I recognized from the phone call hollered at me. "Fran, come in. It's OK. Marco just looks like Frankenstein."

The overhead lights came on. Now Frank was standing in the doorway, a man about five ten, carefully dressed and neatly shaven. His hair looked like it had been styled that morning.

Marco had smiled at the reference to Frankenstein, and I assumed that he took a lot of ribbing about his appearance.

"Marie says you want to know about Sammy's gambling," the Bean said, leading the way into a room full of pool tables. He racked up the balls and offered me a cue.

"I don't know much about pool," I said.

"Give it a try," he said. "I think it should be part of everybody's education. Go ahead. Break."

I lined up the cue ball and shot at the side of the triangle of balls. Somebody once told me to do it that way. It reminded me of bowling, another sport I had to be stubborn to be ignorant of in a town like Cheektowaga. The cue ball hit and the fifteen balls quivered. Hardly what one would call a break.

"Your game needs work," the Bean said, chalking

his cue. He lined up on the cue ball, flicked his wrist, and two balls dropped in the pockets. "You want to play for money?" he asked, grinning.

"No," I said, watching him line up again. "I want to talk about Sammy."

Another ball dropped.

"Did he owe you any money?" I asked.

"No. Sammy always paid. And if he hadn't, his father would have. No problem. Now, my old man would have hung me out to dry." The Bean was cleaning up the table. He never missed.

"Did he gamble much?"

"Much. What's much? Every day? No. Every week? Yes. Not as much in the last few years, but steady."

"Did he win a lot?"

"Average. Everybody wins sometimes."

The conversation went on. Frank dropping balls into the pockets while I watched. I guess he let me break so I would get a turn and be able to say I played pool.

Frank told me the same things other people had told me about Sammy, about his father and mother, about his business, about his wife. Apparently the word wasn't out yet that Karla had left town. But since she and Sammy lived in Orchard Park, the people on the West Side wouldn't see her often enough to miss her.

By the time I got around to describing the woman at the funeral parlor, I began to wonder if Frank the Bean really suffered from the ailment that I'd heard about. But I did have a cold.

"I don't know who it could be. I was at the wake earlier," Frank said. "From your description, it could be any number of women."

"What about old love affairs? Somebody who got hurt?"

"Sammy was a heartbreaker, especially when he was younger. You know, he was like a spoiled kid. His folks always made life easy for him."

"Whose heart did he break?"

"I think Marie's, for one."

"She didn't tell me that."

"She wouldn't. Besides Marie, well, I guess you know about Beth."

"I've heard. But I know it wasn't Beth or Marie at the funeral parlor."

"Then there was Rosie. But that was a long time ago. In high school."

"Rosie?"

"Rose La Polla, a beauty. She was going out with Sammy in their senior year. They went everywhere together. Then, boom, he shows up at the prom with somebody else."

"Was she broken up about it?"

"I don't know; I didn't see her for a while after that. But you know who could tell you about that? Marie. Marie was her best friend."

"But I thought Marie went out with Sammy, too."

"Later. A couple of years later. Sammy dropped her, too. The same way, suddenly. He was like that."

"Sounds like he trampled on a lot of feelings."

"I guess you could say that." Frank had cleaned off the table and was getting ready to rack up the balls again. "Want a drink? Soda, beer, a shot?"

"Ginger ale would taste good," I said. On Frank's signal I took what I figured would be my only turn at the balls on the table. I broke the pack, better this time, but no balls rolled into the pockets.

"Marco, get the lady a ginger ale and get me a drink, too."

Marco lumbered in from the back room and went into the front, where, I assumed, there was a bar.

"When Sammy was going out with Beth, did he gamble more then?" I was remembering what Beth had said about the funny names they made up while they were at play.

"No. But he won more. He was on a streak."

He might have been better off if he'd stayed with Beth, I thought.

Marco brought my ginger ale and a glass of strange-looking liquid for Frank.

Frank tilted his glass toward me and said, "Banana daquiri."

"The astronauts don't eat bananas before a flight." I offered this bit of information before I could stop my-self. Another case of my mouth running when my brain was not in gear.

"Why's that?" he asked, which was a normal thing for him to do.

My face turned colors. I had trapped myself. "It gives them gas," I said, as offhandedly as I could manage. "And you know what close quarters they have in a spaceship."

The Bean looked at his glass in a strange way and put it down on the edge of the table. He missed his next shot.

I took aim at a ball that was standing right in front of a corner pocket, trying to remember how to hit the cue ball so that it didn't roll right in after it. I aimed just under the curve, recalling that it would give the cue ball a back spin and stop it after impact.

It worked, and I got a huge thrill. But that was the end of my streak. And Frank had regained his compo-sure, but he had not touched his drink.

"Do you ever bet the ponies?" the Bean said.

"No. I don't know the first thing about it."

Frank handed me a racing form that had been lying on a shelf near the pool table. On second look, the shelf looked like a desk, one that Frank would work at while standing up. There was a phone on it, and it looked like a window over it opened into the back room. "Look at those lists," he said, indicating six or seven groups of horses' names with numbers after them. "Those are the horses running this afternoon down in New York."

I prepared to glance over the names dutifully and hand the sheet back, but one horse's name caught my eye: "If Looks Could Kill."

Frank saw me pause. "What are the odds on the horse you like?" he said.

When he saw the confusion on my face, he said, "The numbers to the right. What are they?"

"Twenty hyphen one."

Frank shrieked and then broke into a laugh. "Twenty hyphen one," he howled. "That's twenty to one." When his hysteria subsided, he explained how the odds worked.

"You mean if I give you a dollar and the horse wins, I get twenty dollars back?"

"You'd have to give me two dollars," he said. "We don't take one-dollar bets. As a matter of fact we are thinking about not taking any bets under five. So? You want to bet on that nag?"

"I've never bet on a horse before."

"I'da never guessed. But you know, it's fun."

I dug into my purse and came up with two bucks, which I handed over to Frank, who gave me a ticket on "If Looks Could Kill."

"Good luck," he said. "And now I think you'd better clear out. It's almost time for the lunch crowd."

When I made my way back up the alley, I checked my watch. It was already almost noon, and I didn't think I had accomplished very much.

I was logging in my time and mileage and making notes about what Frank had told me when I saw what Frank meant by the lunch crowd.

Out of nowhere a line of men were streaking toward the alley. Some of them had their money in their hands. And when I looked around all the parking places on the block were taken, and a car pulled up behind me, waiting to get into my parking spot.

My next stop would be the house on Ashland. Marie

had hinted that she might be able to give me the name of the woman at the funeral parlor, and Frank had told me that Marie was a close friend of a girl Sammy jilted in high school. Not that a high school romance would lead me to Sammy's killer, but it would help round out the picture I was getting of Sammy. And the picture of Sammy I was getting was one of a self-centered man-child who probably would never have grown up. Of course, that didn't make it legal to kill him, but it might have made someone mad enough to do it.

There wasn't much stirring at Ashland Avenue. I had never been there so early in the day, and I assumed that the women slept late. I saw a movement in the hallway as I approached the leaded glass doors to the vestibule. Good, I thought. Someone's awake and will let me in.

But no one came when I knocked. *Whoever it was was probably sleepwalking*, I thought, and leaned on the bell.

Lina, a tall, skinny, stringy-haired blond, opened the door. "Shhh. Everybody's sleeping. What's up?"

"I came to see Marie," I said. "Isn't anyone awake? It's after noon."

"Is that all?" Lina said. "I'm going back to sleep." And she headed down the hall and went into a room under the stairs.

"Wait," I called. "Where's Marie's room?"

She poked her head back into the hall. "Third floor, second door to the left."

This was the first time I'd been in this house when I hadn't been met at the door by a swarm of women. It was the only time I'd seen the place in broad daylight. Actually it seemed darker at noon, because none of the lights were on and the aged woodwork, which took on a friendly glow in incandescent lighting, looked gloomy and gothic by day.

I listened for signs of activity, but heard none as I walked up the carpet runner on the broad stairs to the second floor. The squeaking of the wood steps rattled in the silence.

At the top of the first flight I heard a rumble and identified the sound as a contented snore coming from the room at the top of the stairs.

The stairs to the third floor were narrower and darker, walled in, while the lower stairs were open. It occurred to me that my cold was subsiding because I was detecting the faint odor of mildew in the stairwell, probably from the carpeting, which was old and worn.

The odor of mildew was replaced by a thick sweet smell as I neared the top of the stairs. The odor grew stronger as I turned to the left and saw that the second door was open. My reluctant feet took me toward the open doorway, even though my mind was telling me what the smell was. Disbelief and denial is strong in a person seeking normalcy.

When I stopped screaming, there was a crowd of women surrounding me, some of them screaming.

Marie was lying on her bed with a kitchen knife in her chest. The blood was still dripping into the puddle by the side of the bed. Several of us noticed the mirror over the vanity at the same time. Written in red, probably lipstick, it said, "Good-bye Natasha."

"Don't touch anything," I said.

"No, nobody touch anything. Everybody get out of here," Valerie said, assuming control.

"Call the cops," somebody said.

"I did," Dot said, coming into the room. "As soon as I heard the screaming, I dialed nine-one-one. Oh, God." And she began screaming.

As Valerie shooed the women out of the room, I looked around. Marie apparently hadn't struggled. If I had to guess, she never woke up when the killer came in the room.

I heard the women in the hall mentioning Natasha.

"If he was after her, maybe we don't want her living

here. Who knows who'll get it next time?" a voice, maybe Jill's said.

"I don't care what anybody else does," someone said, "but I'm clearing out of here."

"Nobody's leaving until the cops are done," Valerie said.

I went back into the hall. "Did anybody hear anything?" I asked. "Did anyone come into any of your rooms?"

"Brrr, no."

"Oh, God, I'm such a heavy sleeper, I wouldn't have heard anything."

The cops were at the door, and Lina ran down to let them in. In a few seconds, who but Ted and his partner, Roland, should come running up the stairs two at a time. When they saw Marie, they called on their walkie-talkies for the medical examiner and the homicide squad.

"Who found her?" Ted said, looking straight at me.

"I did." I felt like adding, I didn't do it, because he was looking at me so accusingly.

"Did you touch the body? Or anything else in the room?"

"No." I guessed Ted was doing his job the way he was supposed to, but he seemed angry at me.

"Did anyone else touch anything?" he asked the assembled women in the hall, who either shook their heads or said no.

Roland started taking the names of all the women in the hall and asking about who else had been there that night. He acted skeptical when the women said that no one but the resident women had been there.

He asked if the doors were locked and who had keys and who was the last one in and did she lock the door.

While Roland asked questions, Ted took notes in Marie's bedroom. Then he came out and asked me what I was doing there, but before I could answer him, detectives Brockway and O'Connor, who had visited my house in the wee hours of the night Sammy died, came lumbering up the stairs.

Brockway's mustache was as jaunty as ever, but O'Connor was wearing a suit that was too small for him, instead of the roomy one he had worn the last time we met. I got the picture of a man who was constantly gaining and losing weight, who only occasionally fit into the clothes he had in his closet.

The detectives sent Ted and Roland and the women to the parlor, but they kept me there and asked me when I had found her and what I had done and how I happened to be there.

I told them that the front door had been locked and that Lina had answered the door.

The way O'Connor talked, I expected them to cuff me.

"Who's Natasha?" Brockway wanted to know.

I explained.

"She takes appointments for these women to go out with men?" O'Connor said.

"Yes. But she just started the job. I used to do it until Mr. Lightfoot left town."

"Lightfoot's dating service," Brockway said to O'Connor, as if he were explaining something to him.

"And who'd want to kill Natasha?"

I told O'Connor about Carlyle shooting Natasha and about all the times he had beaten her. "But I thought he was in jail," I said.

"So, if he got out, why would he come here looking for her?"

"I don't know. That seems funny to me," I said. "Natasha only decided last night to move in here. And she spent last night at the shelter."

"What shelter?"

"The battered women's shelter."

"Where is that?" O'Connor said.

"I can't tell you that," I said. "You'll have to get that information through channels."

O'Connor gritted his teeth and stood close to me, his face about six inches from my face. "What do you mean, you can't tell me."

"She can't tell you," Brockway hollered. "Cops beat their wives, too."

O'Connor backed off, and I thought a secret had just been revealed.

"Bully," I said. I couldn't help it. I was pissed off at the way he had acted.

O'Connor wheeled around as if I had shot off a gun.

Brockway was in between us, talking, before anything could happen. "Mrs. Kirk, officers are permitted some leeway in their actions while interrogating. Now, please wait down in the living room with the others."

I left the room, but before I got to the stairway, I heard Brockway reaming out O'Connor about his short fuse.

When I got downstairs, I asked Roland if I could make a phone call.

"Who to?" he asked.

"Natasha," I said. "If someone's after her, she has to know."

"We'll send a car," he said. "We'll have someone bring her here."

"Hurry," I said. "She's alone in the office and the beauty parlor is closed because of a plumbing problem. She might be the only one in the building. Please. I think I should call her and warn her."

While I called Natasha, Roland dispatched a car to the office.

Natasha locked the office door as soon as I told her what had happened. When she came back to the phone, she said, "Carlyle was in jail the last I heard. The administrator at the shelter keeps close tabs on perpetrators."

"Do you know who else would be after you?"

"He does have friends, but I was put at ease about them by the probation department. They don't think any of them will stick their necks out for Carlyle."

"Maybe he met some new friends in the jail," I said.

"Now that's a comforting thought."

"Don't get comfortable," I said, with some intensity. "I want you to be alert. I don't want anything to happen to you."

"Don't worry, Frances. I am all right. And the policemen are here now."

"Good," I said. "I'll see you soon."

As I waited in the living room, looking around at the women who lived in the Ashland Avenue house, I asked myself: *Who would want to kill Natasha if not Carlyle? How would someone mistake Marie for Natasha? Why would someone think that Natasha was sleeping on the third floor? Would one of the women have killed her and written that on the mirror as a ruse?*

Marie couldn't have been dead for long before I discovered her. It must have been in daylight that she was killed. Therefore, if the killer was after Natasha, he got the wrong information about her whereabouts and he didn't know Natasha.

The more I thought about it, the more I thought that Natasha wasn't the intended victim. Marie was. And the killer wanted to hide the motive. *But what motive? Was Marie's murder related to Sammy's death?* Marie was probably Joe Plata's girlfriend. *Was somebody trying to get at Joe by killing off his loved ones?*

I tried to talk to Ted, but he had his work to do, interviewing the inhabitants of the house. The women were quiet, as if they were making plans.

And they probably were. I figured that by nightfall the house would be empty. It looked like Natasha would have no place to move to after all, and a major portion of the business known as Billy's Dating Service seemed about to evaporate.

It looked like I'd be closing down the office after all. And maybe I'd be checking the want ads for a job with less stress, like short-order cooking, where I'd only have to keep track of who got fries and who got mashed potatoes with their hamburger.

My mind dropped back to a night when a couple of burgers and a large order of fries sat on a formica tabletop chilling as Dick and I looked into one another's eyes and thought we saw happiness ever after.

Twenty-three

I was a long time getting out of the precinct, where the cops took me for questioning. I couldn't blame them. In the past two weeks, I was in places where corpses turned up. And then there were Hauser's capers. If I wasn't a criminal, I was a magnet for crime.

Detectives O'Connor and Brockway were trying to make some kind of unified theory out of everything that happened, despite my protests.

"It's not all related except that it's all connected to my life," I said, sounding not as sensible as I thought.

"Are you sure Sergeant Hauser didn't know anything about this Billy's Dating Service?" O'Connor asked.

"He might have known about it," I said. "But, did he do anything about it? No. I don't think so."

"If he was so interested in you, he might have considered the women in the house some kind of threat to you," Brockway said.

"But the sergeant is in jail," I said. "Marie must have been killed after eleven this morning."

"How do you know that?" O'Connor said, jumping over to my chair. His kangaroo routine was unnerving. So was his tight suit, for that matter. I kept thinking he was going to split one of the crucial seams.

"Because the blood was still dripping when I found the body."

"Who knew Natasha was going to move into the house?"

I took a breath and got ready to answer the question for the fourth time. But this time they got something new. I guess that's why they kept asking the same questions.

"All the women in the house knew; Myrtle from Looks knew; Natasha may have told some people at the shelter, and she told Polly, too, or else I told Polly, I forget which."

"Who's Polly?"

Oh, God, I thought. *Now they're going to drag Polly into this.* "She's the leader of the support group, the battered women's group."

"Oh, yeah?" O'Connor said. I didn't like the look on his face. I was becoming convinced that the man had a big problem with violence. *A wife beater,* I thought. *Probably been through Family Court already.* I worried that he'd take out his anger on Polly.

"I'll call her," Brockway said. And O'Connor dropped it.

I felt like telling Brockway that he was wasting his time taking care of a loser like O'Connor. But people who are into caretaking don't listen until they are sick and tired of all the disappointments that the O'Connors of the world dish out.

When the detectives finally let me go, I barely had time to go home and take care of Horace and then get to the Community Center for the meeting. I made myself a peanut butter sandwich and ate it in the car on the way.

We waited for a half hour and Polly didn't show. Then I told the others where I thought Polly might be, and we sort of started the meeting without her, Natasha and I being the target for the questions.

"How could someone kill that Italian girl thinking it was Natasha?" Minnie said. "You don't look Italian at all, Natasha."

"Thank you," Natasha said with a look that no one could decipher. "But I'd like to know why someone would think I was in a room on the third floor. I've never even been to the third floor."

"That's it," I said, and everybody looked at me expectantly. "If someone knew enough to look for Natasha at the Ashland Avenue house, that someone would have looked for Natasha in Billy's old rooms. You see? It doesn't figure that someone would have one piece of information without the other."

"You conclude, then," Natasha said, "that whoever killed Marie meant to kill Marie."

"Yes," I said. "And that puts us back on the West Side. Probably with someone who knew both Sammy and Marie and probably killed them both."

"Your mystery lady?" Natasha said.

"Who's the mystery lady?" Brenda asked.

I told her about the two times I had seen her, but as I was telling her, a picture flashed through my head. And as the others continued to talk, a conviction grew in me that I knew who she was.

The next time I tuned in to the group discussion, Brenda was saying, "And one of the calls was from Minnie's number, but there was no message from Minnie. But there was someone who got on the line and breathed heavily."

I waited to see what Minnie's reaction would be.

"I'll bet Edgar was trying to frighten you, Fran," she said. "He was really mad at the way you bossed him around on the phone that day."

"He hasn't heard the last of me," I said.

"Oh, please," she said.

I knew he had taken it out on her last time. But I had thought about this. "Why should I let him get away with abusing me?" I said, and left unsaid the part about her letting him get away with abusing her.

"Doesn't Polly say that we shouldn't keep the secrets?'' Brenda said. ''The secrets protect them. Then they get away with it.''

Minnie was on the spot. I could almost hear her sweat.

''I have an idea, Minnie,'' I said. ''I have a friend who is a policeman. Maybe he would go to your house and give him a warning about the phone call.''

''But after he leaves,'' Minnie said, tears running.

''Why don't we all wait nearby,'' Amy said. ''And when he starts hitting on Minnie, we burst in and beat him silly.''

Amy sitting there over her enormous belly and voicing such belligerence, made us all laugh.

''If we beat him up, he probably would be too ashamed to have us arrested for it,'' Natasha said.

Minnie had stopped crying and had started to giggle.

''We could beat up all of them. Give them a taste of their own medicine,'' Amy said.

''Instead of a support group,'' I said, ''we would be a terrorist group.''

''And the violence would continue,'' said Polly from the doorway.

We turned, guiltily, like children caught saying childish things.

''I'm sorry I'm late. I walked in in the middle. Catch me up on what's going on,'' Polly said.

Later that night Minnie made the big leap. She decided to go to the shelter with Natasha and start the legal proceedings that would either break up her marriage or get her husband into counseling and get her some protection.

As we were getting ready to leave, Polly called me aside. I expected that she would voice her displeasure about being called by the cops.

''I was teed off at first,'' she said. ''But the detective, Brockway was it?''

''Yes.''

''He didn't keep me long, and when he was done, I

went over to Ashland Avenue.''

"You went there?''

"You told me I should meet them, didn't you?''

"Yes, but . . .''

"Well, I did. And we had a good talk. I'm going to meet with them at the house regularly on Monday afternoons.''

"You started a group of,'' I laughed out loud. But then, I stopped laughing. "I thought they would be all moving out because of what happened.''

"We talked about that, too,'' Polly said. "They're not moving. But they are going to get better security.''

"Wait a minute,'' I said. "How do they know one of them didn't do it?''

"That was the good part about my meeting them today,'' Polly said, looking smug. "They decided they trust one another.''

I couldn't believe that Polly had established that much harmony among those women who so easily scrapped and argued.

Minnie and Natasha were waiting for me to give them a ride to the shelter. I told them about Polly starting a group with the dating-service women and we all laughed, but we admired Polly, too, for sticking to her notions about the way the world ought to be for women.

After I dropped them off, I went back to the precinct. I had a favor to ask of Ted, who, along with Roland, was doing a double shift that night.

Ted was such a straight arrow, it wasn't easy persuading him to do a little surveillance for me, but finally he agreed that it wouldn't really hurt anyone. Actually, Roland was the one that gave Ted the final push.

"We can do that, Ted. Unless a call comes in for us. It won't take long, and Fran might find her mystery woman.''

Roland found an old coat and hat for me and I got into the back of the squad car.

"If we have to arrest anybody, Fran," Ted said, "You're going to have to get out and walk."

"It's a deal," I said, thinking that Ted was kind of a nice wimp.

Roland drove to Rhode Island Avenue and parked across the street from the Plata house. I hunched in the back, trying to look like someone who had been picked up for some crime.

"Do you guys have any binoculars?" I asked.

"Since when do suspects carry binoculars?" Ted said.

"We do," Roland said. "But don't let anyone see them or you'll blow your cover." Then he giggled. I could tell he wasn't taking this very seriously.

"Nobody's peeking out the windows," I said. "Could you turn on your overheads?"

We sat in the car, and the lights flashed, hitting the windows of the sleeping West Siders. But I was watching the windows at one house.

A front door opened across the street from the Plata house, then a window was cranked open down the block. Myrtle came to her front door, and I pressed myself back against the seat and pulled my hat down, but I kept looking. Joe Plata appeared in the second floor window. Several more doors opened and one of the neighbors came toward the car. Finally I saw her. Behind Myrtle on the front steps. The mystery woman. Myrtle's mother.

"That's her," I said.

The neighbor hadn't gotten to the car yet, and I think Ted and Roland were relieved not to have to talk to him. Roland put the car in gear and drove off.

"So now what are you going to do?" Ted asked.

I didn't know. I was thinking about the time Myrtle grabbed my arm when I started to chase the mystery woman. I decided Myrtle was trying to protect her mother. "I'll go talk to her while Myrtle and her father are working."

"Are you sure you want to do that? Suppose she

killed Sammy and Marie. What's to stop her from killing you, too?'' Ted said.

"I have a hunch that she's not the killer.''

"What good is a hunch?'' Ted said.

"Hunches can be powerful weapons in our game,'' Roland said.

"I'll take my thirty-eight with me,'' I said.

Ted spun in his seat. "You have a thirty-eight?''

I looked at his face and wondered whether this incipient romance of ours was over.

Roland was laughing. "I told you, didn't I, Ted?''

"What did you tell him, Roland?''

"That you had a gun. He didn't believe it.''

"How did you know?''

Roland laughed. "It was a hunch.''

I laughed, too, and Ted reluctantly joined in. But I thought that Roland's hunch was something he developed while he was looking over the gun-registration lists.

"Are you going to tell O'Connor and Brockway about the mystery woman?'' Ted asked.

"Of course,'' I lied. "But they think that as an investigator I'm good at chasing my own tail.''

"That's not so, Fran,'' Ted said. He was starting to sound like the high priest of copdom. "They were excited about those glasses that you found.''

I was so pissed I almost screamed at him. I thought he was going to tell me about the prints on the glasses before he turned them over to the detectives. I was getting the picture of Ted as an eager beaver trying to butter up the guys and improve his chances of getting on the squad. I was even suspecting him of hanging around me to find out what I knew.

Instead of scratching his eyes out, I said, "Whose prints did they find on them besides Myrtle's?'' I controlled myself admirably, I thought.

"Nobody's,'' he said. "I thought I told you.''

Ha. Sure you did. "No, you didn't," I said.

Roland was no fool; he knew what was happening. And he tried to smooth out the feathers. "Well, we had a successful evening. A short stakeout. And Fran found her mystery woman."

"Yes," I said to Roland, "and I appreciate what you did."

Ted said nothing the rest of the ride, and when we reached the precinct, I said good night and got in my car.

What the hell, I said to myself. *You lose some and you lose some. It's not like it was a big romance.*

I went shopping at an all-night supermarket and bought a lot of snack food for eating in front of the TV. If I was going to be spending my evenings alone, I would have brownies, chips and dip, and cheese and crackers to console me.

Twenty-four

Wednesday was cold and blustery and the weatherman was predicting snow. The cloud cover was gray and low, and I could almost see the daffodils shiver.

At nine o'clock, I called the Nevada number and woke up Billy and Karla. It was six in the morning there. Billy was boiling, but he stopped being mad at me when I told him about Marie.

"I don't like it, Fran. Something's going on over there. Joe Plata may know what it is, but he's not going to say even if they are after him."

"Amen," Karla said on the other phone.

"How are you feeling Karla? Aren't you getting close?"

"No. I still have another month. But I'll tell you something. This kid is huge. I'm huge."

"You're twice the woman you were," Billy said.

I could imagine him smiling, the lips drawing up and revealing the big yellow teeth. I wondered whether Karla was smiling back at him and what she looked like when she smiled. All she had ever given me was that tight, little grin. Then, out of the clear blue, I remembered the haircut that Billy got just before he left town. Karla was plying her trade, I figured.

"Karla, when are you coming to supervise the furniture movers?" I said.

"I'm flying into Buffalo tonight." I wondered if she would have told me if I hadn't asked.

"Do you want me to pick you up?"

"Thanks, Fran, but I'm going to rent a car at the airport."

"When are the movers coming?"

"Tomorrow morning, early."

"Where are you going to stay?"

"At the house."

Billy spoke up. "You're going to stay in the house alone? I mean, with all that's happened?"

"Why don't you stay with your mother?" I said.

"My mother is out here with me."

"Oh." This move of Billy's and Karla's sounded more and more like something that had been planned before Joe Plata told them to beat it. "Well, someone else, then."

"Like who? Carmelita Plata?"

I could hear the sneer in her voice as she spoke of her mother-in-law. Billy was mumbling something I couldn't quite make out, but he didn't like the idea of her staying alone.

"Besides," she said, "there's a good security system at the house."

"Fran," Billy said, "do you think you could stay with Karla?"

"I don't need . . ." I heard Karla say, and then there was a deal of whispering.

"I have a dog to take care of," I said. I didn't exactly feel like obliging. I had gone far enough, offering to pick her up at the airport.

"A dog?" Karla sounded aghast.

More whispering.

"I've got to go," I said. "I've got things to do at the office."

"Hold on a minute, Fran, please. Hang up will you

Karla? Listen Fran, I'd like you to stay with Karla. I'll pay you a day's pay and expenses."

I heard more background noise from Karla about the dog.

"And can you get somebody to take care of your dog?"

"Sure. As long as you're paying expenses. That's one of them." *And I'll see what else I can find out about Karla while I've got her alone*, I thought.

Once Karla was reassured that I wouldn't be bringing a hairy animal into the sterile confines of the house in Parkland Heights, she stopped objecting to the idea of my staying there with her. Billy was delighted.

"I owe you one, Fran," he said. "Take good care of her for me."

You owe me more than one, you sneak, I thought. "I will," I said. I should have held out for a hundred a day, the rate Sunset was paying.

When I hung up, I called Natasha to see how she was doing and how Minnie had made out.

"Minnie's down at Family Court this morning with a woman from the Coalition on Women's Security. Minnie's very determined to change things now."

"Good. I hope it isn't too tough on her."

"I think she got her first taste of freedom last night. They let her call him and tell him she wouldn't be home. Of course they stayed right by her so she wouldn't turn tail and tell him where she was and tell him to come and pick her up. But she was great. Not snotty. Very matter-of-fact. That's a sure sign that she's really going to do it. She acted detached."

"That's what happens."

Then Natasha told me that the calls were coming into the dating service normally, despite the murder. People were still calling for their catalogue items and for their dates.

"Dates!" I shouted. "Listen Natasha, get Valerie to check on who is calling for Marie. And especially who is not calling for Marie. Tell her not to tell anyone about Marie. The cops haven't let out much information yet. They've been telling the press that they are trying to locate next of kin.''

"Will do, Fran. Now don't you put yourself in danger trying to find out who killed Marie. That was a nasty business.''

"Speaking of business, is Looks open?''

"Yes," she said. "They found the source of the plumbing problem. Cement.''

"Cement?''

"Yes. Someone dumped cement down the toilet and it hardened in the main sewer line.''

"That's really peculiar,'' I said. "Someone had to do that overnight.''

"That's what the plumber told Gene.''

"Did Gene have any theories about who did it?''

"He thinks he knows who it was.''

"But why? Did he say?''

"Someone he was going to fire.''

"Beth,'' I said. "I'll bet he was going to fire Beth. She didn't fit in with the others.''

"Did she go out with Sammy at one time?''

"Yes. Why?''

"Gene said something like that,'' Natasha said. "But I should get back to work.''

When I stopped in Looks later, Gene told me that he was, indeed, about to fire Beth.''

"And she's not here, she called in sick. A guilty conscience,'' Gene said.

"But couldn't she have done the job with an old sock? Using cement sounds like overkill.''

"If she wanted to do some damage, cost the shop more money, she would do just what she did. I'm running the place now and I've got to show good numbers or Papa Joe will close us up. Beth never liked me anyway, and I haven't wasted any good feelings on her, either.''

His theory made sense, if Beth didn't want to see Gene or the shop succeed. But I was wondering whether this was another stab at Joe Plata. I also wondered whether any funny money went through the books.

"How are your numbers?'' I asked.

"We're not pulling in any twenty-five hundred a day, I can tell you that. Not even on a Friday or a Saturday. And yet, some days we seem to be just as busy as when Sammy was here.''

"Did Joe give you any idea what he expects?'' Gene was either naive or was acting innocent.

"He hasn't said. I'm supposed to deposit the money and checks every day, and he'll send our paychecks every Friday.''

Ah, I thought, Joe or one of his minions runs the account. He can run money through it without Gene being the wiser.

"Does he check up on you?'' I said, smiling.

"Yes, he does. I don't know how, but, yes, he knows what goes on here.''

Myrtle lives next door to him, I thought, and has been on good terms with the Platas for years. And Beth might grind her axe by snooping. Kathy and Dan could be the tattletales, too.

"Well, I'm not the spy,'' I said.

"It doesn't matter. Nobody is cheating him. And that's what he's most interested in.''

I stopped briefly to talk to Myrtle about her experiments on my hair and told her I couldn't make it that night because Karla was coming to town.

Myrtle smiled that strobe-light grin and said, "It's OK. Natasha is going to lend me her head tonight.''

"Great,'' I said. "But I promise you next week you can do my hair twice.''

"You've got it."

The woman who was getting a shampoo from Myrtle raised her arm. "Massage over here, will you, Myrtle?"

Myrtle jerked her head and rolled her eyes at me and began the massage. I left. Looks was understaffed and overworked. I heard Gene on the phone canceling some of the appointments.

So long as Myrtle was occupied, I decided I'd go back to Rhode Island Avenue to see Mrs. Divenzio. But since she was not going to answer the door if she saw me on the front steps, I would wear my gray wig, which I had recently packed into a box in the back seat of my car along with other things that I might need from time to time. And that included my thirty-eight.

I had been in the vicinity when two murders were committed. I could easily have met the killers face to face. I'd been lucky, and I couldn't count on luck if I was going to continue to work for Sunset.

I parked a couple of blocks away from the Divenzio house, put on the wig, put the gun in my purse, and pulled up the collar of my coat, which was a sensible thing to do anyway, since the wind was roaring off Lake Erie and driving snow along with it. I had to tie my scarf around my head to keep the wig from blowing away.

Mrs. Divenzio had let me into the foyer before she recognized me.

"You!" she shouted. "Get out!"

"OK, I'm going. But I don't see why you're so unfriendly. Myrtle likes me. I took her old job at Mr. Lightfoot's place." I tried to talk fast and say something that would connect with her in some way.

"Billy's name isn't Lightfoot," she said.

"Really? That's the name on everything in the office."

"He used to be Boccherini," she said, warming to the role. "But everybody called him Botch. Then he went away and when he came back he was Lightfoot." As she talked she tossed her head as she had in the funeral parlor that night. It was a gesture that I had noticed only recently in Myrtle.

"I didn't know that," I said, which was true. But I also was glad that she was talking to me. "Billy told me that he and Sammy were good friends. What did Sammy think about Billy changing his name?"

"He thought it was funny," she said and then looked guilty. "Come in," she said. "I just made coffee."

Over coffee and a delicious apricot pastry, which she had also made, Mrs. Divenzio stalled and talked about Billy: the odd outfits he used to wear in high school, the deals he used to make with other kids, selling them cigarettes, selling marijuana, getting copies of exams. Finally, she got around to talking about Sammy and she made a big show of telling me why she sneaked into the funeral parlor.

"I used to date Sammy a long time ago. I guess I still had feelings for him and wanted to see him alone." She wiped a tear from her eye with a lace-edged hanky that was embroidered with an *R*. "Then when I saw you there, I was embarrassed. I didn't want to talk about it."

"In high school?" I said. "Did you date him in high school?"

She squirmed. "Yes. I said it was long ago."

"Rose La Polla?"

"Yes," she said. "That was my maiden name."

"It must have been awkward living next door to someone you were in love with."

Her eyes flashed like knives. "I didn't say I was in love with him. I'm a married woman. You are putting too much emphasis on what I said."

I wasn't completely satisfied with her explanation, but it didn't look like I was going to get any more.

"You won't tell Myrtle, will you?" she said. "She's so young. And I wouldn't want her to know that I went out with a man with a reputation like Sammy had."

Myrtle never talked about going out with men at all,

which I thought was odd for a twenty-year-old. Maybe her mother had her scared of men, I thought. I assured Mrs. Divenzio that her secret was safe with me. "I won't even tell her I came to see you," I said.

"Good. I won't tell her either."

I thanked her for the coffee and pastry. "Would you consider giving me the recipe?" I asked.

She thought a second. "I'll try to write it down and send it to you."

I'll bet she doesn't tell me the whole recipe, either, I thought.

I drove the few blocks to Cafe Roma. There was about an inch of snow on the road already. At the back door of the pool parlor Marco was sweeping a path through the snow, probably getting ready for the noontime bettors.

"Frank here?" I said.

"He's outa town," Marco, the monster, said. "Did you wanna make a bet?"

"No, thanks. I'll catch him another time."

Walking in the shelter of the alley next to Cafe Roma felt almost comfortable. The weather was really gearing up for a Buffalo Special. It wasn't like the Blizzard of '77, by whose standards we have measured all of our storms since, but it was starting to look like it would leave several inches and drift badly.

I chided myself for not inviting Karla to stay with me, since my house wasn't far from the airport. But it was too late to change plans. I didn't know what flight or what airline she'd be coming in on. Or whether the flight would be delayed for that matter. And then there was the little matter of Horace, who would no doubt try to snuggle up to Karla while she slept.

The driving wasn't getting any better and I still had to stop at Sunset and talk to Delia and stop at the Ashland Avenue house to see how the women were making out. Then I would head home and make the arrangements for Horace and get what I would need for the night.

Delia was in a snit when I got there. The company was laying off in her department and nagging her to get the work done with fewer people.

"Fran," she said. "Fran," she said again. I knew I wouldn't like what she was going to say.

"Fran, I've got so much work. Can you see what you can do with these two cases in the next couple of days?"

She handed me a couple of folders.

"Sure," I said. "But have you got a minute?"

"Mmm," she said, looking through more folders on her desk. I thought she was going to hand me a few more.

"I've talked to Billy." I knew that would get her attention.

"He called you from Vegas?" she said, showing her hand before she realized it.

"How did you find out where he is?" I asked.

"Well I called the eight-hundred number and left a message."

"And he called you?"

"Not exactly," she said and I knew I wasn't going to find out exactly, but I figured that she had a friend in the phone company, too.

"Did you know his name before he became Light-foot?" I said, wanting to show off the fact that I knew something about Billy.

"Another name?"

"Boccherini. People used to call him Botch."

She smiled. "I guess I like Lightfoot better. When did he change it?"

"He left Buffalo for a while and when he came back, he was Lightfoot."

I could see her doing numbers in her head. Then she nodded, satisfied, I guess, that she had figured out something about Billy.

"Did you have a nice chat?" I asked, thinking that any talk she had with Billy would be tense, to say the least.

"Chat?"

"With Billy when you called him."

"Oh, I didn't call him."

The idea hit me that she had set up surveillance in Vegas, and then I was sure that there was more to her relationship with Billy than mere romance.

"Is there anything official that you want me to convey to Karla?" I said. "She's coming to town."

Delia's well-arched eyebrows rose higher and she pursed her lips as if pondering this tough question. "Yes, there's a form."

"There's always a form."

"She has to complete this before we pay her." Delia had found a form in the third drawer she searched.

"Am I done with the case, then?"

"No. I think there's more we need to know. Have you turned up anything more on the guy who robbed Sammy?"

"No, but I found out that there was a lot more money in the paper bag than Sammy reported to the police."

"Aha!" she said. "I thought so. I mean, I thought he would have asked us to pay the whole amount. How much was there?"

"I don't know."

"Who told you there was more in the bag than he reported?"

"Karla. I don't think she knew the exact amount either. And I don't know whether anyone has audited the books."

"Books, shmooks. They're for the IRS. The real records . . ."

"What real records?"

She clammed up, covering her tracks with something like, "The IRS has the real records."

Delia was in a sweat to get back to work, and signed

my vouchers with barely a glance. I picked up my money and trudged through the snow to my car, wishing I had worn boots.

The traffic was doing its winter crawl, except for the yahoos with four-wheel drive. My defroster was not working right and I had to keep rubbing the inside of the windshield with my glove. I skidded once and almost gashed a shiny Lincoln parked down the street from the Ashland Avenue house.

Workers were already installing a new security system. At least they were trying to, but it must have been difficult for them with so many attractive women, more or less dressed, watching them work and asking questions.

I cornered Valerie and asked her how everything was going.

"Last night was rough, even with the guard we hired. We were all spooked."

"With good reason," I said. "But I'm glad you hired the guard. We'll work out the expenses. I think there's enough to cover in the account."

"We're paying for the security," she said. "It's for us."

She sounded like a woman who had been talking to Polly. "Right," I said, thinking that the whole financial system that Billy had worked out would have to be revised in their favor.

"Did Natasha ask you about the people calling for Marie?"

"Yes, but nobody's calling for Marie. Her friend knows. He's upstairs in her room now. He got there as soon as the cops were through."

"Her friend?" I said, and at that moment I turned toward the stairway, where Joe Plata was descending with his arms loaded with dresses and beads and scarves. His face was streaked with tears.

Nobody said a word. But we all somehow got the same message. I held the door for him, and followed him out to the shiny Lincoln that I'd almost sideswiped. He carried Marie's things gently, not letting them brush against the snow.

"My keys are in the right-hand pocket of my overcoat," he said, choking on a sob.

I fished in his pocket, thinking how odd it was to be in such intimate proximity to this man. I found the keys and opened the trunk for him. But he just stood there.

I began unloading his arms and packing the dresses in the trunk. Before I finished, the women from the house were trooping out with the rest of Marie's things. Still no one spoke, and each of the women packed her armload carefully on top.

Joe just stood there, watching and crying until the women had finished putting everything that was Marie's into the trunk of the Lincoln.

Valerie asked him whether they could get him a drink or a cup of coffee. He shook his head, saluted, got into his car and drove away.

The women found out later that day that the security system had been paid for.

Since sentimentality doesn't hold me in its grip too long, I wondered where he was going to put all that stuff. I couldn't see him marching past Carmelita's kitchen carrying Marie's negligees.

After Joe left, the women told me that the cops didn't think that Natasha was the intended victim after all. They asked me if I would tell Natasha that the women wanted her to come and live at the house, and I promised I'd deliver the message.

The city was shutting down early because of the snow and because the weather reports were now forecasting eight to twelve inches by the next morning. It was beginning to look like stupidity to drive out to Orchard Park, where the snow was usually deeper than in Buffalo.

When I got to the office, I parked on the street in

front of Looks. I didn't want to chance getting stuck in the back lot.

When I called Billy, I got a machine, on which I left a message about the weather and about the unlikelihood of my being able to get out to Karla's place. Then I called the airlines, trying to find out what plane Karla was on. I struck out on that one, too.

Then I told myself that Karla wasn't stupid. She wouldn't try to drive to her house in this weather. But suppose she got in early. *Damn it. I had promised to stay there with her.*

I told Natasha that she should close the office and that I'd give her a lift to the shelter. The sky was so gray that it was getting dark early.

"But I'm supposed to go downstairs and get my hair done," Natasha said. "And I was looking forward to it."

"I thought Looks was closed when I came in."

We closed up the office and walked down the stairs. We had to unlock the front door of Looks to get in.

"Myrtle must be here. She didn't tell me there was any change of plans."

We didn't see Myrtle, but we did see a work station all set up.

"She must have just stepped out for a minute. You go on home, Frances. I wore my boots this morning. I'll walk home."

"While we're on the subject of home," I said, and told her that the women at the house had renewed their invitation.

"But what about . . . ?"

"The cops think Marie was the target all along. The killer was trying to cover his tracks."

The back door opened and a snowy Myrtle came in stomping and shaking the snow off. "It's miserable out there," she said, taking off her toboggan hat and revealing that she had been experimenting with her own hair. The red spikes had been replaced by a blond bob, short and wavy, but still boyish, like her figure. It was a startling transformation and it gave her a sort of style. She reminded me of someone I'd seen before, maybe an actress in a TV series or on an often-played commercial.

"Wow," I said. "You look terrific. So that's how you spent your afternoon."

"Yes," Myrtle said, "People started canceling and the others left early, so I did my hair while I was waiting."

Myrtle stood by the mirror and touched up her hairdo with spray and a styling brush. When she put the brush down I saw the swirls of red and blond hairs mixed on the brush.

"I think she got the color right this time," Natasha said. "She reminds me of Madonna."

"Hmm, maybe."

"So, how is Karla?" Myrtle said.

"I guess she's feeling good, but she says her body is very big."

"And when is Sammy's baby arriving?"

That stopped me for a minute, but I didn't correct her. I guessed that Myrtle's news network hadn't picked up the latest on whose baby was whose.

"In a month."

"I heard she was in Vegas," Myrtle said. Her channels were working somewhat.

"That's what she said. But you know how some people like to keep secrets."

Myrtle laughed a funny little laugh. "Some people think that looks are everything."

At that moment, I was almost certain Myrtle knew her mother's secret.

"And that the truth should be kept chained under the stairs," Natasha said, her mellow laughter bubbling up from deep inside.

"Is Karla flying in tonight?" Myrtle said.

"She said so."

"Is the airport still open? It's getting pretty bad out there," Myrtle said.

"The last time I checked the airport was still operating," I said. "I've got to be on my way. Have a successful coiffeur."

They followed me to the darkened front of the shop. The swirling snow caught in the streetlight was hypnotic. We were mesmerized as we watched the sailing flakes, the spell making me feel peaceful, putting to rest the nagging questions of who killed Sammy and who killed Marie and why.

Natasha said, "It's beautiful even if it is wet and cold."

Myrtle stood between us and put her arms over our shoulders. I looked back at her. The low light had faded most of the color, and the black and white image was startling. I guess I must have made some kind of face.

Myrtle said, "What's the matter?"

"That hair. The hair is you," I said, and she flashed her thirty-two whites.

Twenty-five

It was slow going on the city streets, but the expressway was mostly clear with some slushy spots. I began to feel more optimistic about getting to Orchard Park. Route 219 would get me out to Orchard Park, but once I was off the highway, it might be rough going. The highway plowing crews in western New York were better than in places like New York City or Seattle, where a big snow was paralyzing.

If the plows had been through, I reasoned, I ought to make it. If I had to walk from the entrance to Parkland Heights to Karla's place, I could do it. Of course, I would be taking the chance that by leaving my car on the road, the first plow to go by would bury it and the second would smash it.

I was beginning to feel itchy at the back of my head. The urgency I was feeling about getting out to Karla's was partly rational, partly intuitive.

I ran down my list: Sammy's death, Marie's death, the sabotage, and the robbery at Looks. Could all the violence have been directed at Joe Plata? Who knew whether someone would try to kill Karla with the intent of depriving him of an heir? Not many people knew that Sammy wasn't the father. Wholesale violence could erupt if the power brokers were at war. And I was monumentally ignorant of who wielded the power, where, and why.

Then Delia popped into my head and the funny things she said about the robbery at Looks. She knew something that she wasn't telling me, but I wasn't sure it would make any difference if I knew or whether it had anything to do with Sammy's murder. Money was probably being laundered through Looks, but what did Delia know about it? Did somebody find out about it and decide to break the bank one night?

Myrtle's mother paraded by in my rogue's gallery of suspicious people, or at least untruthful people. Why make such a big secret about saying good-bye to an old flame? She had lived next door to him for years. Surely she had gotten over him. She had married someone else, had a child. Why did she live next door to his family all those years if it was so painful?

Then there was Frank the Bean, who despite his unsavory reputation, seemed almost like a straight arrow; and Edgar, who was yet to be dealt with; and Beth, who was incommunicado, her answering machine giving out a message that sounded out of date when I'd tried to call her earlier.

Gene, Dan, and Kathy, friends and employees of Sammy. They must have suspected something was fishy about Sammy's deposits. They said they had warned him about the paper-bag routine.

Gene knew Marie, but did he know her connection to Joe Plata? Then there were Karla and Billy, who had motive enough, or was it just the opposite: that there was motive enough for Sammy to shoot them?

Would any one of the women at the Ashland Avenue house have killed Marie? Were the murders linked or not?

And then there was that itching on my scalp, those hairs standing up at the back of my neck.

When I got home, there was a friendly and sweet message from Ted, asking me to call him as soon as I got home. He had some information for me that was very important, he said.

When I called him, he told me that the silver car that Hauser was supposed to check on had actually been borrowed by the sergeant the day I saw the car in the woods. I didn't tell him that I already had figured that, but I thanked him.

When Ted made noises about wanting to come over, I told him that I had to stay with a friend overnight. I gave him the rough scenario without mentioning any names.

"It's not a good night to drive, Fran."

"The expressway was in good shape when I drove home. I think it'll be OK."

"But the plows are getting behind on the local streets. Once you're off the highway it'll be rough going. Tell you what. My Subaru has four-wheel drive. I'll be glad to give you a lift and go get you in the morning."

"Really, it's all right. But I'm glad to hear you have four-wheel drive. I'll certainly call you if I get stuck."

"Sure, Fran." He was being put off and he knew it.

"I'll call you tomorrow, I promise."

"I'm working again tomorrow night," he said. "The schedules are screwed up. We got a new sergeant who forgets how many hours are in a day when he does the work sheets."

"I'll cook kielbasa and sauerkraut on Friday. If you want some, you can come over."

His voice brightened. "It's a date. What kind of wine goes with sauerkraut?"

"Ripple," I said.

Thank God, he laughed. "I'll get some German beer."

"Now you're talking," I said, already savoring the tastes.

"And I'll make potato pancakes if I won't get in your way."

"For potato pancakes, you've got the run of the kitchen."

After I hung up, I tried Beth's number again. There was a new message on her tape, so I guessed she got the messages and decided not to return my call. I was relieved that she hadn't been killed or kidnapped. My mind was starting to work like that. I was nervous about everything. I was also carrying my thirty-eight in my bag.

Wally Klune's mom answered the phone when I called.

"Wally's out collecting. You know how slow some people are about paying the paper boy. And I worry about him going around in the evening like this."

"He can come and get Horace and take Horace with him anytime, Mrs. Klune."

"I'll tell him that. I'd feel better if he had the dog along with him at night, and I know he loves that dog." She sounded delighted. I think Wally had told me that he couldn't have a dog because his little sister had allergies.

I gave Mrs. Klune what I thought would be my schedule and told her that I would call her when I got back. Then I pampered Horace while I packed a bag and some snack food, a thermos of coffee, warm clothing, and blankets in case I got marooned.

My calls to Nevada and to the airlines still didn't get me any information on Karla's flight. So I was stuck with the original plan. I had to go to Orchard Park.

The trip did not start well. I got stuck in my driveway and had to shovel out. Maple Street was all ruts and there was no sign of the plow. I threw the shovel into the trunk and picked the tire chains off the peg on the garage wall. I hadn't put chains on in years, but I had faith that I'd remember how if the need arose.

My defroster still wasn't clearing the windshield, although the back window defogger was working perfectly. I stopped at a gas station to fill the tank and asked the attendant if he could fix my defroster.

After he looked under the dash, he diagnosed the problem as a broken switch and told me that without doing any major work he could adjust it so that I would have either heat or defrost, but not both.

I weighed the alternatives, cold feet or no visibility, and put on the heavy boots that I had packed in my emergency kit.

The thruway was clear and salted, and traffic was light. Planes were still going in and out of the airport although according to the radio news some of the airlines had suspended operations. The weatherman was predicting high winds and even less visibility, and a travel advisory had been issued. Although I didn't look forward to being stranded in a snowdrift somewhere, I felt prepared for the elements. The most important thing I had to do was keep the car on the road. Running off the road and into a ditch in weather like this could be dangerous. Your tracks would be covered in minutes, and they wouldn't find you until the thaw.

The thruway and Route 219 between Cheektowaga and Orchard Park were in good shape, and that part of the trip took only twenty-five minutes. It was slower going on the main roads, slower yet when I got off onto the less-traveled roads.

At the entrance to Parkland Heights, the road stopped. The plows had gone no farther, and the snow drifts were four feet high. My headlights picked out about a dozen snowcapped cars parked in a rough clearing just inside the stone pillars that marked the entrance to the development. It didn't look as though any plowing had been done in Parkland Heights for several hours.

That's what happens in a big storm. The plows have to work so hard to keep the main arteries open that the secondary roads get neglected until the storm subsides.

Once I turned off my headlights, I was surprised by how dark it was, realizing suddenly that there were no lights on the street and that very little light was coming from inside the houses. When I got my overnight bag from the trunk, I also grabbed my flashlight and dug around in the trunk looking for anything else that I might find useful in a power outage.

Karla's place was a good walk and there was no path shoveled, so everything I carried would get pretty heavy by the time I got there. I wondered whether one of the cars was Karla's and whether she had walked in all this snow in her condition. I took a brief look at the other cars and did see one that was from Hertz, which was no guarantee that it was Karla's, of course, but it was possible.

I made my way from the impromptu parking lot, walking in the partially filled tracks of those who had gone before. The farther I got from the car, the fewer tracks there were, and by the time I got to Karla's, there were no tracks visible at all. That meant that she wasn't there or that she had arrived early enough for the snow to have covered her tracks.

However, there were no lights coming from the house, either, which meant that she wasn't there or that she didn't have any candles. But she did have candles, I remembered, in fancy holders on the mantel and on the dining room table.

I retrieved the key from the spot behind the light, where Karla had told me it would be. I spent a few seconds looking up the security code that I'd have to use when I got inside before it occurred to me that the security system was probably useless in a power outrage.

Once inside, I started to take off my coat, but stopped when I realized that there was no heat in the house, either. I lit the candles in the fancy holders and that brightened up the dining room and living room. I looked for wood to start a fire in the fireplace, but there wasn't any stacked in the brass log holder.

I stopped in my tracks twice when I heard creaks. But houses do that when they're cooling off. Back in the kitchen I lit more of the decorative candles and then looked around to see if I could find a supply of candles or an oil lamp.

When the phone rang, I jumped a mile. I flashed my light around looking for the phone and found it on the fourth ring.

"Oh, good, you're there," Karla said.

"Where are you?"

"At the airport. I just got in."

"Stay there," I said. "The road isn't plowed inside your development, and the power is off."

"This connection doesn't sound too good, either," she said, just after there was static on the line.

"You can stay at my place and we can call the movers in the morning to see what their plans are. I'll pick you up."

"I've already got a car. They even got me one with four-wheel drive. What's your address?"

I gave it to her and told her to go to the Klunes' house to get the key.

"And if you're worried about the dog, Wally Klune will go into the house first and put Horace in my bedroom."

And then the line went dead.

"Karla?" but there was no answer.

Well, I told myself, *she had the information she needed. Lucky the phone went dead after she called.*

Creak. A creak that sent a chill through me. But no. There were no footprints to the house. I began to walk quietly myself. Quickly and quietly to the front door, where I'd left my bag and the thirty-eight.

I listened, my ears tuned to the slightest sound, my eyes trying to pierce the darkness beyond the circle of the candle light. I reached my bag with a sense of relief, but when I reached inside, the gun was not there.

Did I leave it in the car? I looked through my other bags, but it wasn't there. *Damn. I must have left it in the car*, I thought.

Or is someone here? I tightened my grip on the flashlight and went from window to window, looking at the white expanse outside. Fresh snow. No footprints.

Then I walked back to the kitchen, still looking out the windows, looking for a sign that someone had come to the house. Nothing. But still I listened. I heard nothing, saw nothing.

Not until I looked out the window next to the back porch. There, caught in the beam of my light, prints. Partly drifted in, but clear enough because the porch was sheltered. How old were they? And whose were they?

A deliveryman? A neighbor?

I opened the back door and shone my light into the tracks. They came one way. In. There were no tracks retreating.

And then I heard a rustling. It was behind me and I began to turn, but it was too late. I heard a loud thump and felt the pain and then felt nothing.

I woke up in the dark with my face on a cold surface. My head hurt, but when I tried to feel for the damage, I found my hands were tied behind me. As I took inventory, I realized that my feet, too, were bound.

I sniffed the air and found it damp and moldy and concluded that I had been thrown or dragged or rolled down the stairs to the basement. Were there any other bumps or bruises? I couldn't tell, the pain in my head took precedence. There was a thumping in my head around the site of the wound, but I could make out more thumping.

Someone was moving above me. Whoever hit me was still there, I thought. But suppose it was someone else. *Should I call out?*

I still had not moved, and lucky for me. Just then a door opened and a light shone at me from above. I closed my eyes so that I could see through slits. The stairs were next to my feet, and the light was coming from the top of the stairs.

Probably my flashlight, I thought. *Whoever it is might have my gun, too.* I played possum and prayed for another fifty years of life.

And then the light was gone, and I was swallowed in the darkness. Sounds, like furniture being moved across the floor, filled the air for what seemed like five minutes, but in my state, I wasn't secure in my sense of time. And my watch was behind me. I could feel that. My watch was still there.

Then I heard a huge slam, and knew that it was the front door, and the house grew quiet. I waited, waited for a noise, a breath, a creak, a light. But there was only quiet. I began to wonder whether it was safe to move, to try to free myself. *Was the person gone?*

I moaned, thinking that it was nonthreatening sound for a prisoner to make. Whoever hit me would check on me after hearing the sound.

No light appeared at the top of the stairs. I moaned again, louder, longer, then waited.

I strained at the ropes that held me and tried to change my position. I kicked at the stairs and waited again.

But whoever it was was gone, and I tried in earnest to move. When I turned my head warm liquid ran into my face. *Blood,* I thought; *am I still bleeding?*

The thought of bleeding to death on the cellar floor at Parkland Heights suddenly crowded out any mental activity. Panic took over. I struggled with the bindings on my legs and arms and shouted. But nothing changed, no one heard me. I was still tied up in the basement.

Think, I tried to tell myself. *Calm down, breathe, you are conscious.* A drop of something hit my face and the fear rose again, but this time I knew it wasn't blood from my head; it had dropped from above. I was imagining a bleeding corpse upstairs. I reached for the drop on my cheek with my tongue. Relief. It wasn't salty.

Perhaps a pipe had ruptured. I wondered if some other pipes had already broken and whether the water was damaging the house and Karla's furnishings.

Karla! I had to warn Karla.

I wriggled myself into a kneeling position and then inched to the stairs and sat. I knew there were knives in the kitchen, if I could get there, and if the person with my gun didn't return, I might get lose.

I lifted my butt onto the second step and pulled my feet up to the first step. *Yes, that would work*, I thought, *if I didn't get dizzy and go pitching back down into that blackness*. Butt, feet, butt, feet, all the way up. At the top of the stairs I rested before trying to stand up. It would take all the strength I had in my legs and good balance to get vertical in the tiny space I had to maneuver in.

Maybe standing up is not such a good idea, I thought. I got up on my knees and tried to nudge the doorknob with my face, but that didn't work. Then I clenched my jaw around as much of the knob as I could fit in my mouth and turned my head. The knob turned, the door opened suddenly and I was flat on my face again.

I went through the same gyrations as before and finally got myself sitting with my back against a wall where I wouldn't have to worry about the stairs. I gingerly worked my way up onto my hobbled feet.

By the flickering light of the candles that I had lit earlier I could see what had made the thumping noises I had heard as I came to. The kitchen was in ruins. I didn't doubt that the other rooms had been trashed as well.

Instead of jumping my way across the floor to the cutlery drawers, I inched my feet across the floor which was covered with all kinds of muck. My nose was being assaulted with so many smells that I didn't notice the smoke right away. But there it was. Wafting in from the hallway to the dining room and living room and lending even more urgency to my trip across the floor to the knife that I hoped would be there.

I found the knives in the second drawer I opened, and chose with my eyes the one I wanted before turning my back and taking it in hand. Before I got the knife lined right, I nicked my wrist, and when I sawed back and forth with the blade, I hoped I wouldn't nick myself again when the rope was cut through. The candles flickered and the smoke kept wafting in from the living room.

I felt the pressure let go and my hands were free. It was a wonderful sense of power. Once my hands were loose, I cut the rope on my feet. Then I took a second to assess the damage to my head, which was aching at the spot I got whacked. There was a mucky spot in my hair, but no fresh bleeding. I tried to run the water, but nothing came out when I turned the tap, so I opened the back door, carefully checking this time, and grabbed a handful of snow to hold to my head.

Despite the smoke, I made my way carefully toward the hall, where I had dumped my things inside the front door when I arrived. I had to see if I could still retrieve anything, mainly my car keys.

The mess in the living room was hideous, and the fire that had been started at the base of the drapes had been extinguished by the water from another broken pipe. The rug was still smoldering, and I diverted some of the water puddling next to the wall. I tried not to think what would have happened if the fire had burned as planned.

My bags hadn't been disturbed further by the intruder. The car keys were still there. I grabbed my stuff and left, following the tracks that led from the front door. Two houses up, the tracks veered off, but I didn't follow them. I knew they led to where the intruder's car had been parked. I had some catching up to do.

A phone was the first priority, but I didn't want to stop at one of the other houses. I was bloody and didn't know what kind of reaction I'd get.

I plunged through the snow, deeper than it was before by several inches. It was over the tops of my boots, and chunks of it fell down inside them. My coat dragged in the snow, my bags dragged in it. The clumps stuck to my coat and the bags. The way the snow was sticking to me I felt almost as if I would become a huge ball.

The wind had died down so the drifting wasn't as bad, but the flakes were larger now and wetter, a sign that the weather was warming up and that the roads would be slicker and harder to drive on.

Everything was taking so long, and time was running out. When I got to my car, I started it and let it warm up while I cleared off the windows.

An emergency vehicle of some kind was flashing its light on the road at the other side of a monster snowdrift.

I put the car in gear and hoped I'd get traction. I backed up about four feet before I got stuck. It was time for the Western New York Driving Survival Drill. Forward. Back. Forward. Back a little farther. Finally I blasted out and hoped that when I stopped to switch into forward gear I wouldn't get stuck again.

On the other side of the drift I saw the emergency vehicle. It was a phone company truck. I pulled alongside it, tied a scarf over my bloody head. In the truck, a repairman was sipping a cup of coffee.

I knocked on the truck window. "You have any phone service here? There's none back at my house and I need to call someone fast," I said.

The repairman gave me a flirty look. "Why yes, ma'am. We've just got a line. What can I do for you?"

"Can you patch me in to a number in Cheektowaga?" I smiled at him and batted my eyelashes. "It's very important. I'd be much obliged."

"No problem," he said, and got out of his truck and rang my home phone. After a few seconds, he said, "I'm getting an answering machine, ma'am."

"I guess no one's home," I said. "Thanks for your help."

"Men are so unreliable," he said, his grin showing intermittently in the spinning light from his truck.

There we were in the middle of a huge storm and he was flirting with me. God knows what he expected. Only in Buffalo, I thought. And then, for no reason at all, I recalled a button that some wry Buffalo boosters had made up that said "Buffalo, City of No Illusions."

My car slipped and slid down the hill from Parkland Heights to the main road, and I drove at a crawl into the village of Orchard Park, looking for a pay phone.

Getting hit on the head and lying on a basement floor had made me dizzy but cleared up my thinking. This time I wasn't walking into a trap. I knew someone was out there who would kill again and, as a matter of fact, planned to do just that.

Twenty-six

When I drove down my street, my heart was pounding, but this time I had backup. I knew the killer would be watching my house, but not looking for me. I was supposed to be a shish kebob in Orchard Park.

I hadn't told Karla what had been done to her house yet. I had only told her to stay where she was, at the Klune place, where Mrs. Klune had invited her to tea when Wally couldn't find the key to my house.

Wally was so reliable, it was hard for me to believe he would do what other kids do all the time: lose something. But he did. And he was turning his room inside out looking for the key while Karla waited and made small talk with his mother.

That's where I found Karla and hatched the plan that I hoped would work and wouldn't get me killed.

When I pulled up in front of my house, I was driving Karla's rented car and wearing Karla's coat, a padded belly, and a ratty blond wig Mrs. Klune had found in her attic. Because of the snow, there were quite a few cars parked on the street, awaiting the clearing of the driveways. I saw the two cars I was looking for. One of them was Ted's.

I was sweating as I got out of the car, trying to climb the snowbank as a pregnant woman would, trying to act like someone in an unfamiliar place, and like a person who wasn't scared silly. The snow was still dancing down in big soft flakes, a regular Christmas card, except that it was spring. I scanned the snow, looking for a shadow behind the shrubbery or someone lurking behind a tree.

As I reached the front entrance to my house, I heard a car door slam and had to restrain myself from hurrying. I fumbled with the key even though I knew perfectly well how to use it.

"Karla," a woman's voice said.

I coughed and then replied in a hoarse voice. "Fran, is that you?"

"Er, yes," she said. "You're late."

"Your paper boy couldn't find your key," I mumbled, hoping that I sounded a little like Karla and a little less like myself. I had to keep her talking.

I heard another car door as the woman walked closer. It would only be a few seconds before she realized who I was. I kept my head down, half working at the key and half watching her. I started making small talk about my flight from Nevada, about the airport in Chicago being stacked up, about waiting so long to land in Buffalo that I thought the plane would run out of gas. I chattered and chattered, hoping I was fooling her. And all the while I was watching Ted coming across the street fast.

Before Ted could reach her, she pulled a gun from her purse. It looked like my gun. Her hand was shaking, her eyes were glazed.

"Haven't you done enough killing, Myrtle?" I said.

She stopped. Her mouth dropped open. I thought her hand trembled. She looked confused. Then she shook her head, as if to shake away a fly buzzing around her and stared at my protruding stomach.

Ted was racing up behind her. Then I realized that some other men were converging on the spot, too.

"Sammy will never have another child," Myrtle said.

"No. Wait. It's not . . ."

She aimed at my belly just as Ted lunged at her. The

gun went off and the bullet tore through the padding and nicked my side. I buckled.

Ted had the gun now and was looking at me to see how I was and at the same time was holding Myrtle's arm behind her back.

Myrtle was struggling and shouting. "No more little Platas. I'm the end of the line. Ha. Why should you be happy? He ruined my mother's life. I didn't even know my own father."

"Fran," Ted said. "Are you hurt?"

"She grazed me," I said.

"Fran?" Myrtle said, looking at me, frowning. "How? Where's Karla?"

Ted had stopped looking at me and was watching three men who were coming at him from different directions. Each one was carrying a gun.

Myrtle looked at them and screamed.

One man, a very large man, waved a semiautomatic at me and said, "Get in the house."

I stood up gingerly and decided I was still ambulatory.

Another man was behind Ted sticking a gun in his back. "You get in the house, too," he told Ted, and took the gun that Ted had taken from Myrtle. I was sure it was mine and at that moment I thought of how many sets of prints would be on it.

We did as we were told, and the big man grabbed Myrtle.

"No," Myrtle shouted. "Don't leave me, Fran, don't . . ."

The big man covered her mouth with his ham-hock hands. The other two followed Ted and me inside the house and made us lie down on the living room floor. Horace was behind the gate in the kitchen barking and leaping, outraged at the intrusion into his territory.

I was hoping that the gate wouldn't give. One of those guys would shoot Horace if he came bounding out.

When the men left and closed the door behind them, Ted and I got up and ran to the front window. Ted pulled his own gun, overlooked by the goon who thought he had disarmed him.

"No," I said. "You don't stand a chance."

We watched from behind the blinds as two of the men took Myrtle to a car down the block and drove away. The third man followed them in Myrtle's car.

"You didn't tell me you were going to be dressed like that," Ted said. "I didn't know it was you at first. Damn it, Fran, she shot at you."

"Thanks for the backup, Ted. But she wasn't shooting at me, she shot at what she thought was her future half-brother or sister."

"Half what?"

"Myrtle is Sammy's daughter."

"I'd better call the precinct and tell Brockway and O'Connor what happened."

"You do that," I said. I was getting fed up with his backside-kissing routine. "And when you're done talking to them, give me the phone."

Ted's face turned several shades of pink and the expression on it fluttered from anger to recognition. Then I remembered what I liked about him: He was a decent guy. "Uh, maybe you'd better call them," he said.

O'Connor and Brockway wasted no time getting out to my place. But by the time they arrived, Karla was there, too.

Karla had been none too happy when I told her about the mess her place was in, but when I told her the rest, she seemed ready to let that go.

"I could be out there in that vandalized house, dead," she said. "I'm glad you're OK, Fran."

That had reminded me of the wound on my head, where I felt only a dull ache.

Ted turned quite green when I asked him to clean it up, and Karla took over and finished the job.

"It would be a good thing to have that stitched," she said. "The scar will be smaller."

I had attended to the bullet wound on my side, which really was no more than an abrasion that I could have gotten falling while running.

"Who knew Myrtle was Sammy's daughter?" Karla said.

"Until recently, my guess is that only Sammy, Myrtle's mother, Joe Plata, and of course, Marie, knew. Myrtle may have suspected when her hair started turning gray. But she didn't know for sure until her mother told her, which probably happened when she found out you were pregnant."

"Oh," Karla said.

I knew what was running through her mind. If she had gone away with Billy as soon as she realized she was in love with him, none of the killing would have happened.

"It probably would have happened anyway," I said. "If Sammy had married Beth and Beth had become pregnant, the same strong emotions would have been triggered."

"But how did *you* know?" Ted asked.

"It was all there in the photo album on Mrs. Plata's kitchen table, but I didn't recognize it at first. The pictures of Sammy growing up and turning gray, then the pictures of Myrtle. It started to dawn on me, but I didn't put it all together until I was lying on the cellar floor in Parkland Heights. In the dark, I saw all the pictures again, especially Myrtle's hair at her high school graduation streaked with gray. And then I remembered Myrtle earlier tonight in the half light at Looks. She had bleached her hair, and in the dimness, it looked white. I was startled, but didn't figure out till later what had startled me. She looked just like Sammy. And then I remembered what I had seen in her hairbrush. Blond hairs and red hairs, but the red ones had white roots."

"And Marie knew too much?" Karla said.

"She was Myrtle's mother's best friend. Maybe she said something to Myrtle that indicated she suspected that Myrtle had killed Sammy. Certainly somebody got suspicious or the goons wouldn't have been trailing her tonight.''

I went through the evening's events for O'Connor and Brockway, leaving out the part where I dressed up like Karla. I looked at Ted to see if he would squeal on me, but he held his tongue. I told the detectives that Ted just happened to stop over as I was opening my front door.

Even Karla knew I was lying, but Brockway and O'Connor didn't blink.

"The guys that kidnapped Miss Divenzio," Brockway said. "Did you recognize them?''

I wasn't about to say that one of them was built like Marco from the Cafe Roma. I didn't see his face and didn't want to.

"No," I said. "They had their collars up and their hats pulled low."

The phone rang. It was for O'Connor.

"They found her car," he said when he hung up. "At the airport. She's not in the trunk. But they found two guns."

"That may be the gun she took from me. Is my flashlight there too?''

"I'll ask them," O'Connor said, grinning in a funny way. He looked almost friendly.

"That could mean she's on a plane," Brockway said.

"It might only mean that her car is at the airport," I said.

Brockway and O'Connor both smiled.

"So where do you think she is?" Brockway asked me.

"I don't know, but whoever does know isn't likely to talk about it," I said. "Are you going to question Joe Plata?''

Brockway and O'Connor laughed together.

"We won't be hearing much from Plata in the future," Brockway said. "The feds are closing in on him. Maybe he'll have to lie low."

Karla had been sitting there sort of stunned, and then she said, "I wouldn't want to be in Myrtle's shoes. She killed Sammy, Joe's only child, her father. He won't consider her his blood any longer." Karla stopped, shook her head. "Oh, no, you'll never find her. That's the way it will happen." Karla shook her head again. She seemed to be thinking of something other than Myrtle's plight. Maybe something that had made her bitter about the West Side.

"We already checked on Plata," O'Connor said. "He was home watching television."

"Of course," Karla said.

And then O'Connor and Brockway started asking me questions. What had I seen, when.

Karla suddenly yelped. "Oh, no. The baby." She stood up and water ran down her leg. "I didn't want to have this baby in Buffalo."

Her pains started immediately and they were hard and close together. By the time we had loaded her in the detectives' car and I had called Billy in Vegas, I had my story edited for the version I would give to the detectives.

Epilogue

Karla had twin girls, about four pounds each, at Children's Hospital. Billy was stunned. He smiled a lot.

As Karla predicted, Myrtle has not turned up. I found out why Karla knew what would happen: her father had crossed Plata's group and had disappeared years before. Karla's mother never told her what had happened until after Karla had married Sammy.

Billy had an old beef with Sammy, too. A beef that kept Sammy beholden to him for years. Back when Billy Boccherini disappeared from the neighborhood and came back as Lightfoot, he had been in jail. He had taken a rap for Sammy, for a price, of course.

Ted told me that Mrs. Divenzio cried when she was questioned by the police. She didn't tell the cops that she was the former Rose La Polla, that she got pregnant in high school with Sammy's child, that Joe Plata had arranged her marriage to Mr. Divenzio, because Sammy was too young to get married. She was used to keeping secrets.

She didn't tell the cops, but they found out when Carmelita Plata broke down and told everything she knew, which wasn't everything. Carmelita didn't know who had kidnapped Myrtle that night on my lawn in Cheektowaga.

The media people went wild. I heard that someone was writing a book and a TV movie. Myrtle's picture was on a couple of the crime-fighter programs. Wanted for questioning, they said. But everybody knew that the gun that killed Sammy was found in her car.

The neighborhood was changing on the West Side. Where the storefronts had once featured Italian foods, Spanish foods began to appear. Joe Plata's empire scattered. Marco opened a new Cafe Roma in Blasdell, where Frank the Bean, no doubt, plays pool and the ponies. And while we're on the subject of ponies, my bet on "If Looks Could Kill" paid off. Frank the Bean called me the day after Myrtle disappeared and told me to come over and collect.

Several months later the Platas moved out to Karla's place in Parkland Heights. Joe lives there in between appearances in federal court. The feds followed some of that loose change that went through Looks and some of Plata's other enterprises. They've charged him with filing false income-tax returns so far.

Polly still runs the group at the Ashland Avenue house, where Natasha lives. The Tuesday night battered women's group still meets, too, and once a month we have a picnic, indoors or outdoors, depending on the weather.

Minnie is going to college to become a teacher, and Edgar is paying for it. But they don't live together. Amy's baby was stillborn after her last beating. She moved to the women's shelter, where she's working on her decision. It's status quo for the rest of us.

Sergeant Hauser was charged with attempted rape and two counts of assault, one in connection with his attack on me and the other with his attack on my ex-mother-in-law, Marsha. It took her a while before she told the whole story, but Hauser recognized a victim when he saw one. The cops charged him in connection with Dick's death after one of my neighbors told them that she saw Hauser check Dick and then go back to his car and sit there for ten minutes before he checked Dick again. At that point, she called an ambulance.

Ted and I see one another for dinners, but we haven't made contact, so to speak. I think I'm still too fragile emotionally, and it's still hard for me to trust him, which may be my fault rather than his. We are good friends, though, and maybe someday we'll be more than that.

I'm still working for Sunset, but Delia quit and I report to her old boss. Delia now shares office space with Natasha and me. She's an insurance agent and she has sold me more insurance than I've ever had before. She's also working on curing my technophobia with her penchant for acquiring electronic gadgets.

I finally figured out why Delia was so interested in the robbery at Looks. She suspected that Billy was involved and was worried that her affair with Billy would be found out.

Actually, the cops stumbled on the robber while they were rounding up people for the feds. It was somebody whom Sammy knew, but the cops didn't find out anything more than that.

The office is in better shape than before; Joe Plata installed a lavatory upstairs.

Detective Brockway called me one day to tell me I could pick up my gun and my flashlight.

Looks carries on without Beth and without any more cement in the plumbing. I had a long talk with Gene, and we decided that it was probably Myrtle who gummed up the plumbing so that she'd have an excuse to be off work and could go to take care of Marie that morning. Myrtle's fingerprints were found in Marie's room.

Gene hired a new girl to do the shampoos. I can't look at her without thinking of Myrtle and her boyish body and her Hollywood smile.

And Horace, he's OK so far. No more seizures.

And, yes, Sunset paid Karla the million dollars.

FAST-PACED MYSTERIES
BY J.A. JANCE

Featuring J.P. Beaumont

UNTIL PROVEN GUILTY   89638-9/$4.99 US/$5.99 CAN

INJUSTICE FOR ALL   89641-9/$4.50 US/$5.50 CAN

TRIAL BY FURY   75138-0/$4.99 US/$5.99 CAN

TAKING THE FIFTH   75139-9/$4.99 US/$5.99 CAN

IMPROBABLE CAUSE   75412-6/$4.99 US/$5.99 CAN

A MORE PERFECT UNION   75413-4/$4.99 US/$5.99 CAN

DISMISSED WITH PREJUDICE

   75547-5/$4.99 US/$5.99 CAN

MINOR IN POSSESSION   75546-7/$4.99 US/$5.99 CAN

PAYMENT IN KIND   75836-9/$4.99 US/$5.99 CAN

WITHOUT DUE PROCESS   75837-7/$4.99 US/$5.99 CAN

FAILURE TO APPEAR   75839-3/$5.50 US/$6.50 CAN

Featuring Joanna Brady

DESERT HEAT   76545-4/$4.99 US/$5.99 CAN

TOMBSTONE COURAGE   76546-2/$5.99 US/$6.99 CAN

Buy these books at your local bookstore or use this coupon for ordering:

Mail to: Avon Books, Dept BP, Box 767, Rte 2, Dresden, TN 38225   C
Please send me the book(s) I have checked above.
❑ My check or money order— no cash or CODs please— for $_____is enclosed
(please add $1.50 to cover postage and handling for each book ordered— Canadian residents
add 7% GST).
❑ Charge my VISA/MC Acct#_____Exp Date_____
Minimum credit card order is two books or $6.00 (please add postage and handling charge of
$1.50 per book — Canadian residents add 7% GST). For faster service, call
1-800-762-0779. Residents of Tennessee, please call 1-800-633-1607. Prices and numbers
are subject to change without notice. Please allow six to eight weeks for delivery.

Name_____
Address_____
City_____State/Zip_____
Telephone No._____   JAN 0395